Readers love
the Sucker for Love Mysteries
by K.L. HIERS

Acsquidentally In Love

"This book has a bit of everything I love, a good mystery, magic, romance, humor, and Action. K.L. Hiers has me hooked and I can't wait for more!"

—Bayou Book Junkie

"Hiers rolls worldbuilding mythology, delicious flirting, erotic scenes, and detective work into a breezy and sensual LGBTQ paranormal romance."

—Library Journal

Kraken My Heart

"I am so in love with this series… This is a really good series. It is one that is worth reading over again, just for the fun of it."

—Love Bytes Reviews

Nautilus Than Perfect

"If you're new to the series – WHAT the hell are you waiting for, go and read the first book! Especially if you love *tentacles*."

—Reading under the Rainbow

Just Calamarried

"Sloane and Loch are so crazy in love that you can feel it."

—Book Review Virginia Lee Blog

By K.L. HIERS

SUCKER FOR LOVE MYSTERIES
Acsquidentally In Love
Kraken My Heart
Head Over Tentacles
Nautilus Than Perfect
Just Calamarried
Our Shellfish Desires

Published by DREAMSPINNER PRESS
www.dreamspinnerpress.com

OUR SHELLFISH DESIRES

K.L. HIERS

Published by
DREAMSPINNER PRESS

5032 Capital Circle SW, Suite 2, PMB# 279, Tallahassee, FL 32305-7886 USA
www.dreamspinnerpress.com

Our Shellfish Desires
© 2022 K.L. Hiers

Cover Art
© 2022 Tiferet Design
http://www.tiferetdesign.com
Cover content is for illustrative purposes only and any person depicted on the cover is a model.

Trade Paperback ISBN: 978-1-64108-405-5
Digital ISBN: 978-1-64108-404-8
Trade Paperback published July 2022
v. 1.0

Printed in the United States of America
∞
This paper meets the requirements of
ANSI/NISO Z39.48-1992 (Permanence of Paper).

CHAPTER 1.

"OLEANDER LOGUE." Alexander read the name off the computer screen with a smirk. "There he is. Home address, bank statements, last credit card purchase, and ah, he renewed his video streaming subscription. Registered magic user under a water discipline. What else...." He clicked around. "Family calls him Ollie."

It's a little worrying how easy it is to find someone's personal information online, Rota's voice mumbled inside Alexander's head.

"More reliable than magic."

Mm, true.

"Let's go."

Right now?

"Yes." Alexander stood up from the computer he'd been using. It so happened to be the computer in Sloane Beaumont's office, the private investigator and Starkiller who had given them Ollie's name.

Considering Alexander and Rota had just spoken to Sloane at home with his husband and child, Alexander had known the office would be unoccupied and they wouldn't be disturbed.

They'd visited Sloane's apartment to take possession of a very rare book, and now they were in need of a translator because it was written in godstongue, the language of the old gods.

The situation was complicated.

Rota was the living soul of an old Sagittarian god, one of many ancient deities worshipped by mankind ages ago before their following faded in the wake of a new monotheistic religion. Rota had been forced by the god Gronoch to leave his physical body and have his soul bound to Alexander, a Silenced mortal. Though he had no natural magic of his own, Alexander could channel Rota's immense godly powers through his body like an antenna.

There were a few limitations, but the one plaguing Alexander was that he could not touch Rota nor Rota him for extended periods of time.

That made things especially difficult when two people were in love.

Rota slid a shimmering tentacle over Alexander's cheek, soothing, *Why don't we rest tonight and go over there in the morning?*

Alexander experienced Rota's physical touch like a cold shiver. Other times it felt like dipping himself into a cool bath. It was always fleeting and all too brief.

Rota's physical manifestations varied between these simple ghostly caresses or mere stationary support like acting as a wall or shield. Anything particularly acrobatic risked unleashing the brunt of his full godly might. There was no in between. Attempting even a simple hug exhausted Rota from trying to hold himself back, and there was a high chance of hurting Alexander.

They'd tried.

Oh, how they'd *tried* over and over again, and the result had always been the same.

Disappointment and heartache.

It was why the translation was so important. The book was a collection of poems written by Wilhelmina Pickett, a Sage who was said to have traveled all the worlds between worlds created by the gods. Alexander's research strongly indicated this book could guide them to the location of the Fountain.

Where Rota's body was supposed to be.

"Tonight," Alexander insisted.

Are you sure?

Alexander could feel Rota's hesitation. "You're worried about me."

You haven't stopped in months.

"This is important."

So are you. You're exhausted.

It was very strange to have a staring contest with a soul, even more so being on the losing side. It was more of a sensation than a physical act since Alexander didn't see Rota so much as he sensed him. There was a vague outline of the giant beastly god and his big spikes and tentacles, but it was only a shadow of Rota's true self.

Alexander already knew he wasn't going to win. Not when Rota was being this stubborn.

Well?

"Fine!" Alexander scowled. "We'll go home, sleep, and go see him first thing in the morning."

A side effect of their unique bond was being connected psychically. They could feel each other's emotions, hear every thought and subconscious impulse, and at first it had made for a very stressful existence.

As time went on, they learned to tune each other out and tried to give the other privacy, even if it was only an illusion.

I want to get this over with. I'm tired of living like this. One kiss isn't enough. It's not enough. Not after all these years, not after everything! Alexander hated he had lost control of his thoughts, and he hoped Rota would ignore them.

Rota did, thankfully, but he still reached out to touch Alexander's cheek again.

Alexander shuddered. *Not nearly enough.*

Let's go home.

Alexander directed Rota to teleport them away with a thought. One moment they were in Sloane's office, and then they were gone.

They were puppet and puppeteer, Alexander long since having become a master of commanding Rota's magic. He could use his thoughts to control it or his physical body for a bigger boost. The latter option was dangerous since Alexander was mortal and his body couldn't handle the strain of channeling a god's power for very long.

For those fleeting moments when Alexander did take on Rota's full power, however, he knew they could have made the whole world tremble before them.

But Alexander didn't care about that.

His desires were very simple, practically base, and achievement of them was so close now that he could almost taste it. He was going to be with the god he loved, no matter what.

Home was the name for wherever they were holing up at the moment, and it was currently the penthouse suite of an abandoned hotel. It was a large space once overflowing with old mattresses, broken furniture, and forgotten trash bags. They'd cleaned it up, made it livable thanks to Rota's magic, and Alexander reflected that they'd lived here longer than anywhere else.

Except for Hazel, he thought bitterly, heading to the kitchenette to find something to eat. *That fucking hellhole.*

Where we first met, Rota added.

"I know." Alexander stared into the fridge. "Kinda hard to forget."

Their current circumstances had been far from voluntary. They'd both woken up inside the Hazel Medical Research Facility with no memory of who they were or how they'd gotten there, both victims of Gronoch, who had taken on the body of the company's CEO and lead researcher to conduct his experiments.

Gronoch had wanted to create an army of Silenced mortals like Alexander who could be easily controlled and serve as conduits for a god's power. He'd had the crazy desire to awaken his father, Salgumel, the God of Dreams and Sleep. Salgumel was said to have gone mad in his dreaming, the deep sleep that all the gods had fallen into when mankind abandoned them, and waking him up would certainly mean the end of the world.

Gronoch and other gods like him wanted the old world where they'd been worshipped and adored, and they were counting on Salgumel rising to make it happen. There would be war, naturally, as not all the gods would be happy about this insane plan, and that's where the conduit program came in.

The idea was to take gods they knew would not support the cause and turn them into mortal slaves to fight on their side in the war that was to come.

It was a plan riddled with multiple issues, countless complications, and a staggering body count. The process was pure agony, and few survived long enough to attempt the actual soul binding. Out of hundreds of Silenced victims, Alexander was the only successful conduit.

Do you ever wonder?

"What?" Alexander directed Rota's tentacles to grab a frozen pizza out of the freezer. He wasn't much on cooking, and he was very tired.

Why us?

"You mean, why did our bond work?"

Yes.

"No, I never think about it." Alexander turned on the oven, using a splash of magic to preheat it instantly. "I know you want there to be some special romantic reason, but I don't think there is one. I think it just… happened."

Rota's thoughts turned sad.

"What?"

I want there to be a reason for all of that suffering.

"Have you seen the world? People suffer every day for no reason." Alexander shoved the pizza in, and he patted his pockets, looking for his cigarettes. "We're not special."

You're special to me.

"You're delusional."

You're too young to be this cynical.

"Am I?" Alexander snorted, raising his hands to guide Rota's tentacle over to light his cigarette. "Well, I think you're too old to be this sappy."

Rota laughed.

Alexander grinned, and he leaned back against Rota's invisible body. He could feel him there beside him, firming up so he could get comfortable. This was the limit of the sustained physical contact they could have, and it felt like what Alexander imagined resting on a cloud would be like, cool and weirdly springy.

Maybe I am, Rota mused, *but I can't help it. I want there to be meaning for what happened. Not just to us, but to all those other people. The ones who didn't make it.*

"But there isn't." Alexander took a long drag off his cigarette. "Shit just happens. Gronoch was insane." He took a cautious probe at Rota's side of the bond to see what was wrong. "You know we're not responsible for that, right? It's not our fault."

Oh? It's not? Even though we literally hand-delivered most of them?

"If we didn't do it, Gronoch would have killed me," Alexander said firmly. "We were doing what we had to in order to survive. Then, now, and always, we do what we have to to stay together."

I wish….

Alexander touched Rota's side. "If you want there to be a meaning to all of it to somehow make it all better, I don't think there is one. I'm sorry it happened, but I'm not sorry I did it, and I would do it all over again to keep us safe."

Rota sighed.

"We found each other, right?" Alexander smiled. "In that awful place… you heard me. You came to me."

Yes.

"Now that means something." Alexander kept petting Rota, his fingers moving through the cool silky feeling of what should've been warm skin. "You were there when I was hurt and alone, when I was scared, when I was ready to check right the fuck out. You were the answer to my prayers even after I was too scared to pray because I didn't think anybody was listening. Even if our bond didn't work, I'm thankful for that night."

As am I.

"I know you feel bad because of what we did, because of what I did, but… I did it all because I love you."

And I love you. Rota seemed to smile, though he still felt sad. *Perhaps that's the only thing that matters in the end.*

"It's the only thing that matters to me." Alexander closed his eyes when Rota passed a tentacle over his hand. He tried to fill his side of the bond with the love he felt for Rota in hopes it would comfort him.

Sometimes I wonder which one of us is supposed to be the disenchanted immortal.

"Ha!" Alexander inhaled leisurely and blew out a long puff of smoke. "I happen to like you like this. Rota, God of Sap."

Hmmph. Alexander, Lord of Grump.

"I'm glad you are. Sweet, I mean. Really. Gods know one of us needs to be." Alexander flicked his ashes on the floor and vanished them away with magic. "I don't know why I'm like this…." *And I wonder if I was like this before.*

Grumpy?

"Angry."

However you are is exactly how I want you to be. I didn't mean to upset you. I keep… I can't stop looking back.

"I know." Alexander fidgeted. "You think about it a lot."

Yes. I'm sorry.

"Don't be." Alexander shrugged. "I'm just ready to move on. Gronoch is dead, thanks to Starkiller. The conduit program is over. There's nothing left to think about."

I suppose not.

Rota shifted behind him, and Alexander stood up so he could move away. Rota couldn't go very far, but Alexander could sense he wanted space. He wasn't sure what was bothering Rota so much, but he didn't pry any deeper into their bond.

Alexander left him alone for now, finished smoking, and focused on getting the pizza out of the oven. He ate once it had cooled down, cleaned up the mess, and headed to the bathroom.

He got undressed, ignoring his reflection in the mirror.

There wasn't much he wanted to see.

He already knew his once brown hair was white and raggedly shaved around the sides, his eyes were a murky red, and he was covered from head to toe in the binding symbols, circles with a single arrow running through them. Each one had been burned into his skin, and looking at them only reminded him of the pain.

Then there were the ones he couldn't see, the ones *inside* of him. It had taken hundreds of bindings to attach Rota, and Gronoch had run out of room on Alexander's skin, so he moved elsewhere, including his bones and even internal organs.

Aside from the reminder of the torture he'd suffered, he didn't like how he looked. He was deathly pale and thin, and he didn't think he was very attractive. He looked tired. He'd seen old pictures of what he looked like before the experiments, and he didn't even recognize himself the first time he saw them.

You're beautiful.

"Get out of my head," Alexander chided affectionately.

Sorry. Can't.

Alexander could feel Rota watching him, and he turned on the water for the tub with his tentacles.

You're the most beautiful thing I've ever seen, and one day I am going to make such love to you....

"Promises, promises." Alexander enjoyed the warmth the words gave him. He could feel that Rota was in a better mood now, and he made a show of bending over to check the water's temperature.

He may not have thought very much of himself, but he knew Rota did.

Oh, you cruel boy.

"Me?"

Yes, you. I'm going to remember this and every other time you've teased me.

Alexander was sure he would. He stepped into the tub and slid down into the water, taunting, "I'll be waiting."

I wanted to take you the day Starkiller let us use his body.

"Right there in front of everyone, huh?" Alexander's heart thumped a little faster, and Rota's desire was strong. It took his breath away, and he knew what was coming.

They had limited options for being intimate, but there was one in particular that was always successful. It was a tease in many aspects, but it was all they had.

Yes. Rota was close now. *I wouldn't have cared.*

"Tell me." Alexander closed his eyes. "Tell me what you would have done."

You want details, I imagine.

Hands sliding down his chest, Alexander nodded. "You know I do."

I would have laid you right out there on the floor, kissing you until neither one of us could breathe. I'd want to taste every inch of you, to memorize the very flavor of you, to worship your entire body... I would touch everywhere you were hurt and reclaim it as mine.

"Yes." Alexander shifted in the tub, and the heat between his legs grew. His cock was getting hard, but he didn't touch himself yet. He was imagining Rota touching him instead, touching all the binding marks....

A memory resurfaced of being held down, strapped to a metal table, and the burn of the first mark searing into his skin. The pain had been so great that he threw up, begged, pleaded—

Staunchly ignoring it, he said, "Go on. Keep going, please."

I know you'd be hard then. Just as you are now.

Alexander shivered as a ghostly tentacle teased his thigh, and he took himself in hand, stroking slowly. "Yeah... I'd want... I'd want you to...."

Tell me. Rota's voice was silky and low, as if he was whispering right in Alexander's ear.

"I want you to take me fast. I don't want to wait." Alexander stroked faster. His lips parted as his breath picked up, and he could feel the pressure inside of him winding up tight already. He spread his legs and pushed his other hand back behind his balls, pressing his fingers against his hole.

Alexander. Rota was panting. *Yes. I will. I will open you up, with my fingers, my mouth—*

"No. Your dick. Your tentacles, whatever, anything. I need you in me." Alexander groaned, the tips of his fingers pushing in dry. He hissed at the burn, but he didn't stop, jerking himself off and focusing his strokes around on the head of his dick. "I can't... oh gods...."

Whatever you want. I'll give it to you. I'll give you everything you want. Right there on the floor, I would have taken you—

"Yeah. Please, please, please. Fuck." Alexander kept pushing inside of himself, grunting from the stretch but too desperate to care. The pressure was amazing, and he was getting so close. His face was hot, his heart pounding, and he wanted to come.

All I want is to be inside of you. I want you more than anything. Rota's tentacles glided over Alexander's hips, cool and feathery.

It was such a tease, and Alexander should have asked him to stop. Trying to touch while they did this could be dangerous, but he told himself they wouldn't get too carried away.

It would be fine.

I want to feel you quiver around me, to hear your moans as we make love, to taste the seed you spill as I make you quake—

"Fuck me!" Alexander growled, his eyes flashing open to glare in Rota's direction. "I want you to fuck me! Down on the dirty damn floor, until my back, mmm, until my back is scuffed up and—"

Yes! My love, Alexander. I will. I will fuck you until you're aching and dripping with my seed. I will fuck you until you're weak from screaming in passion—

"Fuck yeah! Give it to me!" Alexander pushed his fingers deeper, holding them there and making himself cry out, his hand a blur on his cock. Rota's tentacles were writhing, hugging his hips and thighs with pressure beyond the usual faint sensation. It should have been concerning, but Alexander was too close to care.

He was right *there*, he could taste it, and his muscles twisted up, readying to melt in climax.

Yes, I will! I will give all I am! I will fuck you until you know nothing but screaming my name! Rota's tentacles tightened down, and the sudden force crushed Alexander's hip.

"Fuck! Rota!" Alexander yelped in pain, grabbing the sides of the tub and fighting back tears.

Alexander! No! I'm so sorry! I—

Alexander held up his hand, unable to speak. *Stop, stop, stop! Don't touch me! Just give me a fuckin' second!*

I love you... I'm so sorry... I didn't mean to....

Sensing Rota's retreat, Alexander summoned him back with a thought of his own: *I need you.* He focused on the bond, guiding Rota's magic through his fingers to heal his hip. It wasn't broken, but there would certainly be a terrible bruise if he didn't take care of it quickly.

Rota's guilt was washing through Alexander in waves, and he was clearly struggling to hold the emotion back.

Any sensual desire forgotten, Alexander's cock wilted, and he tried not to be angry. It could have been so much worse. He held his hand on his hip until the pain faded and he slumped down in the water. His heart was still thudding, and his balls were complaining from the abrupt denial.

Do you.... Do you want to try again? I can leave.

"No. No, you can't." Alexander knew Rota meant that he could distance himself to give him some privacy, but he didn't see the point. The mood was lost, and he was angry at himself for getting so caught up that he didn't tell Rota to back off.

I'm sorry.

"I know." Alexander put his hand back up on the side of the tub, thinking his next words since it was difficult to speak them. *I'm not mad at you. I'm mad at all of this. I want you more than anything, and I'm sick of trying. I'm sick of being hurt—*

I'm here. I love you. Rota hesitantly touched Alexander's fingers, a cool whisper of sensation. *Tomorrow we're going to see Ollie. He will read the book. We'll find the Fountain and reclaim what is rightfully mine.*

"And then we'll fuck?" Alexander attempted a smile.

Yes. Rota smiled. *As many times as you can possibly handle. Even on the floor, if you want.*

"Yeah. Definitely on the floor."

I love you.

"Love you too."

The ache in Alexander's heart lingered long after the frustration of not coming faded, and it was still hurting after he finished his bath and lay down to sleep.

Seven years was a long time to wait. It was a long time to yearn for something so close and yet so out of reach, but now it was right within their grasp. The book was the key to everything, and Alexander dared to hope he would be holding Rota in his arms soon.

He knew sex wasn't everything in a relationship, but being denied it was maddening. It wasn't as if they'd actually chosen to have a celibate romance. Their situation was out of their control, and Alexander longed for a physical connection. Alexander could have taken others to bed, Rota had even given him leave to, but Alexander had refused.

He didn't know if he'd ever been with anyone before he was taken by Gronoch. He couldn't remember, but as far as he was concerned, Rota was going to be his first and last.

Soon, Rota promised. *I will be.*

Alexander drifted off into a restless sleep with those words rattling around in his head. He didn't dream, thankfully, and was able to rest without interruption. When he woke up, he was out of bed and getting dressed before Rota even finished saying good morning.

It was time to go see Ollie.

Alexander grabbed the book and put it in the inner pocket of his trench coat. The pocket was enchanted, a spell of Alexander's own design, and it could have held a small car. He directed Rota to take them over to Ollie's apartment complex, popping up right in front of his door. He could sense powerful protection wards surrounding the frame, and he snorted, reaching out to break them so they could enter.

Knock!

"Why?"

It's the polite thing to do. We need his help. People don't like helping other people if they break into their homes.

"Starkiller helped us."

He is an exception. My point still stands.

"Fine!" Alexander rolled his eyes and banged on the door, thinking, *This is so dumb.*

I know you're impatient—

"I prefer eager."

—but we should try to make a good first impression, all right?

"Whatever. Fine. Good impression. All over it."

The door opened, and Alexander's heart stopped.

Standing on the other side was the most beautiful man he'd ever seen. Alexander said a silent thank-you to all the gods, because the man was shirtless, and his body was sculpted perfection. His skin was fair with smatterings of freckles across his face, chest, and shoulders. Alexander didn't know people looked like this outside of movies and TV.

There was a thick scar over his sternum that had a silver gleam to it, and his eyes were light, maybe hazel or green. His hair was a dark orange, currently arrayed in a haphazard curly mop that indicated he'd recently woken up. His nose was round, his lips full, and when he smiled—still sleepy and a bit crooked—Alexander blushed.

Attractive, is he?

Oh, for fuck's sake. Get out of my head. Ignoring Rota, Alexander said quickly, "Oleander Logue? I'm—"

Ollie happened to glance behind Alexander, and when he did, instant recognition and terror seized him. He screamed, his eyes rolled back, and he crumpled to the floor in a heap.

"Well, shit."

Oh dear.

"How's that for a first impression?"

CHAPTER 2.

AFTER BREAKING the wards, Alexander let himself into the apartment and shut the door behind him. He stared down at the unconscious Ollie and sighed.

"Well, this is off to a great start."

What do you think set him off?

"No idea." Alexander glanced around the apartment, wrinkling his nose.

It was a mess.

Every conceivable surface was packed with herbs and trinkets, and the wicker furniture had certainly seen better days. The windows were decorated with colorful wind chimes and Sagittarian totems, and it was impossible to escape the fermented scent of alcohol and stale cigarettes. Empty bottles and fast-food containers cluttered what little space wasn't taken up by the magical baubles, and there was a suspicious pile of crumpled tissues beside the couch.

"Charming." Alexander stepped over Ollie's body and took a seat in a high-back wicker chair.

Should we wake him up?

"Take a look around first. Those wards on the door? Those were a god's, don't you think?"

Yes.

"If he knows Starkiller, maybe Azaethoth put them there." Alexander glanced back, using Rota's magic to scan Ollie with a perception spell. There was something odd in Ollie's aura. "Huh. What is that?"

A spark of some kind? It does look a bit godly. Maybe he is the one who made the wards. Hmm… I'll be right back. Rota roamed through the apartment to explore.

"I'll be here." When Alexander felt Rota was far enough away, he peeked around the chair again to look at Ollie.

Still unconscious and sprawled out on his back.

Ollie's expression was peaceful, and Alexander got caught up watching his broad chest rise and fall.

Cheeks burning, he quickly turned back around. He was being ridiculous. It was probably leftover frustration from last night, and he tried as hard as he could to smother it out. He sensed Rota returning and asked, "Anything?"

Nothing. He is definitely a Sage… and perhaps a bit of a lush.

"No shit."

What now?

"Let's wake him up." Alexander sent Rota over to rouse Ollie, and he reached into his pocket for a cigarette.

Judging by the packed ashtray, Ollie wouldn't mind.

Not that it would have stopped Alexander.

He raised one of Rota's tentacles with his hand to light his cigarette, flinching when Ollie screamed.

Oh, he's awake!

"Fuck yeah, I'm awake!" Ollie shouted as he scrambled across the floor. "What the fucking fuck?"

Wait. Alexander bolted to his feet and stalked toward Ollie. *He can hear you?*

Apparently.

"And see you!" Ollie snapped. "You big weird fuckin' spikey god dude!"

"How?" Alexander held his cigarette between his teeth, and he reached for Ollie with Rota's tentacles, seeking to probe his body for answers. The perception spell hadn't revealed much, but perhaps if he looked deeper….

Other than Sloane, who had been touched by Great Azaethoth himself, and Gronoch, who had helped create the bond, no one else could see or hear Rota unless Rota revealed himself.

"Nope, nope, nope! Fuck you!" Ollie threw his arms up, and *something* came over him. It was a shield, glowing and bright, and it completely surrounded him in a bubble. "You keep all those squirmy bits away from me!"

Rota's tentacles could not break through it. That was unexpected. Alexander concentrated, using his fingers to focus Rota's magic and find a way to shatter it like he had done with the wards.

What is this magic? It's most curious.

"Who the fuck are you people?" Ollie demanded.

My name is Rota, and this is Alexander.

"Hi." Alexander forced a smile. He kept trying to break the shield, but he took one hand back to puff on his cigarette and flick the ashes.

"What do you want with me?" Ollie had squeezed his eyes closed, and the shield didn't budge. "I swear, if you're thinking about stabbing me, I am gonna be so mad!"

Alexander didn't understand what Ollie was talking about or why he couldn't break the shield. It reminded him of one Gronoch had used to imprison Azaethoth and their sister Galgareth.

But Ollie was mortal and only a weak water discipline from what Alexander could see.

This shield was definitely godly.

That should have been impossible.

"We need your help translating a book," Alexander replied shortly. There wasn't any reason to beat around the bush. "Starkiller referred us to you. We knocked, you screamed, and then you passed out."

"Starkiller?" Ollie peeked up at Alexander. "You know Sloane?"

"Yes."

He's a friend, Rota offered.

Barely, Alexander thought grumpily.

"Okay. Back up those tentacles, okay? Right now!" Ollie managed an indignant glare. "Or else."

"Or else what?" Alexander couldn't help but scoff, though he did withdraw Rota's tentacles to a respectful distance.

"I've got Sloane plus two gods on speed dial, and I will not hesitate to call them to come kick your little ass!" Ollie narrowed his eyes, staring at Rota. "How... how are you doing this? How come you're not all squished up in Alexander?"

I am only the soul of a god who was forced from my body. I do not possess my physical vessel at this time.

Ollie looked to Alexander, and the shield suddenly dropped. He was gawking now with a mix of horror and pity. "Those marks.... Oh fuck. That is o-fahfah-cially the craziest shit I've ever seen." He tilted his head. "Okay, no, not compared to the cult who wanted to sacrifice me or how you're actually supposed to put Pez in the little dispenser, but close."

Resisting the urge to probe him with Rota's magic, Alexander tried again, "Tell me how you're doing this."

"I have starsight."

Alexander flinched.

Oh, that just made things much more interesting.

Magic was classified in a modern system inspired by Lucian beliefs that divided abilities into the four elements and a fifth that encompassed and surpassed them all called divine. Sages referred to this special and rare magic as being touched by starlight.

Sloane was one such witch, and he had also been blessed by Great Azaethoth with a sword of starlight that made him into Starkiller, a mortal who could kill a god.

Gifts like starsight were another blessing from the gods and equally rare, and the abilities ranged from being able to talk to the dead to seeing the future.

What piqued Alexander's interest was the knowledge that such a person who had been blessed by one of the gods could serve as an additional host to Rota. It was how they'd been able to share their one and only kiss, when Sloane offered his body for Rota to take over.

Normally, Rota couldn't possess another body because of how he was bound to Alexander. But someone who had this rare blessing could supersede the limitation and share a soul as Sloane had done for them.

It had something to do with a loophole for the tentacle orgies the gods used to have with mortals, and suddenly all Alexander could think about was Rota taking Ollie's stunning body and—

"Uh, hello. Didn't Sloane tell you?" Ollie cleared his throat. "I mean, isn't that why you're here?"

"He said you were a translator." Alexander willed away his scandalous thoughts and glanced beside him, where he sensed Rota hovering. *I don't remember anything about starsight.*

Neither do I, Rota said. *I imagine this is the gift of seeing all that is hidden, the Eyes of Yeris.*

"Yeah, that thing." Ollie hugged himself. "Long story, but, uh, yeah, I got a big ol' case of it. I pretty much see everything."

And the shield?

"Well. Uh." Ollie fidgeted. "I didn't know any super strong protection spells, and I needed one."

So, what was hidden to you became seen?

"Yeah." Ollie kept his body facing Alexander and Rota as he stood, and he backed toward the couch. "It's not exactly the most predictable thing, but it usually pops up when I need something. I don't really know how to use it. I drink so much because I see way scary weird crap, but it's better than the drugs, and wow, I cannot stop talking right now." He sat abruptly. "Uh. So. You guys are a Silenced dude with the soul of a god bound to him?"

"Yes." Alexander blinked.

How fascinating! Rota sounded delighted. *Of all the gifts of starsight, the Eyes of Yeris is certainly the most rare. This is extraordinary.*

"Okay. Cool. Cool. That's cool." Ollie fumbled for a pack of cigarettes wedged in the cushions. "So, how about I read whatever it is you want me to read and you can leave?"

"Sounds great." Alexander sat back in the chair and pulled the book from his coat. He pushed some trash off the coffee table and set it down, then took a long drag from his cigarette. "That's it."

"Right. On it." Ollie tried to light up, but his hands were shaking.

Alexander sent one of Rota's tentacles over to light it for him, and he couldn't help but gawk again.

Yes, this was extremely important, but Ollie was nice to look at. More than nice—he was *gorgeous*. Alexander was fighting like hell to keep any and all sexual thoughts out of his head, and it was very difficult.

Especially since Ollie having starsight meant....

No, no, no, no. Alexander puffed away, hoping Ollie wasn't actively listening.

"Thanks." Ollie inhaled deep from his now lit cigarette and opened the book. He squinted, took another drag, and looked around on the floor.

"What?" Alexander asked.

"This works better if I'm not... sober." Ollie picked through the garbage to find a bottle of clear alcohol that had about a third left in it. He tipped it back and polished it right off.

Alexander was drawn to the bob of Ollie's throat and the flex of the muscles in his arm as he chugged, and he hated how red his face was getting.

It's okay, Rota soothed. *I'm thinking the same thing.*

Like with Starkiller?

Perhaps we could ask—

No, no, no, no!

Ollie gave no indication he heard anything, and he dropped the emptied bottle. "Okay! Here we go. Which part do you want read?"

"The whole thing," Alexander replied. "We have part of a translation key for Babbeth's tongue. Can't you just zip through this?"

"No." Ollie grimaced. "That's not how this works. A key isn't gonna help. First of all, I'm a terrible reader. Just because I know what it says doesn't mean I can read it quickly! A book this size could take me days!"

"Days?" Alexander gritted his teeth.

"More if there's a lot of big words!"

"I'm not leaving until that entire book is translated." Alexander incinerated the cigarette butt between his fingers. "We need every page. Do you understand?"

"Totally fine, little dude!" Ollie scowled. "But you're not gonna be here for every single second of it. I need time and some serious solitude to do this."

"Not happening. I'm not letting that book out of my sight."

"Then we are at a serious imposter." Ollie leaned back, blowing out a lazy cloud of smoke. He seemed more confident now, and he smirked. "If you want me to do this, then you're gonna have to play nice."

The fuck I am.

Calm down, Rota piped up. *We need him. Don't you see? It's fine. And wait, did he just say imposter? Did he mean "impasse"?*

I... I don't know.

"That's totally what I said!" Ollie protested.

Oh fuck. He's an idiot. Alexander tried to keep his expression blank. Ollie pointed a finger at him. "And you're short."

He can hear us, Rota reminded gently.

"Yup! He can totally hear you, and he wants you to leave so he can get trashed and translate your stupid giant book." Ollie took another long puff. "Remember! Two gods! Speed dial!"

"Two?" Alexander quirked his eyebrows. He was curious, though not especially impressed.

"Yeah!"

I assume one is certainly Azaethoth the Lesser. Who is the other?

"Wouldn't you like to know," Ollie huffed.

Yes. That is why I asked.

"Oh. Right. It's Gordoth the Untouched. Except now he's touched by my uncle, like, on the regular. And he's Azaethoth's uncle—"

"We know who Gordoth is," Alexander cut in. "I don't care if you know a hundred gods. We need the book translated. Now."

"Tough cookies." Ollie was at the end of his cigarette and reached for another, then lit it with the old one. He belched loudly and coughed. "Those are my terms, and I don't make exceptions for gods or cute dudes, okay?"

Did he just call you cute—

"If you don't want to cooperate, I am more than capable of forcing you!" Alexander snapped, breezing right by the compliment. "I don't want to hurt you, but I will if I have to—"

Okay, now hold on, Rota pleaded. *Perhaps we should allow him time with the book as he's asked. We've already waited this long, haven't we?*

"And you want to trust him with the only copy of the one book that can help us?" Alexander hissed. "You're both idiots, then!"

"Hey, that's not nice." Ollie frowned. "He's just trying to de-escalator the situation."

"Idiots!"

Everyone take a moment to calm down—

"No!" Alexander stood up so quickly he almost knocked the chair over. "I'm tired of waiting. We searched the entire world for *months* tracking that damn thing down." He glared at Ollie. "You have no idea what we've been through or what I am willing to do to unlock the secrets that book holds. Now sit down, have yourself another fuckin' drink, and *start reading.*"

Ollie blinked.

"Well?" Alexander growled.

"Is he always this grumpy?" Ollie asked Rota.

No, not always. He's really quite lovely once you get to know him. Great sense of humor.

"Is he hungry? Is this like a hangry thing?"

No, no. He's, mm, a bit impatient, I'm afraid.

Alexander wanted to scream.

Before he could tear into them for being so ridiculous, there was a shift in the air around them, and Alexander turned to see someone standing in front of the door.

It was a young man, definitely not human, definitely *something else.*

He was wearing some kind of glamour magic to alter his appearance, but Alexander couldn't quite make out what it was hiding. All he saw was a man with long dark hair and a nasty sneer who did not look the least bit friendly.

Rota, he thought urgently, summoning a swarm of ghostly tentacles to shield himself.

"Oh, fuck, fuck, fuck, fuck!" Ollie jumped up on the couch, clearly terrified. "The wards! You broke the wards—"

The man leaped forward, and everything slowed down.

He was altering time itself, bringing it to a stagnant crawl, and he was headed right for Ollie. Alexander tried to move, but it was like being trapped underwater, and he couldn't get his limbs to cooperate. He could sense the time manipulation was limited to himself and Ollie, not the entire room, and he knew he could break it.

Ollie was frozen as the man came at him, his expression stuck in an almost comical mask of terror.

Rota! Now! Alexander flexed the tip of one finger, and it was all he needed to unleash a rush of Rota's full power.

I've got him! Rota surged forward, his tentacles breaking through the bubble of time and snatching Ollie out of harm's way while whipping the man back against the wall.

"Oof!" The man grunted as he rolled to the floor, coughing up a splatter of blood and staring in shock at Alexander. "How the hell did you do that?"

Alexander pushed Ollie squarely behind him and stalked toward the man. He'd heard legends of time magic before, but he'd never seen it done. It wasn't very hard to shrug off, which meant this man was either a novice, or the magic wasn't as powerful as the stories had said. "Better question is what I am going to do to you now that your little trick failed."

He teleported in here. Whoever he is, he must have been waiting for a chance to get through the wards. A chance we provided. Rota sounded upset. *He's not here for us. He was going after Ollie!*

"I'm not here for you!" the man protested, confirming Rota's thoughts. "I need Ollie to come with me for a little chat! That's all!"

"Nope!" Ollie shook his head vehemently. "Absolutely not! Negative! Nope to the nope!"

"Sorry, Ollie is a little busy at the moment," Alexander drawled. "Leave."

"If he doesn't come with me, it's gonna be a whole lot worse," the man warned.

"Let me be very clear." Alexander continued to advance. "Either leave now or leave in pieces."

The man threw up his hands as if to cast again.

Alexander sent Rota's tentacles out, curling around the man's neck and chest and squeezing.

"Wh-what?" the man gurgled as he squirmed against Rota's grip. His magic was fizzling out, and he growled, still trying to escape.

Alexander focused on the man's neck, applying enough pressure with Rota's tentacles to block his airway, and waited for his face to change colors before he spoke again. "You will leave now and tell whoever sent you that Oleander Logue is not currently available for… whatever it is you're doing."

"Ugh… ughrl…."

"I'm sorry, what was that?" Alexander smirked. "Is that you saying, yes, I understand?"

"Gurgh…." The man attempted what may have been a nod.

"Good." Alexander released him.

Wheezing and rubbing his neck, the man hissed, "He's… gonna come… you're so fucked."

Who?

"Who?" Alexander asked out loud for Rota.

"Fuck… you!" The man gave Alexander a defiant middle finger before teleporting away in a blink.

Should we follow him? I can track him if we go now.

"No." Alexander frowned. "We should probably put up new wards, though. Something to keep—"

Big, strong arms wrapped around Alexander from behind and squeezed hard.

It was Ollie, hugging him.

"Thank you!" Ollie gushed. "That was so cool! You totally just kicked Nathaniel's ass!"

Alexander swallowed a squeak and forgot how to work all of his muscles. Ollie was so warm, and he smelled like alcohol, cigarettes, and patchouli oil with a hint of vanilla.

"Seriously, that was amazing!" Ollie turned Alexander so he could beam down at him, still hugging him close. "I mean, okay, it's kinda your fault he got in here, but thank you." He smiled wider. "Whoa. Your eyeballs are turning all pink."

Alexander was torn between pushing Ollie away and melting into his arms. The simple affection was making his knees weak, having for so long only experienced physical touch that was designed to hurt. His brain refused to cooperate, and all he could do was stutter, "Y-yeah, they do that."

Who was that man, Ollie?

Alexander slipped away from Ollie, mourning the loss of contact the second he did. He scrambled to get another cigarette. "Yeah, and *what* was he? I've never seen magic like that before."

"His name is Nathaniel Ware." Ollie fidgeted and dipped back into the kitchen, still talking. "He is so not fuckin' human. He's, like, a troll dude with tusks and a long tail."

An Absola? Rota sounded intrigued. *Here on Aeon?*

The gods had created many monstrous creatures before mortals, including a troll-like race of beings called the Absola. They, along with the other so-called everlasting people, were said to have gone with the gods into the dreaming, and neither Alexander nor Rota had heard of any living in this world for thousands of years.

"Yeah, but not, like, all the way?" Ollie mused. "He's like a diet Absola."

"But the Absola don't control time or space," Alexander pointed out. "The Faedra do."

"Whatever! Look, he's a freaky monster guy, and he works for Sullivan Stoker. Do you know who that is?"

"No." Alexander grabbed the book to put back in his pocket and followed Ollie. Unsurprisingly, the kitchen was as much of a disaster as the rest of the apartment.

Ollie was pouring red wine into two glasses as he explained, "He's a crime boss. Like, this big drug lord. And okay, so I may have had a tiny drug problem before. When I first got the eyeballs of Yeris, I had trouble dealing with it." He thrust a glass at Alexander.

"No thanks."

Ollie poured it into his glass and sipped off the excess. "I made okay money translating, but it wasn't enough to keep up with my habit, so I started taking product on credit. Like, so much. And I kinda owe him a lot of money, and he's very unhappy with me. I've been trying to make payments, and he's been chill 'cause my uncle is a cop, but—"

"He's tired of waiting and he's sending goons after you?" Alexander finished.

"Yeah. Damn. You should be a detective."

"How about this?" Alexander crossed his arms. "I'll keep the criminal scum from hounding you in exchange for you translating the book?"

"I, I guess that could work." Ollie frowned. "Will you.... Will you stay here? I need some time to figure out how to deal with Stoker, and, and I'll find a way to make the translating work, okay?"

"Okay. I'll put new wards up, and if anyone is stupid enough to come back, I'll—"

"Where are you gonna sleep?"

"What?"

Ollie scratched his head. "My bed is kinda small, but I guess we could share—"

"Your couch is fine." Alexander blushed miserably. He could not handle the mere thought of being anywhere near a bed with Ollie right now. He had to be going insane. That's all it was. "Once it's cleaned up, of course."

You should take better care of your home, Ollie. It's quite a mess.

"I know." Ollie sighed. "It's so damn bad. I just never have the energy, and I've been really depressed. Like, forever depressed. I died a little, my ex is getting married... it's been a whole thing."

Alexander had the inexplicable desire to reach out for Ollie. It was obvious he was upset, and Alexander wanted to feel his arms around him again. He stayed where he was, taking a step back for good measure, as if the distance would quell the urge.

So, you're single?

"Rota!" Alexander barked, angrily chanting inside his head, *Shut up, shut up, shut up!*

"Yeah. Duh." Ollie snorted and slurped more of his wine. He swayed and leaned against the counter, eyeing where Rota was hovering behind Alexander. He grinned. "Okay, wait. Are you hitting on me?"

I believe we are, yes. We're not very good at it, but we're making an effort.

"No, we're not!" Alexander gritted his teeth. "Hey! You look good and drunk. Book. Now."

Say please.

"Please," Alexander hissed.

"Okay, okay, sure thing." Ollie was still grinning. "You know, if you were hitting on me, I would have to tell you—"

A portal opened up and a hand slid through, snatching Ollie so fast that he dropped his wine. The glass hit the ground, shattering as the portal closed.

Just like that, Ollie was gone.

CHAPTER 3.

"SHIT!" ALEXANDER quickly reached into the air where the portal closed, feeling around with Rota's tentacles.

Oh no! I'm so sorry! We should have put up the wards—

"You think?" Alexander snarled. "You were too busy trying to flirt with him!"

But you're very attracted to him, and he would be a suitable vessel!

"Don't you think I already know that? You're making this weird!" Alexander tried to focus on finding the trail of the portal. It was like having a hair stuck on his tongue, slippery and just out of reach.

I believe he would be receptive to a proposition. He said you were "cute."

"Oh sure! Yeah! That would go great! Let me borrow your body for a minute to have sex with my boyfriend for the first time! Not weird at all!"

Certainly we would request more than a minute?

"Rota!" Alexander snapped. "Help me focus!"

I'm sorry!

Alexander pointed his finger, twirling it in the air to guide the end of Rota's tentacle. He kept spinning in a circle, finger and tentacle together, sensing the trail and making the circle smaller and smaller until—there!

He grabbed the trail and pulled, popping through the path of the portal.

They were now standing in an old theater. No, it used to be a theater, but it had been turned into a strip club. The stage had a catwalk with a pole, and there was a bar with neons. Large carved murals of sea creatures and tentacles were posed above the stage, but they were faded and cracked.

The place looked like it had been through hell.

Standing before them with a very curious expression was a man with graying hair and sharp blue eyes. He was wearing a black suit, was irritatingly handsome, and he reeked of old magic, though Alexander couldn't immediately discern *what* he was.

He doubted he was human.

Nathaniel, the man from before, was cowering behind him. "That's him! That's the guy!"

"This is the one who gave you so much trouble?" The gray-haired man did not appear impressed.

No sign of Ollie, but I sense another portal.

Find it, Alexander directed inside his head. He focused on the two men. "You took something of mine, and I want it back. Now."

"My apologies." The gray-haired man tipped his head. "I'm Sullivan Stoker. That 'something' owes me a lot of money, and he's been very difficult to get in contact with." He stared Alexander down, his eyes narrowing.

Alexander could feel the press of a powerful perception spell. He didn't care that Stoker was trying to figure out what he was or that he was able to cast without speaking or using his hands. It vastly decreased the chances that Stoker was human, but Alexander wasn't worried.

"You...." Stoker seemed curious. "Are very interesting."

"What I am is pissed off," Alexander said. "Return Ollie right now."

"Oh? And if I don't?"

Alexander remained motionless, using his thoughts to send out a wave of magic that rattled the entire building and cracked the bar down the middle. Glasses fell off the shelves and shattered, the stage groaned as the wood warped, and a fresh cloud of dust rained down from the shifting rafters.

He enjoyed seeing Stoker flinch in surprise.

He assumed it didn't happen often.

Nathaniel scrambled to duck back behind Stoker, as if he could hide from all the commotion.

I already found the portal, but it doesn't make any sense. The trail leads here.

What? Alexander used his thoughts to reply, but he kept his gaze on Stoker.

The portal leads right here to this building. It doesn't seem to lead into another world, but it does.

I don't understand.

Watch out, Rota warned. *Stoker is casting something.*

"Well, that was adorable." Stoker's eyes flickered. "My turn."

Rota. Alexander tensed.

With Alexander's psychic guidance, Rota brought his tentacles up in a dense shield. *I've got you, my love. I've got—*

The magic that hit Rota's tentacles was focused, controlled, and very powerful. It blew back Alexander's hair and whipped his coat around, and he had to take a step back to steady himself as he rode out the blast. Yes, it was strong, but this couldn't be everything. He raised his arm to block his eyes and thought urgently, *Something's wrong!*

What?

This doesn't feel right. He's obviously stronger than this. If he wanted to show off—

Portal, portal, portal! Rota screamed in alarm.

Alexander became aware Stoker had magically appeared right behind him, and he'd cast a portal, no doubt about to drag Alexander right through it. *Fields! We're taking him to the fields!*

Got it!

Just as Stoker grabbed Alexander's shoulder, Alexander whipped several of Rota's tentacles around his wrist and pulled him forward. He opened a portal of his own in the floor, letting himself and Stoker fall forward right into it.

Rota released Stoker and wrapped himself all around Alexander to protect him and slow his fall as they dropped to the ground of the new world. Because Rota was invisible, it appeared as if Alexander was simply floating down and landing gracefully on his feet.

The fields was what they called one of the worlds they'd discovered several years ago when they first learned how to portal together. Pocket dimensions like this one existed in between the realm of earth, Aeon, the home of the gods, Zebulon, and the bridge that connected them, Xenon. Most had been created by the gods as sacred places of worship, though it was unclear what they would have done here, as it was nothing but a giant field of dead grass.

Hence the very creative nickname.

Stoker had managed to land safely, and he was standing now and adjusting his jacket. "Well, you continue to be very interesting, Mr....?"

"Where is Ollie?" Alexander demanded.

"Back on that again, are we?"

Alexander advanced quickly, holding out his hands and channeling Rota's tentacles around his wrists to power up a potent charge of magic. "Last chance."

"How is someone Silenced using magic?" Stoker mused. "Unless... ah. I do know who you are. You're L-X-I-X. Gronoch's little toy, aren't you?"

How does he know that?

Alexander didn't reply to either of them, letting his fury boil over from hearing that horrible name—no, not even a name! It was an identifying label for an experiment, not a name for a human being!—fuel his spell. He threw his hands back, cracking Rota's powerful tentacles like whips at Stoker.

Stoker was shielded, something bright and beautiful, but it cracked beneath Alexander's assault. "Ah, sore spot, huh?"

Alexander refocused his efforts, summoning another wave of destructive magic and swinging it at Stoker's shield.

Calm down, Rota soothed. *If you're not careful, you might hurt him.*

That's the fuckin' idea! Alexander continued to wale on Stoker's shield, and he sent Rota around behind Stoker to explore for additional weaknesses. Even as the shield cracked, it held, and that only pissed Alexander off more.

"You are truly astonishing!" Stoker was clearly struggling to keep up his spell, his teeth gritted and his face flushed, but he seemed excited.

"Give me Ollie. Now!" Alexander roared, twisting his fingers to channel more of Rota's power and finally shatter the shield. He swung his arm, blasting a magic missile right at Stoker's exposed chest.

It sent Stoker flying backward, skidding through the grass and fighting to get back up.

Alexander hit him again, letting his hands drop to his sides as he strolled toward him. He allowed himself to feel a little smug. Whatever Stoker was, he was still a mortal and clearly no match for Alexander and Rota's combined strength.

A few more little slaps and they could force him to tell them where Ollie was and get out of here.

Stoker wiped a small smudge of blood from his lip, frowning at it in dismay. His wicked eyes flicked up to meet Alexander's, and he smiled. "You're *precious*."

Wait. He's casting again, Rota cautioned.

He's probably human. Who cares?

He's human, yes, but—

A snap of Stoker's fingers summoned a brilliant wave of raging fire, hundreds of feet tall, that crashed over Alexander's head.

Alexander dropped to his knees, holding out his hands to command Rota's magic to protect him, and he gasped at the heat and smoke clogging up his nose and mouth. It was hard to breathe, and the flames were licking through Rota's shield, burning his hair and clothes. He could feel Rota's magic struggling to fend off the magical blaze, and he'd never seen a fire spell like this before.

He didn't know what Stoker was, not exactly, but he was mortal.

Maybe.

The fire warped into a tornado, now spinning violently around him, and Alexander was getting aggravated. He couldn't move, he couldn't breathe, and the swirling flames were relentless. He kept the bulk of Rota's power in place, but he sent out a single tentacle to find Stoker and sink right into his chest, seizing his heart.

Such a feat required Rota's flesh to remain ghostly to slip deep inside but also keeping the tip solid to make his threat absolutely clear.

Immediately, the fire dissipated, and Alexander gasped for air as the smoke cleared from around him.

Are you all right? Oh, my love.

I'm fine, Alexander promised even as he wheezed. His lungs were burning miserably, and his throat was scratchy from all the smoke. *Next time, we'll just kill him.*

"Well, you continue to be full of surprises," Stoker drawled. His hands were raised in surrender, and he was standing perfectly still. "This… is a very neat trick."

Alexander stood and dusted himself off, glaring at Stoker. "Now. Give me Ollie—"

"Yes, yes, I know. Or else lots of violence and pain. What if I wanted to offer you a deal, LXIX?"

"My name is Alexander, asshole. And you're not in any position to make deals."

"Oh, I don't know about that." Stoker smirked.

Alexander…. Rota gasped.

Alexander didn't immediately understand what was wrong until he felt the squeeze of invisible fingers inside his own chest around his heart. Somehow Stoker had reached in just as Alexander had, and they were now locked in an awful stalemate with their hearts literally in each other's hands.

Well, hand and tentacle, anyway.

"I'm a very fast learner." Stoker winked. "Now, do you want to hear the terms of my deal or not?"

What are the chances of survival if I decide I want to crush his heart like a grape right now? Alexander asked inside his head.

Not very good if he crushes yours at the same time. My love, perhaps we should hear him out. Let us yield and see what he has to say.

Okay. And then I will fuckin' crush it.

Absolutely.

"Fine," Alexander said out loud, keeping his grip around Stoker's heart secure. "What do you want?"

"I need some assistance in investigating a series of crimes," Stoker replied. "Off the record."

"I know a great private investigator. Call him."

"Oh no. I need someone who isn't human."

"I am human, you dick."

"Having the soul of a living god bound to you firmly qualifies you as 'other.'"

"Is that what you are?" Rota asked out loud, his voice a low rumble.

"Oh, hello there." Stoker raised his brows. "You must be the god, yes?"

"Yes."

"May I know your name?"

"Rota."

Stoker's brows arched again. There was no god named Rota, which he obviously knew. Instead of questioning it, he said, "I'm actually not so different from you two. Part mortal—"

"Great, awesome." Alexander did not care. "Now where is Ollie?"

"Does that mean you're accepting my deal?"

"What do you want us to do?" Rota asked. "I'm still curious why you think we qualify as being the best ones to help you."

"Bring me the person responsible for these crimes and I will forgive Ollie's debt. Then he's all yours. How's that?"

"No. Give me Ollie now and I'll return him after he's done what we need—"

Alexander! Rota growled. *You don't mean that.*

Alexander tried to ignore Rota, saying again, "I will return him to you after he's done what we need him to—"

No! Rota interrupted again. *You wouldn't dare! Ollie clearly needs our help.*

"—and then you can do whatever you want to with him!" Alexander raised his voice to hear himself over Rota yacking away in his head.

I cannot believe you. You'd leave him to this man's mercy?

Not our problem, Alexander snapped back with his thoughts. *We need the damn book translated, okay?*

"My apologies if I don't believe you," Stoker drawled. "There would be nothing stopping you from taking him and disappearing. I have Ollie right where I want him. I have no reason to give him up."

Alexander gritted his teeth and resisted the urge to tighten the hold on Stoker's heart. "Okay, fine! If I agree, then what?"

"Then I present you with the evidence of the crimes that have been committed. I will expect results. Quickly."

"And Ollie?"

"I'll make sure you have access to him."

"Full access."

"At your leisure, you will be able to come and go where I am holding him." Stoker narrowed his eyes. "But he will not leave. And I will be expecting results, as I said. If you do not deliver any, I will end your visitation."

I think it is a fair deal, though I do not trust Stoker. It is most unusual he hasn't reported whatever these crimes are to the proper authorities.

More than unusual, Alexander agreed. *It's probably illegal. He's some sort of drug dealer, right? He probably can't call the cops without risking his business. So. Fuck. What do we do?*

I think we should help.

Ugh. Of course you do.

"I take it you're discussing this with your, hmm, partner?" Stoker asked.

Stoker couldn't hear Alexander or Rota when they spoke psychically, so it appeared as if Alexander was standing there silently.

"Yeah. One second." Alexander switched back to his thoughts. *We need that book translated. If Stoker is gonna keep Ollie hostage from us, I don't know what else to do. This is bullshit. We had him, we had him right there—*

I'm sorry. It is my fault the wards were not repaired in a timely manner. I was very distracted.

Oh, right, because you were more worried about getting us laid.

I was trying to help!

"We'll do it," Alexander said at last, biting back his frustration. He withdrew Rota's tentacle from Stoker's chest, and he breathed more easily when he felt Stoker's grip recede. "All right?"

"Very good." Stoker nodded. "Now, if you'll come with me—"

"Take us to Ollie first," Rota commanded. "We want to see that he is unharmed before we do anything."

Alexander rolled his eyes.

"As you wish." Stoker snapped his fingers and transported them all back to the club.

Wait, no, it was the club, but it was different.

It was fully restored, from the intricate murals above to the lush carpet under their feet. Gone was the crusty bar and catwalk, replaced by couches, chairs, and the stage was full of tall bookshelves. There was a fluffy cat lounging in a nearby chaise, which was hardly the weirdest thing here, but was impossible not to notice with it being a brilliant shade of neon green. There were several patrons milling about, but none of them seemed too interested in Stoker and Alexander magically appearing.

And the patrons....

None of them were human.

Some had long tails or colorful skin, a few had claws and sharp teeth, and there were ones with tentacles and slithering bodies and wings. They were all varying degrees of mortal and beast combined, and it took Alexander several seconds for it to register what he was looking at.

They were variations of the everlasting people, the monstrous races created by the gods before mankind. The Absola, like Nathaniel, were trolls with big tusks and long tails; the Faedra were behemoths with little wings; the Vulgora were giant aquatic worms.

On and on, Alexander saw them all in bits and pieces of the people here.

They're the everlasting races. Rota was amazed. *This is incredible.*

"Welcome to the Hidden World, Alexander and Rota," Stoker said.

"What is this place?" Alexander asked firmly. "How are you doing this?"

"It's an altered plane of existence I've created to keep them safe," Stoker replied. "They're all descendants of the everlasting people who stayed on Aeon after the gods went into the dreaming. Some bloodlines can go generations without ever knowing their lineage...."

"Until one day a baby pops out with a tail?"

"Exactly so." Stoker crossed his arms. "They needed a place to live where they would be safe from harm, far away from mortals, where they can be themselves without having to hide beneath glamour magic. I provide that for them."

"For a price, I imagine." Alexander scoffed.

"It takes a lot of magic to maintain this and make sure it stays hidden," Stoker said casually. "When I first started, it was only the theater. But as we grew and more people found their way here, we had to expand. Now it's almost the whole—"

"Where's Ollie?"

"Right to business, hmm?" Stoker eyed Alexander. "Brisk little thing, aren't you?"

"I don't care about you or your little hideaway world or any of the people here." Alexander scowled. "You can save the tour for someone who gives a fuck."

Alexander, you're being very rude, Rota scolded. *You don't think this is the tiniest bit fascinating? All of this tucked away right under our noses, and we had no idea.*

Alexander ignored Rota. "Ollie. Now."

Brat.

"Very well." Stoker shrugged.

The theater vanished, and they were now standing in a small hotel room. From the feel of the magic around them, Alexander surmised they were still inside the Hidden World.

Ollie was curled up in bed, and he lifted his head, gasping when he saw Alexander.

Ollie! Rota greeted. *You're all right!*

"Hey, guys!" Ollie got up and then bolted forward to snatch Alexander up in a bone-crushing hug. "I can't believe you're here!"

Alexander grunted, but he managed to hug Ollie back this time, his heart pounding away. "Uh. Hi."

It was then Alexander knew he wouldn't have left Ollie with Stoker, not really, and he wasn't sure what to do with that. Even thinking about it now made him feel guilty, and he awkwardly patted Ollie's very bare, very muscular back.

"You came to rescue me!" Ollie was beaming. "That's so very cool of you."

We were worried about you, Rota said. *Have they been treating you well?*

"Yeah, no, I'm okay." Ollie avoided looking at Stoker. "Just a little freaked out. The last time I got kidnapped, I died? So the bar has been set real low."

Check around the room, Alexander silently commanded Rota. *There's a lot of magic here. Probably wards. Find them.*

Why? Rota seemed to be frowning.

Just do it.

"You died?" Alexander finally caught back up to what Ollie was saying.

"Only a little! My uncle saved me." Ollie was still hugging Alexander. "I'm really happy you're here. Thank you." He sniffed. "Why do you smell burnt?"

"Don't ask."

"As touching as this is, Alexander has some work to do," Stoker spoke up.

"Work?" Ollie frowned.

"He's helping me with a private business matter," Stoker explained.

"No," Ollie said. "Look, you don't need to get them mixed up in any of this." He squeezed Alexander's shoulders. "Please, don't do this—"

"We need you to translate that book," Alexander said harshly.

Ollie flinched, clearly hurt.

That alien feeling of guilt rolled back through Alexander's gut, and he tried again, "Big book, right? Might take you days to read? You can't do that if you're stuck in here."

Ollie's expression softened, and he was smiling again. "Yeah, sure. Right."

We won't leave you here. We promise, Rota assured him.

Did you find the wards? Alexander asked quickly.

Yes. They're quite innovative—

Stoker cleared his throat.

Shit. Alexander offered a strained smile. "We'll talk soon, okay? Be back as soon as we can."

Okay, don't get mad at me. It was Ollie's voice inside Alexander's head now.

"What?" Alexander was shocked at hearing Ollie speak like that.

So, my starsight did a thing, and I have an idea. Ollie drew Alexander in close, tilting his head downward. His eyes were hooded, and his lips had parted in a very inviting pout.

Alexander didn't understand what was happening until Ollie's lips pressed against his. He jerked, his hands tightening into fists against Ollie's chest. *What are you doing?*

Stoker isn't stupid, Ollie thought back quickly. *He's gonna know you guys are sitting here talking inside your heads, okay? We can't just stand here staring at each other.*

Oh... right... I.... Alexander awkwardly kissed back, his heart up in his throat. He forgot what they were supposed to be talking about, and Ollie's hands on his waist felt really, really good.

Stoker sighed, but he was polite enough to turn away.

The wards, Rota said. *They're like nothing I've seen. Stoker or another very talented witch must have made them. They effectively block all teleportation and portal spells. Stoker must have a key of some kind to pass through, perhaps a phrase or an object.*

So there's no way to get me out of here? Ollie's kisses were soft, gentle, and he seemed confident taking the lead. He was good at this kissing thing, and wow, there weren't any signs of slowing down yet.

Alexander's brain still hadn't come back online, and his hands were trembling as they finally unclenched to slide up Ollie's broad chest. This was only his second kiss, and it wasn't Rota. He should have been more concerned about that, but all he could focus on was the sweet taste of Ollie's lips and the strength in his arms as he pulled him close.

I didn't say that. We will just need more time to examine them. They can be broken. Rota sounded very smug. *How did you figure out how to talk to us?*

It was hidden to me, and I needed it. Ollie tilted his head the other way, reconnecting his lips to Alexander's with another sweet kiss. His tongue darted forward, and he groaned. *I'm so very super sorry. I couldn't think of anything else to do.*

Tongue! That's tongue. Alexander gasped.

Oh! I'm sorry.

It's okay. It's totally okay. I... I....

You couldn't perhaps find a way to break those wards, could you? Rota pressed.

No. I'm sorry. Ollie sighed quietly. *I'm telling you it doesn't work that way. It just, well, it just happens. It kinda has a mind of its own.*

Stoker cleared his throat again, louder this time.

"Right." Alexander pushed away. His face was bright red, and he suddenly couldn't catch his breath. *We need to go. Right now.*

Please don't be mad, Ollie thought urgently.

It's all right, Rota soothed. *We'll be back as soon as we can.*

Stoker must have been tired of waiting because he transported them away without another word. The last thing Alexander saw was Ollie's crooked little smile and his lips, still pink and slick from kissing.

Alexander barely had time to process what had just happened before he was caught up, looking over their new surroundings with a grimace.

They were standing in a morgue, surrounded by bodies hidden beneath white sheets.

"Now." Stoker strolled over to the closest table, whipped back the sheet, and revealed the mutilated corpse under it. "What I need you to do, Alexander, is to catch a murderer."

CHAPTER 4.

ALEXANDER CONTINUED to grimace. "Oh? That's all?"

Are you okay? Rota asked. *Are you upset about the kiss?*

I'm fine, Alexander lied. He didn't want to think about kissing Ollie while he was surrounded by corpses.

There were five bodies, and the one Stoker was showing them was not human. Judging by the broken tusks and greenish skin, Alexander assumed this person was the descendant of an Absola like Nathaniel was.

"I believe the everlasting people are being hunted." Stoker flicked the sheet back with a flourish of his hand.

"Here?" Alexander asked as he approached and then impatiently pulled the sheet off again so he could look.

Stoker quirked a brow, but he continued, "No. This was Eric Grimes. He was killed a few blocks from a bar I own, Dead to Rites. They left him in an alley." He gestured to the next body. "Lucy Myers. We found her two weeks later in a dumpster behind a local restaurant, the Hot Pot. Then there was Brady Lincoln. Killed in his car outside of a grocery store a week after that. Baxter Yeun was also murdered in his car, in the parking lot of the Crosby-Ayers Funeral Home after Brady's wake. Lacie Briggs, car, parking lot of a gas station a few days later."

"The kills escalated," Rota observed out loud. "Your killer is getting more bold."

"Or sloppy." Alexander walked over to the next body and lifted the sheet.

This one was missing most of its face, and its hands were severed, its skin glittering with scales.

"Eric was an Absola. Lucy and Brady were both Vulgora," Stoker continued to explain as Alexander looked at the rest of the bodies. "Baxter was a Deverach, one of the tentacled goblins. Lacie was an Eldress. She could almost pass for human."

Alexander noted the two holes in the top of her head, asking, "Horns?"

"Yes."

"All of them were everlasting, and whatever made them unique was removed?"

"Yes."

"This is why you didn't call the cops?"

"Exactly so. It's critical to their survival that no one knows they exist. Even the Sages think they all fled to Xenon or went into the dreaming with the gods. An autopsy on such a person would be difficult to explain."

"How were they disguising themselves?"

"Glamour, either charms or incantations." Stoker followed behind Alexander and fixed the sheets again. "Only a very powerful witch would have been able to see through them."

"How were you able to get to them before the police?" Rota asked.

"Watchman spells," Stoker explained. "My version is very advanced and allows me to track where all of my people are at the same time. Additionally, it lets me know if they're hurt or—"

"Dead?" Alexander cut in.

"Yes. Then I can teleport directly to their location."

"And you never saw anything? Nobody sneaking around?"

"If I had, why would I be asking you to help?" Stoker raised his brows. "I never saw anyone. No prints except ones belonging to the victims. No magical residue or physical evidence that would point to a suspect."

He's wrong, Rota said suddenly.

Alexander could sense Rota hovering around the bodies. *What is it?*

Two of the bodies have what looks like some kind of incense.

Incense?

Move your hand over here. Rota gently nudged Alexander over to one of the tables. *Don't let him see.*

"Why do you need us?" Alexander asked. "You could do this investigation yourself."

"I've encountered a specific problem," Stoker replied. "The staff at Dead to Rites. I've only recently taken ownership of the property, and they have not been exactly cooperative. Nathaniel, the Absola you met, was eager enough to work for me, but the others? Not so much."

"And you think they have something to do with the murders?"

Rota's ghostly tentacle slid over Alexander's hand, and Alexander leaned on the edge of the table, slowly working his fingers under the sheet.

"The first body was very close to the bar, and all the other victims were patrons." Stoker paused. "Ah, except Mr. Yeun. He wasn't much of a drinker. He was friends with Brady, however, who was a regular."

"So, you want me to what?" Alexander kept sliding his hand down. "Go to a bar and knock some heads around?"

"No. I want you and your little godly companion to talk to them. I want you to figure out what I've missed." Stoker shrugged. "Do well and I will allow you all the time you want with your little boyfriend."

Alexander almost started to ask who Stoker was talking about until Rota gave him another nudge. "Right. My boyfriend." *Who would be great to have down here to look at these bodies.*

We can't let Stoker know about Ollie's ability. If he knows, he may not ever let him go. Now, move your hand here. Rota pushed Alexander's hand again.

Alexander tried not to make a face when he felt cold fingers touching his own.

"That's who he is, isn't he?" Stoker tilted his head. "I imagine his companionship is what you needed him so desperately for?"

"Yes, and that's why he's coming with me," Alexander said quickly. *What?*

"What?" Stoker said at the same time.

"You heard me," Alexander said firmly. *Shit, shit, shit.*

Why did you say that? Rota hissed.

I don't know! Just go with—

"Why would I do that when I have him exactly where I want him?" Stoker drawled, overlapping Alexander's thoughts.

"Because I don't trust you." Alexander stepped back from the table and stalked toward Stoker. "I saw your wards back there where you were keeping Ollie. No way in or out unless it's with you, right?"

Why are you telling him? Rota was alarmed.

Shut up. I got this.

"I'm actually impressed." Stoker clapped.

"Even if I do what you want, I have no guarantee I'll get Ollie back." Alexander stopped right in front of Stoker and glared up at him. "You've got those fancy watchman spells, right?"

"I do."

"Tag him with one. Let me take him with me."

Stoker peered down at him, curiously looking him over. "Were your eyes always red? I imagine not. At what point did that happen, hmm?"

Alexander's upper lip twitched, and his rage was instant. He was so furious he was shaking, and he wanted to tear this entire place apart with everyone in it—

Alexander.... Rota's voice was full of sorrow. *Please don't.*

"Let me take him with me," Alexander repeated between clenched teeth. "You can use your stupid spell to take him back whenever you want, right?"

"As long as he's not anywhere with wards that would prevent me," Stoker said with syrupy sweetness. "I told you that I expect results before you get anything, and—"

"Incense on two of the bodies," Alexander snapped as he held up his hand.

Stoker stared a moment before scoffing, "It's nothing. It's dried marigold petals."

Rota? Alexander prompted. *What the fuck is this?*

"Which is also used in Lucian incense for their crowning sunrise rituals," Rota rumbled. "This residue also has the breath of fire in it. Whatever it came from was either burned or was meant to be."

Stoker looked again in disbelief. His eyes narrowed and then widened. "Well, then. Look at that."

Was that a test, or did he really not know? Rota wondered.

Who cares? Alexander refused to back down. "Time to go visit some churches, don't you think?"

"Not yet." Stoker shook his head. "Bar first."

"Whatever. Now give me my boyfriend."

"After he's tagged. I will still be expecting very timely updates. Do you understand me?"

"Yeah."

"You do understand I'm taking quite a risk here. My hope is that you'll work more efficiently if you're not stressing over your precious little beau." Stoker leaned in close, his voice barely above a whisper as he hissed, "If you try to cross me, I'll make whatever Gronoch did to you look like a picnic."

"If you keep *fucking* with me," Alexander immediately bit back, "I'll show you what he did to me."

Stoker smiled wide. "Deal."

The world moved, and Alexander was standing back in Ollie's apartment in the kitchen.

Alexander's hands were still shaking from the earlier rush of adrenaline, and he rubbed them together with a sigh, trying to ease the tingling feeling away.

Not that I'm complaining about us winning Ollie's freedom, Rota said cautiously, *however temporary it may be, but why did you tell Stoker he's your boyfriend?*

It just popped in my head. That's all.

And why did you tell Stoker what we found? Like with the wards?

"He needed to know we're serious. Both about Ollie and the investigation." Alexander opened the fridge and made a face when there wasn't anything nonalcoholic to drink except soda. He reluctantly grabbed a citrus flavored one. "If he doesn't believe we're going to try, I don't think he would have let us take Ollie."

Fair.

A very confused Ollie appeared beside him.

Ah! Hello, Ollie! Rota chirped. *Good to see you.*

"Whoa." Ollie blinked. "Is this a dream?" He looked down. "Huh, I still have my pants on."

"I made a deal with Stoker." Alexander backed away to give himself some space. "You're marked with a watchman's spell, but you don't have to stay in his hotel prison."

"Right. Cool." Ollie looked around. "So…."

"Stoker wants help solving some murders." Alexander popped the can open and took a sip. "Someone has been killing everlasting people. Five so far, happening more and more often, more public spots."

"Oh. Like a serious killer?"

"Serial?"

"That too."

For fuck's sake. Idiot. "Yes."

"I can hear you."

"I can't stop what I'm thinking, especially since it's true."

"That's no way to talk about your boyfriend, you know." Ollie grinned.

"What?"

"Stoker said he was sending me to my boyfriend, which makes you my boyfriend."

"I just said that to convince Stoker to let me take you." Alexander hated how hot his face was getting. "It didn't mean anything. Like that stupid kiss didn't mean anything!"

"Hey, I thought it was a good idea!"

Personally, I thought it was great, Rota cheered.

"The only benefit is now Stoker thinks he can use you against me," Alexander ground out.

"How is that a benefit?" Ollie fished around for a bottle of liquor and found one in the sink that still had a little left that he immediately turned up.

"Because he can't." Alexander chugged the soda and crushed the can into a tiny ball, his fingers trembling as Rota's tentacles swarmed around the thin aluminum. "I don't care what happens to you as long as you translate that fucking book."

Ollie nearly choked, and his eyes glimmered. "Wow. You're a real jerk, do you know that?"

"So I've been told." Alexander rolled his eyes. "I'll leave the book. Have a few drinks. Go read. I have to go to some stupid bar."

"No, I'm going with you." Ollie slammed the emptied bottle down. "Jerk or not, Stoker thinks we're dating."

"I am not doing this."

He's right. Rota sounded nearly gleeful. *What if Stoker comes to check up on us? Don't you think he will find it odd if Ollie is not with us?*

"No." Alexander scowled. "Because if I actually was dating Ollie, I would want to keep him out of danger."

"Wouldn't the safest place be with you?" Ollie grinned again.

Clever boy! Rota hovered near Ollie. *With us is the safest place you could possibly be.*

"Cool! So, it's settled. I'll find a shirt."

Alexander glared at them. "What the fuck is happening right now?"

I believe you're being outvoted.

"Besides, you said bar." Ollie smirked. "And what do you know? I could use a drink."

"You're both idiots." Alexander threw his hands up. "I am surrounded by fucking idiots."

"Hey, I'll be right back!" Ollie hurried off toward his bedroom. "Don't you guys leave without me!"

Alexander scowled.

Don't be so angry, Rota soothed. *This could be fun!*

"It's not supposed to be fun. The fun part was supposed to come later after that stupid book gets translated, or did you already forget, huh?" Alexander wanted to scream.

I want us to have a backup plan.

"A backup plan for what?"

Just in case.... Rota's invisible tentacles slid gently over Alexander's cheek.

You don't think your body is there, Alexander realized.

We have to consider that Gronoch lied.

"I am not considering shit until I'm standing there taking a piss in that fuckin' fountain!"

"The Fountain of the Kindress?" Ollie piped up as he walked back out. He was still wearing his sweats, but he'd added flip-flops and a hideous Hawaiian print shirt with big green flowers and little frogs.

Alexander flinched. "Yes?"

"The guys who killed me talked about that place."

"Why can't you just say normal things?"

What happened to you? Rota asked gently.

"This is the kind of conversation that really needs a drink." Ollie smiled, but it was sad. "Maybe we can all start over?"

That sounds like a wonderful idea, Ollie.

Alexander's heart thumped. "Okay, whatever. Let's go." He quickly directed Rota's magic to transport and blink them out of the apartment.

He had a vague idea of where the bar was, and he was able to bring them a block away, appearing at the corner of an alley and the street. Without even a second look to Ollie, he walked toward the big sign that said Dead to Rites.

"You ever been here?" Ollie asked, jogging a few steps to catch up.

"No."

"I have. It can be a little rough. Some poor guy drowned in the alley out back a few weeks ago."

How did he drown in an alley? Rota asked.

"You see, water got into his lungs, and then he couldn't breathe. So, then he died."

"So, you know the people that work here?" Alexander cut in.

"Yeah. Jackie Cheese anyway."

That's... a person's name? Rota asked.

"Yeah!" Ollie laughed. "His brother's name is Ashtray."

That cannot be real! Rota chuckled. *There must be a very interesting story behind how they got those awful nicknames.*

"I'm tellin' you, it's legit!"

Alexander ignored the funfest behind him and shoved open the front door of the bar.

In a previous life, it had been a funeral home. The chapel was crowded with chairs and tables instead of pews, and drinks were served from a converted pulpit. The walls of the viewing rooms had been knocked down to make room for pool tables and a jukebox.

It was sticky, dirty, and reeked of cigarette smoke and rotten flowers. Above the end of the bar hung a magnificent statue of Azaethoth the Lesser, his twisted dragon form taking the place of the Lucian star. It was carved in a style eerily similar to the murals at Stoker's club. There were flowers, stale peanuts, and emptied shot glasses left as offerings at his clawed feet.

A lone square table by the bar was set with old high-back chairs and a lush chaise that was likely original to the building when it was still a funeral home.

There were no other patrons, probably because it was so early, and Alexander made a beeline for a table in the corner by the jukebox.

"No, over here." Ollie pointed to the table with the fancy chairs. "Sages' table." He plopped down in one that was puffy and green.

Alexander took the chair across from him, and he immediately hated it.

He and Rota didn't go out. They couldn't. They couldn't sit down in restaurants or bars. They couldn't go to movies or take walks or any of the stupid meaningless dating crap that suddenly meant so much when it wasn't fucking possible—

"Wow, okay." Ollie cringed. "Look, maybe if we just start talking, that'll make you feel better?"

"What? You felt that?" Alexander grimaced.

"Your brain kinda screamed at me." Ollie offered a gentle smile. "So, uh, hi. I'm Ollie. This one time I died."

Is that how you gained your starsight? Rota asked. *It's often been said that mortals gain the gift through overcoming great adversity.*

"No, I guess you could say I really had to su-fahfaher to get it." Ollie's smile faded.

Alexander ignored the throb in his head. "What happened?"

"Short version? Well, it's—" Ollie paused when a stocky man approached the table. "Oh! Hey, Jackie!"

"Hey, Ollie." Jackie had gold teeth, braids in his beard, and he was definitely not human. "Been a long time."

Now that Alexander had an idea of what to look for, he could see the glamour like before with Nathaniel. He wasn't sure what Jackie was, but there were definitely wings and tentacles hidden somewhere beneath his human visage.

"Yeah. You know." Ollie fidgeted, squeaking his chair loudly. "I've been hanging out. Lots of hanging. At my place. Alone. Super alone."

"Ted?" Jackie asked sympathetically.

"No! I'm so over him!" Ollie scoffed. "Totally. Don't even think about him. Nope to the nope."

Jackie did not look convinced.

"In fact, this is my new boyfriend." Ollie beamed, his inner voice pleading, *Please just go with it. Please, please, please—*

"Right. Boyfriend. That's me." Alexander flashed his teeth.

"Oh!" Jackie was surprised. "Nice to meet you… uh?"

"Alexander."

"I'm Jackie Cheese." Jackie smiled. "Haven't seen you before. You new around here?"

"Yes. New."

"Well, uh, what can I get you guys to drink?"

"Captain and Dr Pepper, double," Ollie replied. "And whatever my dear snookums—"

"Alexander," Alexander grumbled.

"—Alexander wants."

"I'm fine. Thanks." Alexander didn't see the point in screwing around. "What I would love is to talk about the dead body that—ow!"

Ollie had kicked him under the table.

Jackie arched his brow. "Uh, what was that?"

"Nothing!" Ollie laughed nervously. "He meant, uh, he's on a diet. To keep his body dead. Uh, drop-dead gorgeous. So… uh, just a Diet Coke for him?"

"Sure thing." Jackie frowned, but he headed back to the bar to get their drinks.

"First of all, I do not like soda," Alexander snarled low. "Second of all, I'm here to investigate a bunch of murders. An investigation, by the way, I'm only doing to keep you away from Stoker so you can translate that book!"

How about we all calm down, hmm? Rota nudged Alexander's shoulder. *Ollie, why don't you tell us how you died? I'm very interested in hearing what happened to you.*

Thank you, Rota, Ollie thought smugly.

I hate you both. Alexander sighed. *This is so stupid.*

Shush. Enjoy this…. Rota's love was seeping through his side of the bond. *Please.*

"Fine." Alexander didn't know why Rota wanted this so much, but he decided to humor him for now. "Ollie needs to be drunk anyway, right?"

"Very." Ollie nodded.

"Go on, then."

"Well, I should probably tell you guys about how I got starsight, 'cause that's why I was killed." Ollie took a deep breath. "So, short version. Super condensed. I asked my boyfriend to marry me, he sorta drowned trying to save this kid he was real mean to, and then I brought him back from the dead."

Alexander blinked. "A resurrection."

"Bless you."

"You performed a resurrection?"

"That thing, yeah." Ollie shrugged. "I didn't know how, and I was really upset. I just…." His cheery demeanor slipped. "I know I'm not exactly the brightest spoon in the drawer. For once in my crappy life, I didn't want to be stupid. I wanted to be able to do something right."

And that's when the blessing came to you? Rota asked quietly.

"Yeah." Ollie brightened up when Jackie brought their drinks over. "Thanks, dude. Keep 'em coming."

"You got it, Ollie." Jackie smiled at him, but he gave Alexander a suspicious glare.

Alexander smiled sweetly but sneered as soon as Jackie's back was turned. He looked back to Ollie. "So, where is your miraculously alive fiancé?"

"Getting married to someone else." Ollie tipped his glass back. "He told me no, and somewhere between the drowning and driving home, we broke up."

Did you not tell him what you'd done for him?

"No, I didn't." Ollie twiddled with his straw. "I didn't want him to know. I was afraid he'd make that into the reason he stayed with me."

You wanted him to stay because he loved you. Rota sounded sad. *Not because you'd saved his life.*

"Yeah. So." Ollie coughed. "Fun side e-fahfahect of bringing someone back from the dead? Can't be sacrificed to wake up a god!"

Pardon?

"There's these guys trying to wake up Salgumel," Ollie explained. "They're led by a fuckhead named Je-fahfah who kidnapped me and stabbed me because he needed a heart from someone with starsight. I died, but my heart isn't whole."

Life for a life. Rota gasped. *The scar on your marvelously sculpted chest.*

"What?" Alexander grunted. He was trying not to get too invested in this pointless conversation, but he was actually quite curious.

And okay, the mention of Ollie's chest got his attention.

That's the price of resurrection. Life for life.

"I gave part of myself, my heart, to bring my boyfriend back from the dead." Ollie took another drink. "When Je-fahfah stabbed me, the ritual failed. No wakey up Salgumel, which was super cool."

"Cultists?" Alexander frowned. "Starkiller asked us to keep an eye out for them while we searched the worlds between worlds."

"Yeah, those assholes. That's them."

How did you come back? Certainly you didn't bring yourself back to life.

"My uncle saved me." Ollie grinned. "Him, Azaethoth, Sloane, and Gordoth. 'Cause we were between worlds, my soul hadn't run o-fahfah, like, all the way yet? So my uncle did this fire thingie and called my soul back while Azaethoth and Gordoth healed me."

That's incredible!

"Yeah. It was pretty intense." Ollie paused to drink. "That's really it, I guess. Since the whole starsight thing happened, I don't come out much. Keep seeing super weird stu-fahfah." He tapped the table. "Last time I was here? I saw this kid with the face of an angel but he was all dead inside. Like straight rotten."

Oh my. That sounds horrific.

"It was very not cool."

"So, the bartender. Jackie?" Alexander tilted his head. "You can see what he is?"

"Yeah. Duh. Just like I can see Rota." Ollie twirled his straw around his glass. "He's a lot nicer to look at than Azaethoth or Gordoth, though. They look super weird when they're in their micro modes."

Why, thank you... I think.

"So, what about you guys?" Ollie smiled. "How did all of this happen to you?"

Alexander did not want to answer.

Gronoch did this to us. Rota hesitated. *It's complicated.*

"I just kinda spilled my guts out to you guys. Feelin' a little crazy." Ollie frowned. "I mean, I don't wanna make you uncomfortable."

"After my parents' research indicated my blood type would make me more receptive to soul binding, Gronoch killed them and kidnapped me," Alexander replied curtly. "I woke up in a small room with no memory of who I was, and I was tortured, physically and mentally, for years to become a conduit for a god. There. Super condensed version. Happy?"

"No." Ollie reached over the table to touch Alexander's arm. "No, that's terrible! Fuck. I'm so sorry."

Alexander could feel Ollie's concern—fuck, that was weird—and he didn't pull away from his touch. He wanted another hug, maybe more, and he tried to control his wild thoughts.

"I know I can't exactly understand what kinda messed-up shit you've been through, either of you, but I'm really sorry that happened to you guys." Ollie squeezed Alexander's arm and offered his hand. "Seriously."

Alexander frowned, but he took it, his pulse fluttering when their fingers laced together. "Uh. Thanks."

We appreciate that, Ollie. Very much.

"Is that why you guys need the book translated?" Ollie asked. "Something to do with your bond?"

Gronoch told us my body is hidden at the Fountain of the Kindress. That book may be the only record of how to reach it.

"Ohhh, wow. Damn. Je-fahfah would, like, give his left nut for that thing." Ollie slurped the last of his drink. "When him and his rude dudes kidnapped me, they were talking about finding the Kindress to wake up Salgumel or something. I can't remember exactly. Drank a lot since then and, you know, died."

"They won't get the book," Alexander promised. "Once we're done, we'll destroy it."

"Okay, cool." Ollie's cheeks were flushed now. "So, solve murders, translate magical book, find Rota's body. We can totally do that."

That's actually something I wanted to ask you about, Ollie. About the lack of a body situation we have. I have a proposition for you.

"Rota," Alexander warned.

"Oh?" Ollie grinned. "What kinda preposition?"

You see, Alexander and I haven't been able to… oh. Alexander, we may have trouble.

"What now?" Alexander turned to where Rota nudged him, and he saw Jackie coming from behind the bar with two large men.

They were whispering spells, something destructive and probably involving fire, and they were all glaring at Alexander.

"Hey, Jackie! Hey, Ashtray! Hi, other big guy I don't know!" Ollie waved, totally oblivious. "Are you gonna bring me another drink? I'm on empty, dude."

"That depends," Jackie replied icily. "When were you gonna tell me your little boyfriend works for Sullivan Stoker?"

Ah shit.

CHAPTER 5.

"Uh." Ollie's eyes bugged out. "Oh yeah. Well. Uh. You see...."

"Look, kid," Jackie grunted. "I know you've gotten in some trouble with Stoker. I'm not stupid. And I've got every idea this guy ain't actually your boyfriend."

"He's totally my boyfriend. We kissed. With tongue."

"Enough." Alexander stood from the table and faced the three men. "I don't work for Stoker. I'm helping him with his investigation—"

"You're talkin' about the murders? Ha!" Jackie scoffed. "It's all Stoker's fault they're dying!"

"Oh? Care to elaborate?"

"No." Jackie scowled angrily. "You've got ten seconds to leave before I start burning holes in you."

"Oh well. We tried!" Alexander started to the door. "Come on, Ollie. Let's go."

Alexander, wait! Rota pleaded.

"Can I get a drink to go?" Ollie asked hopefully.

"You're not going anywhere," Jackie said. "Sit down. We got you, kid."

Alexander stopped midstep, sighing as he turned back around. "See, that's where you're wrong. Ollie is coming with me."

"Yeah, Jackie, it's totally okay." Ollie grinned anxiously. "I'll go with him. But maybe just pour me a few shots—"

"What has he done to you?" Jackie whispered and scanned Ollie with his hands, fingers together to form the triangle of a perception spell. "You're marked! No way! We're getting this thing off you and you're staying here."

"Can we please not fight?" Ollie begged.

Alexander sighed again. He was not in the mood for this, and he didn't want to mess with any more fire today. "Fine. We'll do this the easy way."

Alexander? Rota was very concerned.

I'm not going to hurt them, you big baby. Alexander surged forward, swinging his hand back and bopping each man in the forehead. He moved as fast as lightning, using Rota's power to propel his speed as he placed a silencing ward on each of them.

"What the…?" Jackie sputtered and tried to cast, but his spell fizzled out in his hands. He stared at Alexander in shock. "I checked you out! You're Silenced!"

"And many other things." Alexander reached into his jacket for a cigarette. With Rota's tentacles sliding up his hand, he used his fingers to light it and take a long drag. "Now, are you guys done? Or you want me to show you what else a Silenced person can do?"

"Please, guys. None of that." Ollie was up and pushing himself between them, though he stumbled a little. "I'm serious, Jackie. Alexander is okay. I swear he's cool. He's trying to help me, okay?"

"Start talking." Jackie was furious, and he pointed a thick finger at Alexander. "Now."

Careful. Rota was floating around the three men. *Yes, they're silenced for now, but one of them is trying to use a truth totem of some kind.*

"Ollie got into debt with Stoker," Alexander replied carefully. "I agreed to help Stoker to pay off his debt, but he will only let Ollie go if I can find out who is behind the murders."

Jackie glanced back at the bigger man, who gave him a nod. "What exactly did Stoker tell you?"

"I have a list of names, crime scenes, and a vague timeline." Alexander smirked. "I was told you all were not being cooperative, and he asked me to come here first."

"Fuck Stoker," the bigger man said.

"That's my brother, Ashtray," Jackie said. "Other guy is Marbles."

"Care to share why you're so sure Stoker is responsible now?" Alexander asked.

Jackie and Ashtray exchanged a look for a few tense moments, and Ashtray nodded.

"There was this Lucian missionary who used to come in here all the time," Jackie said at last. "Trying to spread the Litany, you know. Name's Tim. Never drank, only ordered coffee, tipped well. We'd let him hang for a bit during the day and then always give him the boot when we got busy. But when Stoker took over? Stoker flipped."

"How so?"

"Said he couldn't stand having some Lucian mouthpiece hanging around one of his properties. Dragged the poor idiot outside and roughed him up real bad. Haven't seen him since. A few days later, Eric Grimes was dead."

"Bit of a stretch, don't you think?"

"I think Tim saw what he was. I don't know how to explain it, but I think something happened when Stoker hurt him."

"Like he had some sort of awakening," Ashtray spoke up. "You know, like the kind that maybe lets him see stuff?"

"You think Stoker gave the Lucian missionary starsight by beating the shit out of him?" Alexander drawled.

"Look, man." Jackie shook his head. "Tim has worked funerals at the same funeral home where Baxter was killed. He works part-time at the grocery store where they found poor Brady taking bags out for little old ladies. That gas station? Lacie? Right by his house."

That plus the incense we found is certainly suspicious, Rota mused. *It's not as if we have any other leads.*

"Any connection to the restaurant?" Alexander asked.

"Not that we know of, but I'm sure he's eaten there," Jackie replied. "It's a pretty popular spot."

"So, why didn't you tell Stoker that you think Tim the missionary did it?"

"Because one, fuck Stoker, and two, we're gonna handle it ourselves. As soon as we find him, he's toast."

"I happen to be very good at finding people. Let me find this man and take him to Stoker for you."

"No fuckin' way!" Ashtray snapped. "We want fuckin' dibs on him. He killed our friends! Our family!"

"You don't know that for sure yet," Alexander said smoothly. "And I can't help Ollie unless I give Stoker a nice warm body to play with."

"You bring him to us first," Jackie insisted. "We'll make sure there's still some twitch in him before you take him to Stoker. Fair?"

"Whatever." Alexander did not care. He had a name now, and the rest was going to be easy. He just had to go find this idiot and—

"Hey, Jackie!" Ollie called from behind the bar where he'd slipped off to. "Where's the Dr Pepper?"

"Ollie!" Jackie scolded. "Get outta there! I'll get you your damn drink!" He glared at Alexander. "You gonna unsilence us now?"

Alexander removed the wards with a thought, and he headed back to his chair.

"How did you do that?" Marbles demanded. "I've only ever seen Stoker cast magic like that."

Alexander eyed Marbles for a moment.

Big, broad, with a layer of scales hidden beneath his glamour. His nails were absolutely filthy.

"I'm not like Stoker," Alexander replied firmly.

"Whatever. Freak." Marbles laughed. "Good to know you."

Was that a compliment? Rota wondered.

I have no idea. Alexander looked up as Ollie returned with a new drink and a triumphant grin.

"Hey! Look at that!" Ollie beamed. "I got to help!"

You certainly did. Thank you. I'm not sure if we could have smoothed that over without you.

"Finish your drinks and then get outta here," Jackie said, watching them from his perch back behind the bar. "If Stoker is keeping an eye on you, I don't want his eyeballs anywhere near here. Got it?"

"Got it!" Ollie raised his glass and took a big gulp.

They seem nice.

"Oh, they are. Little rough, but they're good guys. Never looked down on me for being human."

Oh? They don't like mortals?

"Not really." Ollie scratched his chin. "They don't hate them. I mean, okay, some of those guys do, but it's just if normal people knew what they were? It wouldn't exactly be a happy ending. Kinda hard to like people who might wanna kill you if they knew what you really were."

"Like what they believe ol' Tim is up to?" Alexander asked. "Destroying abominations in the name of the Lord of Light?"

"Maybe." Ollie tipped his glass back. "I've met Tim. He was an okay dude, I guess. But if Jackie is right and he can see the shit I see…?"

You think it's enough to make someone kill?

"It was enough to make me a little crazy. And I'm a Sage! I actually recognize some of the weird stu-fahfah out there. Tim? Being a Lucian? If it's true, he probably thinks he's seeing demons or something."

"Tim have a last name?"

"Tim Bateman."

"You have a computer?"

"Yes?"

"Good." Alexander could feel Jackie and Marbles staring at him, and he defiantly flicked his ashes on the floor. "Finish your drink."

"On it."

The front door opened while Ollie chugged, and a thin young man walked in. He didn't look much older than sixteen, and the first thing Alexander noticed was the mask he was wearing. It covered most of his face, garishly painted to resemble a normal human visage. He had dark wavy hair combed over to help hide it, and the one eye Alexander could see was a bright gray.

"Hey, Jackie! Hey, guys!" the young man said, waving as he hurried up to the bar.

Curious, Rota noted.

Huh. Alexander watched the boy, and he used a perception spell to check him out. *Let's see what we have, shall we?*

The young man was a mortal with a surprisingly strong alignment to water, but that was all. There was no glamour or any other trickery Alexander could detect.

The young man was busy chatting away with Jackie, and he handed him something from his pocket.

Oh, that's Will! Ollie piped up, looking very pleased with himself he could now add to the psychic conversation.

Alexander did not like that one bit. *Who is he?*

I dunno. Ollie blinked. *He's Will?*

What is he doing here?

Oh! Right. Ollie nodded. *He works for Mrs. York, the lady that runs the oddities shop?*

I don't think we're familiar, Rota said.

"Mrs. York is a Sage," Ollie whispered loudly. "Wait, I said that. I didn't think it. I mean, it's not like it's a big secret. She sells weird things and maybe *other* things." *Like, things for ghouls. Wink wink, nudge nudge.*

"Ah." Alexander understood immediately.

Ghouls were people who had died and whose souls had been bound to a ghoul vessel, an empty copy of their original bodies. The process had to occur before they actually passed on, so it was not true necromancy, but it was the only way anyone in present times knew to extend someone's life.

Well, other than Ollie, of course.

The problem with ghouls was their new bodies would inevitably rot and required very special medicine to slow the process. The witches who provided this service were called ghoul doctors, and they tended to keep a very low profile since ghouls were extremely illegal, as was aiding them.

Alexander took a second look at Will, curious if he was a ghoul and he'd somehow missed it, but he was definitely alive.

"Mrs. York's daughter actually works with Marbles over at the funeral home," Ollie went on. "He's in, like, the crematory or something. She's a funeral director, and she's, like, part of this big secret underground ghoul thing." *They help ghouls survive and keep them hidden, you know, so they don't get ratted out.*

That's rather nice of them. Rota was smiling.

And what is he doing here? Alexander asked. He didn't care about sweet and sappy stories. He wanted to know what a baby-faced criminal was doing with other potential criminals.

I dunno. I just have starsight. I can't read minds. Ollie shrugged, swirling the ice around his empty glass. *He's giving Jackie some kind of little rock. I think it's rose quartz. It's got some sort of protection charm on it.*

What's with the mask?

It's a real messed-up story. Poor little guy. They say—

"Hey, Ollie!" Jackie called out.

Yeah? Ollie turned toward him. *What's up, Jackie?*

You're still talking with your "inside voice," Alexander drawled.

Ollie cleared his throat. "Right. Uh. Yeah, Jackie?"

"Thought you and your, ahem, boyfriend were leaving?" Jackie glared hatefully at Alexander.

"Boyfriend?" Will grinned, gasping as he waved excitedly at Ollie. "Really?"

Oh God. Alexander cringed. *He's gonna come over here, isn't he?*

"Really really!" Ollie exclaimed, speaking to Will and giving Alexander an apologetic look.

"Hey! That man needs another drink, Jackie!" Will laughed as he headed their way. "Will you bring me my usual?"

Jackie's mean mug softened. "Isn't it a little early, kiddo?"

"Never too early," Will teased.

Ollie stood to give Will a friendly hug. "Hey! How are you?"

"Good!" Will replied with a warm smile. "How the fuck are you? Haven't seen you in months!"

"Oh, you know." Ollie scratched the back of his head. "Uh. I've been… around." He sat back down, quickly gesturing to Alexander. "This is Alexander, my new boyfriend!"

"Hey!" Will offered his hand. "It's nice to meet you!"

Very reluctantly, Alexander shook Will's hand. "Hi."

He seems nice, Rota observed.

Whatever, Alexander grumbled in his thoughts.

Jackie arrived with drinks in his hand and set them down in front of Ollie and Will. Ollie got an additional glare. "Last one, then you guys are going. Right?"

Will frowned. "Why?" He looked to Ollie. "You guys got a big date or something?"

"Something," Alexander confirmed dryly.

Ollie tipped the glass back and hummed. "Yeah, we got, you know, boyfriend things to do."

"Say no more!" Will laughed, raising his glass to take a big gulp. "Still, uh, working from home?"

"Yeah. The translating stu-fahfah keeps me real busy."

"Oh? Then how did you meet this hottie?" Will winked at Alexander.

Did he…. Did he just wink at me? Alexander pressed his lips together in a thin line. He was already over this. It was far more social interaction than he cared for, and he wanted to leave.

He's cool, I promise, Ollie thought insistently before saying out loud, "Oh! Well, he brought me a book to translate for him, and uh, the sparks just flew."

"I'm seriously happy for you, man." Will smiled. "That's awesome."

"What about you? Any exciting fellows in your love life?"

"Ha! You know!" Will's smile wilted. "Gotta beat 'em off with a stick."

Ollie appeared concerned.

"It's an expression, Ollie." Will chuckled lightly. "Oh, and hey! The doc might need your help with some tomes she got."

"All she has to do is call me."

"You know how she is. Wants to beat her head against the wall for a little while first. Stubborn ol' bat."

"I'll tell her you said that!" Jackie shouted.

"Fuck you, Jackie!" Will snorted, rolling his eyes affectionately. "Well, hey, look. I gotta run, but it was real good to see you, man."

"It was good to see you too!" Ollie grinned.

"Nice to meet you." Will smiled at Alexander. "You take care of that guy, okay? He's a special one."

"In many ways," Alexander said sweetly.

Alexander! Rota scolded.

Alexander ignored him.

"See you guys later!" Will waved farewell, calling out to Jackie, "Bye, Jackie! Holler if you need me, but try not to need me!"

"Bye, kiddo!" Jackie bid farewell. He waited until the front door shut before he snapped, "Now! You two. Drink up and go."

"I'm all over it!" Ollie turned the glass up and chugged.

So, the mask? Alexander pressed. *What happened?*

Will's dad put a fuckin' fire trap on the bathroom door when he was a little kid. Ollie kept chugging. *Wouldn't let him or his brother use the bathroom except for certain times of the day, the sick fuck, so he trapped the damn door. Little Will really had to go this one time and went to go open it and boom.*

"Fuck," Alexander whispered. He had not been expecting that.

Ollie set the empty glass down and smacked his lips. "Yup."

Magic could not save... his.... It couldn't save... well.... Rota seemed to be having trouble articulating the obvious question.

His face? Alexander said bluntly.

No. The fire? It was Baub's Rage. Ollie shook his head. "Piece of shit wanted to make it hurt. Doctors did what they could, but fuck, he was lucky he lived at all."

"Certainly he could go to another healer? Use glamour?" Alexander raised a brow. "There doesn't seem to be a shortage of it around here."

Ollie shrugged. "I dunno. I never asked, he never says."

I'm sure he's quite lovely without the mask, Rota insisted.

"I bet." Alexander tried not to sound as sarcastic as he felt. He had no room to talk about physical appearances, especially since he was in love with an ancient tentacle god. "Can we go now? Before your little friend burns holes into the side of my head with his eyes?"

"Jackie can't do that." Ollie frowned slightly. "I mean, I don't think he can."

"It's definitely time for us to go."

"Oh yeah." Ollie picked up the glass to chew on some of the ice, crunching away as he said, "I almost forgot! What was the preposition you wanted to ask me, Rota?"

Oh! Yes.

"Oh no," Alexander countered.

You see, Alexander and I have been together for many years, but—

"We're leaving right now." Alexander immediately transported them back to Ollie's apartment.

Ollie ended up on the couch with his drink still in his hand. "Hey!" He pouted. "You made me steal this!"

"Where is your computer?" Alexander demanded. *We are not having that conversation! Not now, not ever!*

"What conversation?" Ollie asked. "The one where you apologize for making me a *thief*?"

The one where I ask you to be my vessel!

"Rota!" Alexander shouted, roasting the cigarette butt in his hand into ashes. "You ridiculous asshole!"

"Vessel for what?" Ollie blinked.

Physical relations.

"Oh!"

Do you understand what I mean?

"Sex." Ollie felt around on the floor, and he found another bottle that had a few sips of a brownish liquid. He poured it into the pilfered glass. "You're talking about having the sex."

Exactly so.

Alexander wished he could melt into the floor. Maybe he could open a portal and leave, never come back and have to see Ollie ever again.

You said Alexander was cute, and he finds you quite attractive. We have been unsuccessful—

"I hate you so much right now." Alexander scrubbed his hands over his face. "Please stop."

—but you having starsight would allow me to use your body as a vessel—

"Stop now."

—and materialize my natural reproductive appendages for mating!

"For the love of…!" Alexander clenched his hands into fists and stomped out of the living room. He had no idea where else to go, and he ended up in the kitchen. "Rota! You bastard! I told you no!"

And I told you there's a chance Gronoch lied! Do you think he really put my body there? Do you?

"What the fuck! It's the only lead we have left, and he was dying at the time. He had no reason to lie!"

Except to be cruel, something he loved.

"What are you saying?" Alexander scowled, and an inkling of panic crept up his spine.

I love you. I love you with everything that I am. I want to be with you. No matter what. But I do not want to wait chasing a pipe dream when we have a viable opportunity right here!

"No, there's no way—"

"Hey!" Ollie shouted, having raised his voice to be heard over their bickering. "I said I'll do it!"

"What?" Alexander felt like he'd been punched in the stomach. He didn't think he'd heard Ollie correctly.

"I said I'll do it?" Ollie was up now, moving to meet them in the kitchen.

Thank you! Rota gushed.

"Wait, wait!" Alexander held up his hands. "Seriously? Just like that?"

"Yeah." Ollie nodded as he finished his drink and set the empty glass on the counter. "You are super cute, like so cute, and Rota is really nice. I think you're nice too. Like, deep somewhere underneath that crunchy shell. And well, uh, it's not every day a god asks you to be his vessel."

Alexander swallowed anxiously. "I'm sorry. I'm having trouble processing this."

"It's kinda been a while for me?" Ollie scratched the back of his head. "So, I'm sorry if I'm not better."

I'll be in complete control, Ollie. You won't have to worry about a thing.

"Oh! Cool." Ollie shrugged. "I'm down whenever you guys are."

"You've been drinking," Alexander accused. "You're in no shape to make a decision."

"Good thing I can magically sober up." Ollie rubbed his hands together and coughed into them until a large ball of liquid appeared in his palms. He dropped it back in the empty glass with a smug smile. "Saving you for later."

"That's disgusting."

"That's saving alcohol, thank you."

"Why do you want to have sex with me so badly?"

"Technically, it's not me doing the sex. It's Rota using my body for the sex."

"Oh, by all the gods." Alexander groaned. "Stop calling it 'the sex.'"

"Look, I haven't been with anybody since me and my ex broke up." Ollie reached out to take Alexander's hands. "That's, like, forever ago. So long ago. I never wanted to go out and just, you know, do it with a stranger. I want sex to mean something. And this? Letting you and Rota be together? It means something."

"Ollie, this isn't—"

"I've kinda peeked in on your bond, and I'm super sorry I did that, but it happened when we kissed?" Ollie cringed. "I know how much you two love each other. I know what you've been through. Sort of. It was just a peek, I swear! Don't get mad. I just… let me do this for you?"

"What are you getting out of it?" Alexander demanded, still unconvinced.

"Well, uh, I get to have sex with a totally good kisser and his nice god boyfriend?" Ollie grinned shyly. "I mean, it's not like it won't feel nice for me too."

Alexander could feel nothing but absolute certainty and affection coming from Ollie, and he was weirdly touched. It was an insane situation, but maybe Rota was right. Maybe they did need to take this chance while they could.

They might not have another one.

"You really thought… I was a good kisser?" Alexander licked his lips.

"Wicked good," Ollie confirmed sweetly.

"Okay." Alexander huffed. "Yes. Now. Let's go."

"Oh? Like *now* now? Cool! Yeah, we can go now." Ollie's eyes widened. "Wait. No. Uh. Wait here!" He took off toward the bedroom, nearly tripping over his feet along the way.

"Are you sure about this?" Alexander whispered to Rota. "Right now?"

We've already waited for so long. Yes, one day I will make love to you with my own body, but this… I don't want to squander such a chance. And he is more than willing, obviously.

Alexander's blood was racing, and there was a pleasant drop in his gut like he was falling. He didn't want to change his mind, not now, and he took a deep breath to steady himself. "What, what do I need to do?"

Nothing, my love. I am going to take care of everything.

"I love you."

And I love you.

There was a loud crash.

"Should we… should we go check on him?"

Might be for the best.

Alexander headed to the bedroom door and knocked politely. "Everything okay in there?"

There was a small delay before the door opened. Ollie was grinning, beckoning Alexander in. "Sorry! I wanted to clean up a little. You know, try to make it nice for you guys."

The bedroom was small, but the floor was devoid of trash, unlike the rest of the apartment. Alexander could see a bit of a bottle and some wrappers peeking out from under the bed and suspected that's where the rest had ended up. There were clean sheets on the bed, candles lit at the bedside, and tiny white petals sprinkled around the pillows.

"Okay, so, I didn't have any roses, so those are daisies." Ollie grinned shyly. "Hope you like it."

"It's… it's perfect." Alexander gathered his courage and stood up tall to kiss Ollie's cheek. "Thank you."

Thank you, Ollie. Really. We cannot express our gratitude enough.

"Hey, it's no big deal." Ollie shuffled his feet, turning a very lovely shade of pink. "You just, uh, take care of my body, okay? Don't get it dirty or nothin'."

I promise I will return it in pristine condition.

"So." Alexander fidgeted. "What do we do?"

Well, Rota asked, *are you ready, my love?*

"So fuckin' ready."

Then let's begin.

CHAPTER 6.

ALEXANDER WAS trembling in anticipation, and he could hardly believe this was happening. He was scared, excited, and his hands were shaking in Ollie's gentle grasp. He didn't care about finding Tim or translating the book. He definitely did not care about Sullivan Stoker.

Nothing else mattered if this truly meant he was finally going to be with Rota.

"Aw, your eyes are that pretty pink color again." Ollie grinned down at him.

"Yeah…." Alexander actually felt a smile creeping up on him from the adoring way Ollie was looking at him. No one had ever looked at him like that except Rota. "It happens when… when I'm happy."

"If you're happy, I'm happy, little dude." Ollie raised Alexander's hands and kissed each one. "Let's do this."

I'm going to take you now, Ollie, Rota said, pausing for a moment. *It may feel… strange.*

"I'm good with that. Go ahead." Ollie's lashes fluttered, and Alexander could feel the moment Rota slipped into him. There was something familiar in those eyes now, an ancient and powerful presence he knew well.

It was the god who loved him—the god who had saved him from himself when he was at the edge of oblivion and called him back with a promise to always be there for him, to care for him and adore him until the end of time.

To be in his presence now only for the second time was overwhelming, and Alexander forgot how to breathe.

"Rota?" Alexander's voice sounded so weak to his own ears.

"I'm here," Rota spoke using Ollie's voice. It had a definite rumble now, unmistakably Rota's. "Gods, look at you."

Alexander's heart twisted when Rota framed his face with his hands—Ollie's hands—and he gasped when they kissed. There, yes, this was his god. Rota's energy was buzzing directly into his skin, and he grabbed a hold of him and never wanted to let go.

He could feel Rota's love seeping through their bond, and there was an unexpected undercurrent of lust. Rota wanted this as badly as he did, and that level of desire from a god was both humbling and exciting.

The kiss was clumsy at first, but it heated up quickly as they found a beautiful rhythm, their lips sliding against each other's passionately. Alexander couldn't seem to catch his breath, and everything was tingly and overly sensitive.

The mere press of Rota's hand against his hip made him writhe, and the friction between their bodies was creating frantic waves of pleasure he didn't know what to do with.

Oh, but he had some ideas.

He pulled at the buttons of the shirt Ollie was wearing, panting, "Now. Please."

"Alexander—"

"Do you remember what I told you?" Alexander's fingers got caught on the last button, and he popped it impatiently, pushing the shirt down and off. "What I would want from you?"

"I don't want to rush this, my love."

"Says the guy who couldn't wait for us to find his body," Alexander argued. He was already shrugging off his coat and pulling his own shirt over his head. "No, I want you inside me. *Now*."

Rota's lust increased tenfold, crashing into Alexander like a freight train. "Then you will have me."

Alexander gasped as a thick bundle of Rota's tentacles materialized, seemingly out of thin air, and wrapped around his arms and legs. They were a dark red with purple mottling along the underside, and they were even more beautiful than Alexander could have ever imagined. The pressure of their grip was fantastic, and he kept waiting for it to vanish like it always did.

But it didn't. Not this time.

Rota carried Alexander to the bed and laid him there, his tentacles reverently working off the rest of his clothes. He was moving fast enough not to draw Alexander's ire, but he still paused to kiss every inch of revealed skin, focusing his attention on the bindings that held them together.

When Alexander was fully bared, Rota gazed down at him with a longing sigh. "By all the gods, mm, look at you. You're so beautiful."

Alexander was trying to relax, but he was already itching to tackle Rota to the bed. His cock was hard and leaking, and all of the frustrations from the last seven damn years were a tidal wave swallowing him up. He didn't want slow. He didn't want to take his time. He wanted to have sex, and he wanted it now.

He reached up and grabbed the back of Rota's neck, pulling him down into a deep kiss. He locked their lips together, and he found he still had some control over Rota's movements. He immediately directed one of his tentacles between his legs.

"Wait," Rota gasped. "Not like that."

"What?"

"Not that one." Rota presented Alexander with a thick tentacle that had a particularly phallic slit at the tip. "Remember. Only some of my appendages are used for coitus."

"Then give me one of those!" Alexander hissed impatiently.

"I will give you everything," Rota promised, silencing Alexander's complaining with another kiss. He moved up between his thighs, using hips to pin Alexander to the bed.

Alexander growled, but he did really like the kissing, so he allowed it for a few more moments. He was hot, his legs awkwardly seeking somewhere to rest as he dragged his hands up Rota's firm back.

God, those *muscles*.

Ollie had a fantastic body. Alexander told himself that he wouldn't have cared what form Rota was in when they did this, but he was secretly gleeful it was such a lovely one. The tentacles were gorgeous in their own right, and the slick sensation against his bare skin took his breath away.

The pure love and joy flowing through every pore from the tentacles' touch was overwhelming, and his eyes stung with tears. His heart pounded through his ribs, and he could feel it in the head of his dick. Rota was touching him all over with hands and tentacles, tracing over the marks cut into his skin, and it took everything in Alexander not to sob outright.

"I love you," Alexander whispered urgently. "Please, please. Don't make me wait, don't—"

"I won't." Rota kissed him again, and one of the slitted tentacles slipped between them, probing against Alexander's hole.

The sensation of something other than his own hand there made him jerk, and Alexander struggled to stay still. It was weird, a little awkward, but he wanted it so badly that he ached down in the very core of his being.

This was it. It was real and hot and finally happening.

The first press inside was soft, wet, and Alexander experienced the strange feeling of being stretched from within. It had to be Rota doing this to help ease the way. The pressure was intense, though not painful, and he inhaled sharply to work through it.

"I've got you," Rota whispered right next to his ear. "Relax, my love. I've got you."

"Mmmph." Alexander couldn't manage any words, but he nodded, petting Rota's back encouragingly.

The tip of the tentacle pushed in a little deeper, and it made Alexander squirm. It was going much farther than his fingers ever had, and he whined as the resulting pressure made him tremble. He panted through it, trying to memorize every sweet second, and he gasped as Rota pulled the tentacle out a few inches.

When he pushed back in, Alexander's entire body lit up with sensation. The shivers that rolled through him made his nipples hard, and he clung to Rota's shoulders with a low cry. This was it, Rota was fucking him, the tentacle moving in and out of his body in slow, gentle thrusts.

"Rota," he whispered brokenly. "By all the gods... yes... ah... yes!"

"My love," Rota groaned, sliding his arms beneath Alexander's shoulders and holding him close. He buried his face there in the crook of his neck, kissing and sucking along his shoulder. *You feel perfect. You're so warm and tight, like you were made only for me. You're everything I ever dreamed of....*

"And more." Alexander closed his eyes, and a tear slid down the side of his face. "You're everything I dreamed of and more."

Alexander allowed himself another loud gasp as the tentacle slammed into him with more force, his nails digging into Rota's back as he braced himself. Rota was fucking him harder, the tentacle making the most fantastically lewd sounds as it pounded his wet hole. There were quick bites of pain at first, but they were overshadowed by the incredible bliss.

He couldn't tell how much he was taking, but it felt enormous. His body was so wonderfully full that he wondered if he might burst, his insides pushed to their limits and each nerve firing away in pleasurable pulses. It was beyond anything he could have imagined, and yet he still hungered for more.

"Rota," he urged. "Come on... fuck me... I can take it."

"Alexander." Rota's voice was a low grumble, rough with desire.

"Fuck me!" Alexander snapped as he cracked his hand down on Rota's ass. "Now!"

Rota slammed the tentacle forward, making Alexander yelp loudly. He halted at once. "Wait, are you all right?"

"Don't stop, don't you dare stop! Don't you dare—ah!" Alexander whipped his head back against the pillows as Rota slammed into him again, gritting his teeth and growling. He raised his legs to ease the deep stretch, finally letting out a deep moan of pleasure.

"Ohhh, my love." Rota's voice joined Alexander's, and his tentacles coiled around Alexander's thighs to offer support and spread him wide.

"Ah, ahhh, oh fuck!" Alexander braced himself against the headboard, not even caring how hard it was rattling against the wall. Being speared perfectly on Rota's fat tentacle was the only thing that mattered, and he was smiling like a fool, giving himself over to the beautiful act completely.

Countless moments of heartache and failure, a river of miserable tears, and a lifetime of longing were finally being relieved, and Alexander wanted this ecstasy to last forever.

There was another tentacle moving over his body, also slitted, now swallowing every inch of his cock. No, he wanted this to last, he wanted it to go on and on—fuck!

Alexander came with a sob, flashes of light dancing across his vision as he bucked up into the tentacle sucking him so eagerly. Everything was too sensitive and incredible, and he groaned when the tentacle inside of him suddenly swelled. There was heat and a rush of being filled, and he pulled Rota into a fierce kiss as they came together.

There was something else, a new feeling, something warm and beautiful rolling through them both like a wave of sunshine. It made Alexander's head throb, and he wanted another taste of it, but it was already fading away.

You're perfect, I love you, I want more, I want everything, I think I might pass out, fuck, it was perfect, it's so good—

I love you, Alexander, you're my whole world, you're the stars in my sky, the love of my life, you're all I could ever want—

I love you, I love you—
I love you so much.

Their thoughts collided, overlapping as their lips met and parted with breathless kisses. The energy between them remained wonderfully charged, and though the heat was simmering down, it did not dissipate. Alexander was a little sore, but not overly so, although it was definitely weird when Rota pulled out and left him empty.

"Again."

"Already?" Rota laughed and kissed him. "Mmm… yes, my love. As many times as you'd like."

"We'll never leave this bed," Alexander mumbled.

The slitted tentacle that was sucking Alexander now took its place between his legs, easily slipping back inside his hole and thrusting deep. It was slower this time, as some of the earlier urgency had faded, and Alexander let himself relax and enjoy the steady pumping.

"Tentacles," he murmured. "How many again…. Five?"

"Yes, I have five used for mating," Rota replied. "There are four that are open for penetrating and receiving, and one that is only designed for penetration."

"Where is *that* one?"

"Mm, you're so greedy." Rota chuckled and pushed the tentacle in particularly hard. "We'll get there, my love."

The depth made Alexander grunt, but he didn't want to give up yet. He rubbed Rota's hip, urging, "Come on. I can take more. You know I can."

"Do I?" Rota smirked. "I should have known you were going to be insatiable, even for your first time."

"Had a lot of time to think about what I want."

"Fair…." Rota glanced over Alexander's lips. "Would you like… would you like to taste me as I pleasure you?"

"Is that gonna get me closer to having your big magical penetration-only tentacle?"

"Yes. I was also hoping you'd enjoy it."

"Bring it on, then." Alexander laughed as a slitted tentacle almost instantly appeared in front of his mouth. "I guess you've been thinking about this a lot too, huh?"

"Yes."

Alexander wrapped his fingers around the tentacle, enjoying the smooth texture and the heat. It was so different from the ghostly touches, and he knew he never wanted those again, not after having this. He licked the tip slowly, following the same rhythm of the tentacle still moving gently inside of him, and he loved how Rota moaned for him.

Determined to hear more of those lovely sounds, he took a deep breath and slid the tip into his mouth. He couldn't take much, but he sucked and twirled his tongue around like it was a lollipop, swallowing back the spit that pooled.

"Alexander... I...." Rota couldn't even speak, reduced to stunted whines and gasps. The tentacle inside of Alexander thrusted a little faster, and soon a second one approached, rubbing around his already full hole.

"Mmm...." Alexander sucked harder and tried to push down, desperate to take on another. He felt reckless and eager, and he wiggled impatiently, daring to take Rota's tentacle deeper into his mouth just to hear him cry out.

The second tentacle at his hole pressed in, the tip squirming inside of him until it could thrust. The new stretch made Alexander almost choke, and he had to stop sucking so he could breathe. His body was caught between pulling away from the added intrusion and grinding down on it, and he fought to take it.

"F-fuck.... Rota...." Alexander squeezed the tentacle in his hand, and he whimpered as the two appendages inside of him moved as one, fucking him in deep, passionate thrusts.

He didn't know if he was actually a virgin before this, but he was certain even if he wasn't that no mortal man could compare. The two tentacles were twisting and pounding, hot and slick, and the pleasure was miles beyond anything he'd ever been able to give himself.

Rota ran a hand over the side of Alexander's body, tentacles and fingers lavishing his skin with bold caresses, bowing his head to kiss Alexander's shoulder and chest. He fucked Alexander even harder, diving into his body over and over, groaning brokenly, "My love... I'm...!"

"Come on!" Alexander urged as he stuffed the tentacle he'd been sucking back into his mouth. *Give it to me. Give it all to me. Fuck me up, make me come, make me come again, please, fuck, I wanna come—*

Rota let out a roar like Alexander had never heard, loud enough to shake the glass in the windows, and he pulled the tentacle right from Alexander's mouth to crash their lips together in a ferocious kiss.

Alexander threw his arms around Rota's shoulders, and he moaned when the tentacles inside of him flooded his hole. There was so much come that it was gushing out with every thrust, and the resulting wet friction pushed Alexander over the edge. He came even harder than before, his back curling right off the bed as his hips jerked with each hot pulse. "Rota!"

All he saw was stars and light, and the ecstasy made him want to sob. His orgasm wasn't ending, instead going on with endless waves that took his breath away and made his cock twitch helplessly. Just as he thought the insane bliss was dwindling, Rota sent the cock Alexander had been sucking on to join the other two, pushing its way inside to deliver another thick load.

"Oh fuck! Ahh, Rota!" Alexander did cry then, his entire body overwhelmed by another mind-shattering orgasm. All three tentacles flexed inside of him, and he buried his face against Rota's chest as he rode out the incredible storm of passion.

"I love you," Rota whispered, wrapping Alexander up tight. "I love you, my beautiful, beautiful boy."

"Love you," Alexander managed. "My beautiful god."

One by one, Rota carefully removed his tentacles and placed a lingering kiss on Alexander's lips.

Alexander couldn't stop smiling, and sweet bubbly energy thrummed all throughout their bond. That new sunshine feeling was still there, and it only added to the tender moment. Even though he was sweaty and sticky and his muscles were way too heavy to lift, he'd never been so happy.

Everything was perfect.

"I think I'm ready for the big one," Alexander teased.

"We will get there, my love…." Rota's eyes closed, and he sighed. "But first I need to rest. I'm so sorry."

"What? What's wrong?" Alexander frowned as he felt Rota leave Ollie, and his insides clenched with the awkwardness of having Ollie pressed against his naked body.

I'm sorry, my love. Rota sounded far away. *I'm absolutely exhausted. Possessing Ollie for so long was much more tiring than I was expecting.*

"It's okay," Alexander quickly reassured him. He didn't want Rota to feel guilty when what they'd just shared had been incredible and beyond his wildest dreams.

Could have done without the giant dopey redhead still on top of him, though.

"Wow." Ollie had the biggest, dumbest smile on his face as he beamed down at Alexander. "So, uh… that was awesome."

"Were you… aware?" Alexander cringed, trying not to imagine Ollie there watching him and Rota have sex.

"Well, yeah." Ollie rolled onto his side and offered an arm out to cuddle. "I mean, I could feel what Rota was feeling. And you. Like, through the bond. You couldn't feel me?"

The wave of energy that felt like sunlight…. Rota smiled. *That was you?*

"Yeah." Ollie glanced between his legs with a goofy laugh. "Uh, yeah. Kinda explains the very wet spot in my sweats. Somehow, like, I came with you guys. That was pretty wild." He quirked his brows at Alexander. "You didn't feel me, though?"

"I don't think so." Alexander regretted the lie, but he had to stick to it. He didn't like what was happening at all, and he felt filthy now. What should have been an intimate act seemed tainted.

I felt it…. Rota sounded exhausted but very happy. *It was beautiful.*

"Yeah. It totally was. Thank you, guys. For, you know, letting me be a part of it." Ollie smiled, leaning in to kiss Alexander.

Alexander froze. "I thought we were done. Rota needs to rest."

"Oh, uh, I guess?" Ollie pulled back immediately. "I'm sorry. I thought… I like you, and I like Rota. We just shared this crazy awesome thing, and I wanted—"

"To what? To have some of me for yourself?"

"No! I wanted… uh…." Ollie floundered. "Cuddle?"

Alexander, please, it's all right.

"Ollie, I want you to leave," Alexander said firmly.

Absolutely not! Alexander, what are you doing?

"No, it's okay." Ollie respectfully pulled away. "You guys need some time. It's special, I dig it."

Ollie….

Alexander rolled over, putting his back to Ollie and staring at the wall. "Thanks for understanding. Now go."

"Thank you, Alexander." Ollie smiled. There was the sound of a dresser drawer opening and closing. "You too, Rota. It was super cool to feel that kinda love again."

"Yeah. Whatever."

The door shut, leaving Alexander and Rota alone.

Alexander! Rota was furious, barking, *Why did you do that? You had no reason to be so cruel to him after what he did for us!*

"It was fucking weird," Alexander argued fiercely. "This was supposed to be our first time, just me and you, and all I can think about is him watching me get fucked!"

I'm sorry, my love. Truly. I would never wish any sort of discomfort upon you.

"I'm sensing a 'but.'" Alexander sat up, using Rota's tentacles to grab his jacket so he could get a cigarette.

But that was still very mean of you. You can feel him too. I know you can. And so you know as well as I do that Ollie's intentions were not so lecherous. He wanted to share in our happiness—

"See, there's the problem. It's *our* happiness. A fuckin' happiness we've waited years to have! I don't wanna share shit."

Why did you lie about feeling him through the bond?

"Hey! Get out of my head," Alexander warned, glaring as he lit up. "I lied because… because…." He was flustered, and he took a deep drag before his thoughts took over to finish the sentence. *Because it felt like it belonged with us, like the most natural thing in the world, and I don't want anyone else. I only want you.*

There is nothing wrong with being attracted to Ollie, Rota soothed. *He is very handsome and kind—*

"He's an idiot."

Ah, but a very sweet one! You like him and you don't want to admit it.

"We've barely known him a day. Chill." Alexander ran a hand through his hair, flicking his ashes away.

Alexander….

"Stay out of my head, Rota. There's nothing else to talk about, and it's not happening again."

Hmph. Rota sounded like he was smiling. *All right.*

"What?" Alexander didn't understand why Rota was so happy about that. He'd expected more of a fight.

I'll remember you said that.

"Smug bastard."

Brat.

Alexander smiled, and the tension brewing between them faded. He didn't like fighting with Rota, and he was truly thankful to Ollie for allowing them to have this intimate time together.

But he didn't care how right it had felt—Ollie didn't belong with them.

After finishing his cigarette and cleaning up, Alexander got dressed. They still had work to do, like catching a murderer and translating the book still tucked away in his trench coat pocket.

The sooner, the better.

He stepped out into the living room, and he didn't immediately see Ollie.

Kitchen, Rota said.

Alexander headed there, stopping short when he saw....

Ollie was *cleaning*.

"Oh, hey!" Ollie flashed a bright smile, loading the last of what had cluttered the sink into the dishwasher. He was wearing a fresh pair of sweatpants and nothing else. "You hungry?"

"What are you doing?" Alexander noticed a frying pan on the stove he hadn't been able to see before because of the trash. Something yellow, maybe eggs, was cooking.

"Well, okay, it's dorky, but there's always, like, breakfast the morning after?" Ollie popped in a tab of soap and closed the dishwasher. "You know, the morning after the sex. And I know this is still like, the afternoon, but I thought you might... maybe want to eat something. Uh. After that."

Alexander's stomach fluttered, and he ignored a nudge from Rota. He crossed his arms. "Thank you."

Thank you, Ollie, Rota gushed. *That's so very thoughtful of you. Isn't that thoughtful, Alexander?*

"I said thank you," he muttered.

"I figured after we eat, we could go look up Tim like you talked about and go see him," Ollie suggested.

"And what are we eating?" Alexander peered around Ollie and frowned at the stove.

"I'm making scrambled eggs."

"Sure about that?"

"Yeah, why?"

"The pan is on fire."

"Fuck!"

CHAPTER 7.

THE EGGS could not be saved, but luckily Ollie had more.

While Ollie began again on a fresh batch of scrambled eggs, Alexander used Ollie's laptop to look up Tim Bateman. Tracking him down through the Lucian church directory was laughably easy, and it wasn't long before Alexander had all of his personal information, including his home address.

"Oh yeah. That's Tim!" Ollie said as he brought over three plates balanced on his arm. He plopped right beside Alexander, setting them down around the coffee table and pointing at the picture of a middle-aged man with graying hair. "That's him."

"I know. It has his name under the picture." Alexander scooted over purposefully. "Why are there three plates?"

"There's three of us?" Ollie scoffed and took a big bite of eggs, shaking his head.

"Rota doesn't eat."

It's still very thoughtful. Rota was smiling, and it sounded like he was trying not to laugh.

"Well. Fine." Ollie picked up the extra plate and dumped it on his own. "Hmmph."

Thank you, Rota said. *I appreciate it.*

"You're welcome." Ollie kept on eating. "So, we gonna go after this?"

"No." Alexander picked at his plate. "Rota and I are. You need to stay here."

"Wait, I thought I was going with you."

So did I. Rota was frowning now. *What's wrong, Alexander?*

Alexander had to fight to control his thoughts, and he replied hastily, "It's not safe. We don't know what sort of person Tim really is, and Ollie needs to get lit and translate a book." *Lala, nope, nope, lalala, nooope.*

Alexander....

"You don't want me to come because of the sex?" Ollie asked bluntly, picking right up on the very thing Alexander didn't want him to hear.

Dammit! Alexander groaned.

Are you still upset? Rota asked.

"No! I mean, yes! I just…." Alexander dropped his fork and stood up in a huff. *I can still feel where you were inside of me, and it's weird having him right here. It's all fucking weird, and I don't like feeling this out of control.* "I want to go."

Ollie either didn't hear Alexander's frantic thoughts or, more likely, chose to ignore them. "No, yeah. I can hang back, uh, I gotta translate. Book. On it."

No, Rota argued. *Ollie, you're coming with us.* He turned on Alexander, sliding a tentacle along his arm. *You know he isn't safe here, and Stoker may come back to check. We talked about this.*

Alexander gritted his teeth.

"I mean, I could… I could go with you." Ollie fidgeted and shoved another bite of eggs in his mouth. "Um. If you wanted me to. I could, uh, help. Look around and stu-fahfah."

"Okay, why do you do that?" Alexander snapped.

"Do what?" Ollie blinked.

"*Fahfah.* Why do you do that?"

"Because there's two *F*s."

"That doesn't make any sense!" Alexander threw up his hands. "You don't actually have to say both letters. That's *stupid*. It's so stupid!"

"But—"

"No! You don't say you want bu-*tahtah*-er on toast, do you?"

"Well, no—"

"You don't say you need a ru-*bahbah*-er band, huh? Huh?"

"No." Ollie held his head high. "Because those aren't *F*s. So, ha!"

"For fuck's sake." Alexander sighed loudly.

Alexander? Rota pressed. *You know Stoker is going to be expecting results, yes? Which means he will probably be checking on us at some point—*

"I know," Alexander muttered.

—and since he placed that watchman spell on Ollie, he will be able to take him again if he so chooses. I know you do not want that to happen, do you?

No, Alexander reluctantly admitted.

Then sit down right now, finish your eggs, and let us all go together find a Lucian priest to accuse of murder!

"Damn, Rota," Ollie whispered in awe. "You're kinda hot when you're bossy."

Alexander refused to acknowledge the accuracy of that—especially when his face was turning as red as his eyes, thinking about other areas to apply that surprising dominant streak—but he did sit back down and grabbed the eggs. "Whatever."

Good boy, Rota said smugly.

For fuck's sake. Alexander ate as quickly as he could, and then he had to wait for Ollie to put more clothes on.

When Ollie came out of the bedroom with a neon green tank top and a blue jacket that was printed with little snowmen to accompany his gray sweats, Alexander didn't say a word.

That is, until he saw the sparkly purple jelly sandals.

"What are you wearing?"

"Clothes?" Ollie shrugged. "What?"

"I can't believe I'm going out in public with you. Again."

"Hey, we can't all dress like cool little vampires."

"*Vampire?*"

Ollie raised two of his fingers up to his mouth to mimic fangs and hissed.

"Ohhh, you big idiot—"

Now, now, Rota scolded. *You both look very handsome. Alexander, your trench coat is very dashing. Ollie, I love all the colors, and your shoes look very comfortable.*

"Thank you." Ollie beamed. "They are."

"Let's fuckin' go." Alexander raised his hand to direct Rota's magic. "First stop, the church."

Lucian churches were nearly always white brick or stone with lots of windows and tall steeples. The Archersville First Lucian Solis Church was no different than any other one Alexander had ever seen, and he made a face looking up at the big glass doors. He knew he had been raised Lucian by his parents after seeing some of his own personal documents at Hazel, and there was a very good chance they might have worshipped right here at this very church.

Then again, there was no way to know for sure. He didn't remember. A familiar ache resurfaced, and he hated not knowing.

I'm right here, Rota soothed, sensing his discomfort.

I know. Alexander charged forward with Ollie behind him, and he pulled open the doors.

The sanctuary was well lit from the many windows, and the pews were all clean and neat. There was a large sunburst hanging above the pulpit on a red velvet upholstered plaque. A quick scan revealed Lucian protection wards above the windows and doorways, and Alexander sneered.

All magic originated from the Sagittarian gods, and spells like wards were written or spoken in their language of godstongue. Over time, the Lucians—who claimed magic came from their Lord of Light and not the heathen gods worshipped by Sages—altered spells by adding in their own symbols and words. These additions were ultimately meaningless, and the result was comparable to a bus parked up in the branches of a majestic oak tree.

Not only did it weaken the original spell, but it was hideous to behold for anyone who could read godstongue. Alexander was hardly fluent in any dialect of the sacred language, but he knew enough to recognize how awful it was.

"May I help you?" a polite voice asked, piping up from back behind the pulpit.

Alexander recognized the person speaking as Tim from his picture. He walked toward him with his hands clasped behind his back. A quick perception spell revealed Tim as human with a faint earth aura. "Oh, I think you can."

Tim frowned at that, and he looked past Alexander to Ollie. His face lit up with recognition, and he laughed. "Oh! Ollie! Hi! How are you?"

"Hey, Tim!" Ollie waved. "I'm doin' okay. Look, uh, me and my boyfriend need to ask you a few questions if that's okay."

"I suppose so?" Tim stepped out from around the pulpit. He was wearing the white-and-gold robes of the Lord of Light, and he offered a timid smile to Alexander. "What can I do for you?"

"Hold still," Alexander replied.

"Pardon?"

Alexander commanded Rota's tentacles to surge forward, wrapping around Tim's neck and waist. He cast the most powerful truth spell he knew, coating it over Tim's body from head to toe. He then pushed him up against the vaulted ceiling and held him there, calling out, "I

need to ask you about the deaths of Eric Grimes, Lucy Myers, Brady...
something.... Shit, what was it?"

Tim screamed hysterically, kicking and swinging his arms as he
tried to escape Rota's hold.

Brady Lincoln, Rota supplied.

"Right. Brady Lincoln," Alexander continued. "Baxter Yeun, Macy—"
Lacie.

"*Lacie* Briggs." Alexander crossed his arms. "Know anything
about them?"

"Put me down, please!" Tim hollered. "Please, for the love of all
that is touched by the Lord's sacred light! I don't know what you're
talking about! Please!"

"What are you doing?" Ollie gasped in horror.

"Finding out if he's a killer or not?" Alexander frowned. "What do
you think I'm doing?"

"Why are you being so *mean*?"

"Look." Alexander swung Tim from one end of the church to the
other, dragging him along the peak of the ceiling. "We need to know if
he did it or not. I don't have the time or patience to sit around and have
a long in-depth interrogation, and I definitely don't want to give him a
chance to lie."

"Please, I pray the Lord of Light's radiance washes over me and
protects me from this fiend of the abyss," Tim babbled above them. "I pray
our Lord's light finds him and purges the wicked ways in his heart!"

"Yeah, fat chance of that," Alexander mumbled. "So? Nothing?
You don't know anything?" He gave Tim a hard shake when he didn't
respond. "Hello!"

"Oh, Lord... I... I don't know!" Tim cried. "I-I prayed over Brady
Lincoln at his funeral! His, his aunt is Lucian! A fine woman! She asked
me to come. And, and I knew Eric from, from the bar!"

"That's it?"

"Yes! Please! I heard people talking about the deaths at the funeral!
I didn't even know Eric was dead until I worked the service! Same with
Lucy!" Tim was calming down, as much as someone could who was being
held forty feet in the air, and he took a deep breath. "I confess I did not
know Baxter, but I did know Lacie. Are you telling me she is dead too?"

The spell is not detecting any deception, Rota said. *He appears
to be telling the truth. There is some faint residue of that incense on*

his robes, however. Although, I must confess, it's also all around us in the aisle.

Great. That doesn't help us at all. Alexander lowered Tim back down to the ground, but he did not release him. "Do you know of anyone who would want to hurt them? Any of them?"

"N-no." Tim shook his head urgently. "They were all very kind. They would let me pray for them, and Eric even let me recite the Litany to him once." He looked to Ollie. "Please, Ollie. You can't think I had anything to do with this! You know I couldn't hurt anyone. Never!"

Ollie frowned. "I know, Tim. You've always been real super cool. But we found some stu-fahfah that kinda makes it seem like you did it. I mean, or like, somebody here at the church."

"Please help me!" Tim begged. "I-I don't know who hurt those people! I cannot think of anyone who would! If I did, I swear I would tell the police at once!"

Still quite truthful, Rota mused. *I believe our friends from the bar were mistaken, and Ollie is right. The incense is hardly conclusive, and it could belong to anyone who came to this church or any other Lucian service in the city.*

Fuck. Alexander finally released Tim. "All right, thanks."

Tim nearly fell over, and he leaned against one of the pews to steady himself. "Wait, that's it?"

"Yes. You don't know anything. And this has been a giant waste of time."

"We're really, really, super sorry!" Ollie grimaced.

"See!" Alexander whirled on Ollie. "That's what I'm talking about. You said 'sorry,' not so-*rahrah*-ry. It's ridiculous!"

"But those are *R*s," Ollie argued indignantly. "You don't say them that way, little dude!"

"Are you sure? Like rea-*lahlah*-ly sure?"

Ollie folded his arms and pouted. "You're making fun of me."

"You... you just assaulted me!" Tim exclaimed, pointing at Alexander. "I should be calling the authorities—!"

"Oh, right." Alexander turned back to Tim and held out his hand, aiming a tentacle at Tim's forehead. He bopped him hard, using the magic to reach into his mind and pull out the memories of their encounter. He curled his fingers into a fist, the tentacle withdrawing and crushing them. "There. Let's go."

Tim was shaken, and he clumsily sat down in the pew. He looked around, clearly confused, and his face lit up again when he saw Ollie. "Ollie! Hey! How are you doing?"

Alexander snorted, turned to leave, and marched to the door.

"Uh, hey, Tim." Ollie waved awkwardly. "I'm good. Hope you are. Good to see you! Gotta go, bye!" He ran to catch up with Alexander, hissing under his breath, "What did you guys do?"

Alexander rolled his eyes as he walked outside. "What? Your magical starsight didn't show you?"

"I wasn't paying attention. I was trying to look at your butt."

Alexander almost fell down the steps, and he had to throw out Rota's tentacles on the railings to catch himself. "Excuse me?"

The coat really is not flattering at all, Rota said. *The pants, however, are quite nice.*

"You turned around to talk to Tim," Ollie said with a shy grin, "and I'm super sorry, but I got destructed."

"Distracted?"

"That too."

Alexander was immediately defensive, certain it was a cruel joke, but he could only sense a tender affection in the new bond that had formed between himself, Rota, and Ollie.

And he didn't know what to do with it.

That big dopey smile of Ollie's was not the least bit adorable, and there was absolutely nothing about the way Ollie looked at Alexander that made his heart race faster. The malapropisms weren't endearing in the slightest, and he certainly didn't want to hold his hand again or kiss that stupid smile right off his perfect face.

Shit.

"We're leaving," Alexander said quickly.

Where are we going? Rota asked. *We don't have much to report if you're thinking of seeing Stoker.*

"What about the crime scenes?" Ollie suggested. "I mean, it's worth a peek, right? I could look around."

"Holy shit, you had a good idea. Awesome, great," Alexander agreed right away. "Let's go."

They'd already been to Dead to Rites, and Alexander didn't know exactly where the body had been found. The next place that popped into his head was the grocery store, the Jitney Jungle, and he took them there.

The parking lot wasn't too crowded, and no one noticed when they magically appeared by a shopping cart return stall.

"Okay. We're here. Let's look around." Alexander marched forward, summoning Rota's magic for a strong perception spell.

"Got it. Looking around." Ollie followed, and he scratched his head. "What are we looking for?"

"Anything weird or out of place. Clues, Ollie. We are looking for clues."

"Huh. All right. Well, you lemme know when we've found some."

Alexander scanned over the rows of cars, ducking between them as he searched. There wasn't much here. He saw a woman wearing heavy glamour to hide some wrinkles, one man who was carrying a silencing totem, and a young lady who had traces of lavender from an anxiety spell on her hands.

He saw no trace of the marigold incense—wait.

"Over there." Alexander headed to the front of the grocery store and took a hard right toward the corner where he'd spotted the glimmer.

That's it, Rota confirmed. *Marigold with fire.*

"But the guy got killed over in the parking lot, right?" Ollie asked. "This is not the parking lot."

"Maybe our killer was hiding over here." Alexander glanced around the corner, and he saw the side of a big green dumpster. Movement caught his eye, and he walked toward it.

"What is it?" Ollie had to jog to keep up with him.

"I thought I saw...." *Rota, go!*

On it. Rota pushed ahead in a flash.

Alexander stopped at the next corner, and he grunted as Ollie ran right into him. *Watch it! We're trying to be covert here, for fuck's sake!*

"Sorry!" Ollie whispered anxiously. "I didn't see you stop!"

"Shut up!" Alexander groaned, forgetting to use their bond to speak. He took a deep breath to calm himself, asking Rota, *Hey, anything?*

Yes, lots of marigold incense all over the dumpsters, and Will is here.

Will? Alexander frowned. *The kid from the bar?*

Yes.

What's he doing?

He's.... Rota sighed. *He's going through the dumpsters for food. He's taking what I assume must be expired products from the store and loading them into a large bag.*

Alexander felt a pang of sympathy. He and Rota were no strangers to scavenging for food. *Do you see anything else?*

No, Rota replied.

"Wait here." Ollie boldly stepped around Alexander.

"Wait, what are you doing?" Alexander hissed.

"Just wait a second!" Ollie hissed back, and he headed toward the dumpster where Will was.

Alexander knew he looked very obvious, but he couldn't help but peek around the corner to see what Ollie was going to do. He saw him approach Will, who seemed a little startled to see him, but he didn't run and allowed Ollie to speak with him.

Ollie reached into his wallet and handed a protesting Will some cash. They hugged briefly, and Will ran off into the alley behind the dumpsters with his scavenged food and the money. Ollie watched him for a few moments and walked back to Alexander with his hands in his pockets.

Ollie, that was very kind of you, Rota said. *Is he all right?*

"Yeah, I think so?" Ollie shrugged. "Kid's lived a rough life. I wish I had more, but I never carry much cash."

"For all you know, he's gonna spend the money on drugs." Alexander rolled his eyes. "If you really wanted to help him, you should have taken him inside and bought him groceries."

"Maybe I will sometime," Ollie argued, "but right now we're sort of in the middle of a big ol' investigation, yeah? It wasn't that much money, and who cares what he does with it? Sometimes it's just nice to be nice, you know."

"People will take advantage of you."

"I know, but just because something bad might happen isn't a good reason to stop trying to be kind."

Alexander snorted. He had absolutely no rebuttal to that, and meeting Ollie's gaze was uncomfortable. He looked away, mumbling a quick, "Whatever," before transporting them to the next crime scene.

The parking lot at the funeral home wasn't much more helpful than the grocery store. There didn't seem to be a funeral going on, since it was almost empty, though a peek around the back of the building revealed more of the marigold incense on a rear exit door. Other than that, they found nothing, and Alexander took them to the next location.

The Hot Pot was a restaurant a few blocks away from the hubbub of downtown Archersville, and Alexander brought them into the alley just next to it to avoid being seen. Without waiting for Ollie, as usual, he walked out and around to the front of the building.

It was sleek and modern-looking, with black drapes obscuring the windows and a large flaming fountain burning inside an elaborate rock garden that stretched from one end to the other. More flames flickered in two big lanterns set up on either side of the front door. There was an open patio on the other side, and it was very crowded from what Alexander could see.

"Hot Pot?" Alexander read aloud as he peered up at the sign. "What kind of place is this?"

"They do hibachi!" Ollie replied once he caught up. "Like, if you sit inside, there's these giant tables where you can sit down and they'll cook everything right in front of you! It's super cool."

I've never.... Alexander tried to resist finishing the thought, and he turned around to head back into the alley to find the dumpsters.

"We could eat there if you want," Ollie offered.

"What?"

"You know. If you wanted to. I could take you there. To eat. With me."

Oh! Rota sounded excited. *That could be fun!*

"Yeah!" Ollie grinned. "The chicken is awesome. And oh! The noodles? And the white sauce? Oh my gods, I'm gonna drool if I think about them for too long."

Would you like that, Alexander? Rota asked politely.

"Maybe later." Alexander shook his head. "We've still got a lot of work to do."

"Yeah, okay." Ollie was clearly disappointed. "Well, if you wanna try it later but maybe not deal with all the people, we can always order it and have it delivered."

Alexander frowned, and he glanced back at Ollie. "Seriously?"

"Well, I know what it's like not to get out much." Ollie shrugged. "Today was the first time I've been out of my apartment in weeks."

"Why?"

"Seeing the stu-fahfah I see… I can't quiet it down, it never stops, and it honestly scares the hell out of me. I dream about that rotten angel guy constantly, and almost being sacrificed was a pretty big downer. But today? Being with you guys?" Ollie smiled. "I wasn't scared. And I thought maybe treating you to some kickass hibachi would be a nice way to say thank you."

"I...." Alexander blushed and scrambled to walk away as fast as he could. *Okay, yes, that would be nice, but maybe later, like tonight, okay? Fuck, I can't believe I'm saying yes to this. But later. Not right now.*

"Yeah! Totally!" Ollie was beaming, bright as ever, and he easily caught back up with Alexander to walk beside him. "It's a date, then."

Alexander choked on air. "It's not a date! It's food!"

"It's dinner."

It does sound a lot like a date, Rota said innocently.

Alexander swore he could feel Rota smirking at him.

Ollie, the doofus, looked like someone had given him a new puppy.

"All of my hate!" was all Alexander managed to get out before he stomped off toward the gate of the fencing surrounding the dumpsters.

"I think he's happy, but I can't tell when he makes that face," Ollie whispered loudly to Rota.

He's much happier than he's letting on, I'll say that.

Alexander ignored them and whipped the gate open, stopping short when he saw someone digging around in one of the dumpsters. He was surprised to see anyone going headfirst into trash, but it was also a surprise because they'd just seen this person earlier.

It was Will.

If that wasn't odd enough, a closer look at the bottoms of Will's shoes as they dangled out of the dumpster revealed something Alexander hadn't noticed before:

Marigolds.

CHAPTER 8.

"WILL?" OLLIE blinked as he peered over the top of Alexander's head. "What are you doing here?"

"Ollie?" Will scrambled out of the dumpster and then dusted himself off. "Uh. Looking for food, what does it look like?"

"But that's what you were doing at the grocery store," Alexander accused. He cast a truth spell with a thought, and he was ready to grab Will—

No shaking! Ollie pleaded inside his head.

Ugh.

"Wow, you're super observant, huh." Will snorted. "I scavenge from a lot of places. You know there's a lot of people who need to eat, okay?"

"People where?"

"Around." Will stood up straight. "Don't you worry about that. I'm just here to get the food and use it to fill some hungry bellies." He frowned at them. "What are you guys doing here?"

"Looking into the murders," Alexander replied without hesitation. "You know one of the victims was found in these dumpsters."

"Yeah, I know." Will's frown was sad. "I found her. Lucy."

I thought Stoker was the one who found them all because of the watchman spell? Rota asked suspiciously. *That didn't register as a lie, so he must be telling the truth.*

"I thought Stoker found all the victims?" Alexander asked out loud.

"He was late getting to Lucy, I guess." Will shrugged. "I had just flipped open the lid when boom, there she is, and then boom, two seconds later, here's Stoker. He gave me a pretty rough time, asked me a bunch of questions, then let me go."

If Stoker vetted him, why does it feel like you want to accuse him of murder? Rota asked. *Because of what you saw on his shoes?*

Yes. Alexander crossed his arms. "So, you come here to look for food and over at the grocery store. You run errands for Jackie at the bar, and I've heard you work for someone over at the funeral home too."

"Alexander?" Ollie touched his shoulder. "Hey, wait, what are you saying?"

"I'm saying it's very strange that he just so happens to regularly visit the same places where some of the victims were found."

Will scowled.

"Please don't shake him," Ollie pleaded. "You don't have to do that."

"I also live over by the gas station where Lacie Briggs was found." Will turned so he was staring at Alexander head-on, his one visible eye narrowed. "You gonna try and pin that one on me too?"

"Maybe." Alexander cocked his head, and he debated on whether to grab Will and toss him around. He was hesitating because of Ollie's plea, and he didn't like that.

"I wouldn't hurt my friends," Will insisted. "They've been good to me, better than any other normies have."

"Explain the marigold incense on your shoes."

"The what?" Will blinked. "The marigold...." He stared down at his feet. "I don't use any marigold incense."

I did sense something burned or intended to be burned, Rota said quickly. *Not to be tacky, but maybe it's not actually incense. Perhaps the essence of the burned...?*

Is him, Alexander agreed in his thoughts. *Because he was burned.*

"Oh!" Will snapped his fingers. "It's my body powder."

"Excuse me?" Alexander drawled.

"I use a body powder for my burns that's infused with marigold and aloe that Doctor York made for me." Will cringed. "Except I dropped it last week and the bottle shattered on my bathroom floor. I tried to clean it up, but it's a really fine powder. It's probably all over my shoes."

"But it's not on *you*," Alexander said as he scanned Will again.

"Well, no. Duh. I just told you I broke the bottle." Will quirked his brow. "I had to start using a different powder until Doctor York can make me a new batch of the other stuff."

Still being honest, Rota said with a long sigh.

Will gestured expectantly. "Well? Are you happy now? Or am I still a suspected killer?"

Alexander thought for a moment. *Maybe I can shake it out of him—*

"No shaking!" Ollie shouted.

Will stared at Ollie. "Are you okay? You're kinda freaking me out."

"Since you've just so happened to be at every single crime scene or in the vicinity, is there anything useful you can tell us?" Alexander asked briskly.

"No." Will reached up to adjust his mask. "I already told Stoker this same crap. I found Lucy, but I never saw anyone. I didn't see shit. I know the guys at Dead think it was that missionary guy, but I don't think he'd hurt anyone. Even if he knew what they were."

Alexander pulled out a cigarette and lit up, inhaling deeply and exhaling as he rubbed his temple. He was getting a headache.

They'd found two great suspects and eliminated both in a single day.

This was not going well at all.

"We were at the church a little while ago and talked to Tim," Ollie said with a faint grimace. "Trust me. It wasn't him."

"Well, it's gotta be somebody that hates the everlasting people, don't you think?" Will glanced between them. "What other motive could there be?"

"There's certain spells that you need, uh, parts like that for." Ollie made a face. "But—"

"Let's go." Alexander turned to leave, stalking down the alley and trying to gather his thoughts as he puffed away at his cigarette.

Five victims, all descendants of the everlasting people, all patrons of the bar except one, Rota rattled off what Alexander was already thinking. *Marigold on two of the bodies with the essence of having been burned or intended to be....*

Ollie called out a hasty goodbye to Will, jogging over to catch up with Alexander. "Hey! Wait! Damn, you guys are always leaving me!"

My apologies, Rota said. *He's very focused right now.*

Yeah, focused on what a total shitshow this is! Alexander lashed out and smacked at the alley wall with one of Rota's tentacles, leaving a sizable hole and scattering bits of brick everywhere. The urge to keep pounding away until it disintegrated into nothing was strong, and his anger was bubbling up in heavy waves.

The entire situation was stupid. He and Rota should have attempted to translate the book on their own instead of getting involved with any of this, and Alexander wished they could just leave. He wasn't a hero or a detective, he didn't like helping people, and he definitely did not have the patience for this.

And it was far too familiar.

Working for Stoker for Ollie's sake was way too much like being enslaved by Gronoch again because there was no escape. Alexander couldn't take the book and leave with Rota because things had become weirdly complicated with Ollie now.

Not only would Rota not forgive Alexander if he made them leave without helping him, but Alexander didn't think he could forgive himself.

How could so much have gone so very wrong in a single day?

"You didn't even say bye to Will." Ollie reached for Alexander's arm. "Hey! Hang on a second, please?"

Alexander's immediate instinct was to pull away, but he could sense Rota was with Ollie now. The touch on his arm was Ollie and Rota together, and he turned to face them both.

It was strange to look up into Ollie's eyes and see Rota with him in there, stranger still to feel both of their concern for him. He knew it was Ollie pulling him in for a hug, but it was Rota who kissed him.

We're going to figure this out, Rota promised as he held the kiss. *We've already made much progress. You and I can do anything together. We took on a god.... This is nothing to us, my love.*

Alexander flicked away his cigarette and curled his hands in the lapels of Ollie's snowman jacket, letting the kiss soothe his anger. Rota's love was a wonderful balm, and his adoring kiss eased the familiar rage he always struggled with.

I'm here too. Ollie's thoughts were quiet but earnest. *We'll get it done. You're a smart and powerful little dude, and you and this fuckin' god here got this.*

I fear this "fuckin' god" is still quite tired.... Rota chuckled. *But we shall persevere. Together.*

Alexander felt when Rota left Ollie's body, leaving his lips locked with Ollie's.

Ollie's hands, now under his control, moved up to a more respectful height on Alexander's waist, but his lips lingered.

Alexander didn't know why, but he didn't stop kissing Ollie. He knew it wasn't Rota, but he could hear Ollie's thoughts, and in that moment, they were the most beautiful thing he'd ever heard.

I know this crap with Stoker is because of me, and I'm so sorry, and I wanna make it up to you so bad. I just wanna see you smile, hear you laugh, do whatever I can to make you happy and take all that pain away.

Let me take you to dinner. Let me cook for you! Okay, wait, no, it depends on what I'm cooking, because I almost killed a small dog accidentally—

Ollie. Alexander sighed, his grip tightening on his jacket. *Shut up.*

Right. Shutting up. Except it's my brain? And I can't shut it up. And wow, your lips are soft, like, wow they're, like, super soft, and I love how you smell. Not like it's a bad smell like you smell bad, but really good like dirt—

And you ruined it. Alexander pushed away, turning sharply to dart out of the alley to clear his head.

Alexander! Rota tried to warn him.

It came a moment too late, and Alexander smacked into a large man on the sidewalk. He ducked his head down to step around whoever it was, but a thick hand landed on his shoulder to stop him.

"Hey! Watch it!" The person grunted angrily.

Alexander was set on using Rota's magic to remove that hand very violently, but he paused when he saw who it was.

Marbles, one of the men from the bar.

"Oh! Hey, Marbles!" Ollie was there now.

"Hey." Marbles relaxed when he saw who he'd run into, and he laughed. "You guys again!"

"Move your hand before I tear it off." Alexander scowled.

Marbles did so with a frown. "You're the one that bumped into me!"

"And yet you're the one who's about to have a very unfortunate accident."

"Sorry!" Ollie reached for Alexander and pulled him back while laughing nervously. "He's so cranky. Low sugar."

"Right." Marbles cleared his throat. "Did you guys find Tim?"

"Yeah. We had a super exciting chat, but it wasn't him, okay?"

"The fuck it ain't." Marbles scowled. "Maybe you didn't ask him *politely* enough."

"Oh no. It was not polite at all." Ollie grimaced and shook his head. "There was a lot of shaking. So much."

"Hmmph...." Marbles didn't seem impressed. "Well, you just make sure you talk to Jackie and let him know what's going on—"

"Whatever." Alexander rolled his eyes and kept on walking down the sidewalk.

He didn't answer to Jackie Cheese or anyone else.

Fuck this, fuck everything, fuck—

Alexander, Rota suddenly spoke up. *We need to go home.*

Why? Alexander asked.

I believe I know what the killer is planning now. Go back and get Ollie.

Ugh. Fine. Alexander went back, finding Ollie still standing there with Marbles, chatting away.

"I've been tellin' Jackie to keep out all the damn mortals like Tim for months," Marbles was saying. "Shit wouldn't have happened if he'd just listened to me."

"Marbles, come on." Ollie frowned. "We told you it wasn't Tim! And hey, you guys let me hang out there!"

"Maybe we shouldn't. No good comes from us mixin' with you normies."

"Not cool, Marbles!" Ollie pouted. "Not cool, dude!"

"Let's go." Alexander grabbed Ollie's arm and dragged him away.

"Hey!" Ollie stumbled along, waving bye at Marbles. "Okay, try to maybe be less of a jerk! Try hating people less! See ya' later, dude!" He tugged at Alexander's grip. "Fuck, you're strong. Uh, where we goin'?"

Home, Rota said. *The parts taken from the victims? I think you were right, Ollie.*

"I was?" Ollie grinned. "Hey, cool, I was!" He frowned. "Wait, about what?"

I believe they may be ingredients for a spell, Rota replied. *The horns, the scales, all of it. We need to make a list of what was taken and we can reverse engineer what sort of spell or ritual they might be needed for.*

Alexander waited until there was another alley to duck into before teleporting them back to the hotel he and Rota had been living at.

"Whoa." Ollie looked around with big eyes. "Is this… is this, like, your secret hideout?"

Something like that. Rota chuckled.

Alexander headed right for books stacked up by the bed and grabbed two. He and Rota had gathered dozens upon dozens in their search for the Fountain. He propped himself up on the pillows, set both books in his lap, and opened them.

"What are you doing?" Ollie asked.

"Reading." Alexander scanned the first page of the book closest to him, waiting for Rota's nudge to turn the page of the second book.

They'd read this way together often, and it worked well when they had a lot of ground to cover.

Naturally, Rota read faster, and he was already nudging for a new page before Alexander had finished half of his.

We need a spell with two Eldress horns, Rota said. *Perhaps Vulgora scales or cheeks or both. Oh! And the tentacles of a Deverach and the tusks of an Absola.*

"So, uh, you guys just gonna keep reading?" Ollie asked curiously.

"Yes." Alexander glanced up. "You know, you could be reading too." He pulled the poetry book from his pocket and dropped it on the bed.

"Cool. Right." Ollie fidgeted. "Got anything to drink?"

"Kitchen."

There's a small cabinet there full of liquor, Rota added helpfully.

"That's cool, thanks." Ollie headed that way, humming to himself as he explored.

Alexander ignored the sounds of Ollie bumping around the kitchen and tried to stay focused on reading.

"Wow. Where did this all come from?" Ollie asked as he pawed through the booze. "There's, like, a million bottles in here."

"I wanted to try alcohol," Alexander replied briskly.

"There's, like… maybe a shot missing from these?"

"It all sucked."

"Oh."

Alexander turned a page for Rota, and he got settled back down to read again. He flinched as Ollie continued to make noise in the kitchen, and he had to start a sentence over.

"Hey, are you hungry?" Ollie called out.

"What?" Alexander snapped his head up.

"Dinner?" Ollie had a bottle in his hand as he walked over toward the bed. He grabbed the book of poetry and plopped down next to Alexander.

"What about it?" Alexander's pulse fluttered at how easily Ollie invaded his space, and he wanted to push him off the bed.

"Well, I wanted to take you out—"

"We're not leaving."

"Right, but I could order food from the Hot Pot and get it delivered if you'd like." Ollie paused to chug some liquor. He'd selected a dark whiskey Alexander had found particularly vile. "It's not as cool as seeing them cook it in person, but it still tastes super good. If you think you'd like that. Or we can get somethin' else. Whatever you want."

"Whatever." Alexander tried not to smile, keeping his eyes on the book.

That's his way of saying "Yes, thank you, Ollie, and I love chicken," Rota said sweetly.

"Cool." Ollie glanced around. "So, uh, where are we exactly?"

While Rota gave Ollie the address for the hotel, Alexander went back to reading.

Or at least he tried.

It was hard not to steal glances at Ollie chatting away with Rota, the two of them discussing the diverse menu Ollie had brought up on his phone and picking out food to share with Alexander.

Ollie's smile lit up his whole face, and he blushed so prettily when he messed up the name of a dish and had Rota gently correct him.

It was… cute.

He noticed Rota had slowed down reading, based on the lack of nudges to turn pages, also distracted by Ollie's company.

After the order was placed, Ollie got to work on reading the book. He mumbled each word out loud, pausing when he stumbled over one and repeating it a few times before he moved on.

Alexander was sure it would annoy him, but listening to Ollie soon became comforting. He'd spent so long with only Rota's voice in his head, and he found he liked having someone else here.

When Ollie was ready to go downstairs and grab their food, Alexander gave him a spell to transport him back and forth to this floor so he wouldn't have to deal with the stairs. The elevator hadn't run in years.

"Thanks, little dude." Ollie gave him a wink right before he disappeared that made Alexander's heart thump.

You do like him, Rota accused.

"Shut up." Alexander stared back at the book. He'd barely made a dent. "He's a distraction."

Because you like him.

"This was your great idea, wasn't it?" Alexander gestured at the pile of books. "We still have at least fifty more we need to look through."

Yes, yes, I know. I'm just… amused.

"Amused?"

Yes. Because you like him.

"I'd like him a lot more if we weren't in this shitshow because of him."

We shall figure this out, my love. Once we know the nature of the potion or spell, we may understand the killer's intentions better.

"I hope so."

Ollie reappeared, two big bags of food in his arms. "Whoa, that was trippy. Uh. We eatin' in bed?"

"Sure." Alexander gave up reading for now. He was hungry, and whatever Ollie had ordered for them smelled good.

Alexander ate while Ollie only lightly nibbled and drank heavily, trying to finish fast so he could get back to reading. It was chicken and rice with savory noodles and fried crisp vegetables and so many different delicious things that Alexander was afraid he was going to burst if he ate another bite.

He gave himself a break to read a little, though he paused often to snag another forkful.

Ollie was still reading out loud, and so far the poems didn't sound that helpful. The one Ollie was on spoke of the gods' grace and beauty and blah blah blah, not so much a description of any magical world but only of the poet's adoration for the divine.

Boring.

Alexander was getting tired, and he was having trouble keeping his eyes open. Each hour dragged on more than the last, and they hadn't found squat. Rota nudged him back into the pillows, promising to keep Ollie company and wake him should they find anything useful.

He was too sleepy to fight for once, and he drifted off, full and content. When someone pulled the blankets over him and kissed his hair, he wasn't sure if it was Rota or Ollie or both.

Alexander woke up a few hours later, his heart thudding with dread and the clutches of a terrible memory still gripping him.

LXIX, now hold still. You're already bleeding all over the place. Stop it. Stop it right now. If you don't hold still, this is really going to hurt....

A nightmare.

He was curled up in a ball with Ollie's arms around him, holding him flush against his chest like a teddy bear. He tried to pull away, but Ollie held fast, and Alexander decided he could tolerate the closeness for a little longer.

It was very early, judging by the lack of sunlight peeking in, and going back to sleep wouldn't be the worst thing.

Hello, my love, Rota's voice greeted him quietly. *You should be sleeping still.*

Morning, Alexander replied. *Mm, working on it.*

Are you all right?

Same old bad dreams. He smiled when he felt Rota's touch moving within Ollie's arms so that both of them were hugging him. *Gods, that's nice.*

Do you like feeling me...?

Yes. Alexander closed his eyes, arching back into the embrace. It stirred something in him, creating a rush of heat between his legs that made his cock twitch.

Do you want me, my love? Rota slid Ollie's hands down Alexander's hips. His desire was palpable through their bond, and his fingers moved to open Alexander's pants.

"What about Ollie?" Alexander asked. "Is he still out?"

"You're good," Ollie mumbled drowsily. "Go ahead. I'm going back to sleep."

Thank you, Ollie. Rota took full control, and he grabbed a hold of Alexander's cock and squeezed.

"Mmm, yes." Alexander pushed up into Rota's hand, gasping sharply. Ollie's strong body grinding behind him felt good, and Rota's tender strokes were amazing.

"My love," Rota whispered. "I want to wake up with you like this every morning."

"Mm-hm." Alexander gasped again as one of Rota's slitted tentacles replaced his hand on his cock, sucking softly. He shoved his pants and underwear down to his knees, and he pushed back into Rota's hips.

"So greedy...," Rota murmured as he sent one of his other slitted tentacles up between Alexander's legs to tease around his hole.

"Seven years," Alexander growled. "Seven years of wanting, wishing, and having fuckin' nothing. I will take everything I can get whenever I can get it."

"And you shall have it," Rota promised, the tip of the tentacle slipping inside Alexander. "You shall have it all."

Groaning, Alexander panted through the stretch. It burned a little, but it was worth it to feel Rota so deep inside of him. Magic eased the sting of penetration, also offering lubricant and relief from the discomfort as Rota fucked him.

"Is that good, my love?" Rota murmured, thrusting steadily.

"Gods, yes…."

Fuck, you feel so good, Alexander…. Ollie's thoughts came bubbling through the bond.

"Ollie," Alexander breathed. He could feel Ollie there too, warm and bright as before, and his desire nearly rivaled even Rota's.

Ollie's cock was hard, digging into Alexander's thigh, and when his hips grinded forward, it was definitely Ollie's will that had moved them.

Mm, you're so damn hot…. Ollie sighed longingly. *I want to be in you too….*

"Do it," Alexander whispered, reaching back to grab at Ollie's pants. "Give it to me."

Alexander. Rota groaned lustfully. *Are you sure?*

"Yes." Alexander growled, impatient as always. "I want you both. Now."

Rota and Ollie moved together to pull out Ollie's cock and then guide it toward Alexander's already stuffed hole. They rubbed the head around in all the slick, and Alexander could feel how much they both wanted him. It was overwhelming, almost as much as the new wave of pleasure Alexander felt when Ollie's cock slid inside of him.

Ollie wasn't anywhere as big as Rota's tentacles, but the added girth made the already intense stretch even more fantastic. Knowing it was Ollie brought another unexpected level of pleasure, and Alexander moaned when they thrusted together.

Fuck, Alexander…. Ollie sounded out of breath. *Fuck, you feel so fuckin' good. You're perfect. Gods, I can feel both of you….*

I'm here, Rota soothed. *I'll take care of* both of you… *just relax.*

Alexander gasped as Rota rolled him over on his stomach and draped himself over his back, driving his tentacle and Ollie's cock deeper inside of him. Rota was thrusting them both at the same time, in sync with the roll of Ollie's hips. Alexander's hole was aching, and the stretch in this position sent delicious waves of blissful sensation right to the head of his throbbing dick.

He realized he could feel another tentacle moving now between Ollie's legs, and it was probing at Ollie's hole. He could feel everything

Ollie was feeling, and it was near maddening to be so connected to someone else.

Yes, please, Ollie groaned. *Take me too. Fuck, please, Rota.*

Alexander? Rota asked.

"Do it," Alexander commanded. "Now."

When Rota slipped the tip of that other tentacle inside Ollie's body, Alexander cried out, because he could feel it. He could feel the wet heat surrounding him as if it was his dick in there, and he could feel the insane pressure of being penetrated again by slick flesh.

Ollie's mouth on Alexander's shoulder was his and Rota's together, and Ollie's hands were being guided by their mutual desire as they moved both cock and tentacle inside Alexander's body. They were moving together perfectly, and Alexander was aching with the need to come.

He couldn't tell who was touching where, and everything felt so good, and all he could hear and smell and taste was Ollie and Rota. Nothing else mattered except this blissful moment and the sensation of hot skin on skin. The pressure inside his loins was building, his lips numb and tingling, his cock throbbing, and—

"Ahem."

Alexander jerked, staring over his shoulder at Stoker, now standing there at the foot of the bed.

"Well," Stoker said cheerfully, "that's certainly one way to start the day off, isn't it?"

CHAPTER 9.

"WHAT THE fuck?" Alexander snarled as he pushed away from Rota and Ollie, forcing them to pull out as he scrambled to grab a blanket to cover himself. He hadn't even felt the wards break, and he cursed himself for getting so distracted.

Oh dear. Rota slipped out of Ollie's body, quickly scanning the room. *He shattered everything. Our protection sigils, the wards we created, all of it!*

"Hey, Stoker!" Ollie waved. "Good morning!"

Alexander had never been so mortified in his entire life, and he'd suffered some pretty horrible indignities prior to this. Somehow, nothing managed to top having Stoker walk in on him having sex with Rota and Ollie.

Oh Gods. He was having sex with Rota and Ollie, not just Rota.

Oh *fuck.*

"Come on." Alexander threw some of the blanket over Ollie's lap. "Will you please put your pants back on?"

"Right. Sorry." Ollie grinned, reaching underneath the blanket to wiggle his pants back into place.

"I'm assuming if you have all this free time to mess around that you've discovered who the killer is and were just on your way to come tell me once you were done cuddling?" Stoker drawled. He'd turned his head to give them some privacy while they got dressed, but it was clear he wasn't planning to leave.

"Something like that." Alexander fixed his clothes quickly, slipping out of bed and straightening himself out. He was still wet and open, and it felt weird as he moved around. He tried to ignore it. "We talked to your men at the bar."

"And?" Stoker pressed.

"They pointed the finger at a man named Tim, a missionary you apparently gave the boot to. We checked him out, put some pressure on him, and he was clean. Didn't know anything. We also had a little chat with Will, since he has a bad habit of hanging around crime scenes."

"I know it's not Will," Stoker said sourly. "I already talked to him myself."

"After he found a body that you claimed to have found." Alexander crossed his arms. "Any other details you've left out that you wanna tell us about?"

"No." Stoker smirked. "So, that's it, hmm? That's all you've managed to accomplish? Roughing up a priest and harassing a vagrant child?"

"We're checking into the pieces that were taken from the victims. Could be that they were being targeted for parts. Rota and I have a pretty big collection of books. Might be able to figure out what it's all being used for and get an idea of what our killer wants."

"That's almost clever... if I hadn't already thought of it and looked through my own library for the very same thing."

Fuckin' dickweed in a fuckin' three-piece. Alexander narrowed his eyes. "Yeah, well, fuck your library. You don't have the books we do."

"No, I see that now." Stoker walked over toward the haphazard stacks. "Several first editions, some family grimoires.... You may find something useful in there after all." He snorted. "If you can keep it in your pants long enough to do some real work."

"Fuck you."

"We're going to try this again." Stoker ignored the cursing. "I will be expecting a timely report from you regarding your progress with the books. If I do not receive one by this evening, I'll be more than happy to remove Ollie from your company and consider our deal forfeit. Am I making myself clear?"

"Yeah. I got it."

"Find the killer, Alexander," Stoker commanded. "Now if you'll excuse me, I have a city to run."

"Bye!" Ollie waved again.

Stoker vanished.

"Son of a bitch!" Alexander raged, smacking his hands together violently and rebuilding the wards with a wave of magic that rattled the windows. "He just came waltzing up in here and smashed up all of our shit like it was nothing! Bastard! Fuck, I hate him!"

Easy, my love, Rota soothed. *It's all right.*

"No, it's not!" Alexander snapped. "This is supposed to be our home! Our safe place! Just us!"

"Hey." Ollie got out of bed and cautiously approached. "I'm sorry this happened. I didn't think he'd—"

"Barge in like he owned the place? Like I didn't matter? Like my privacy didn't fuckin' matter?"

"Alexander, hey—" Ollie touched Alexander's arm, and he flinched as a memory flashed between them.

Hey, LXIX, time for your medicine! Come on now. Let's get those clothes off. You must be real dirty after what you were up to last night, you filthy little boy. Oh yeah. We see everything, you know, and we know what you were doing—

Alexander pulled away to sever the connection. "Stop."

"Oh, by all the gods...." Ollie was horrified, and he yanked his hands back. "I'm so sorry. I didn't know... I...."

"I don't expect you to understand," Alexander said quietly. "Having a place that is my own, that is mine, is very important to me. Stoker took that away from me in a second and had no idea and wouldn't have cared if he did. It's...." He closed his eyes. "*Violating.*"

"I'm sorry," Ollie murmured. "It doesn't feel like that's enough... but I really am."

Alexander could feel Ollie's sincerity through the bond, but it did little to comfort him. "I just want to get this over with and get you and him and everyone else the fuck out of my life." He stomped toward the bathroom without another word.

He knew he'd hurt Ollie, and he tried not to care. He felt filthy, vulnerable, and he wanted a hot shower immediately.

Alexander? Rota was following him. *Please wait.*

"Go help Ollie with the book," Alexander snapped. "He gets stuck on anything with more than two syllables."

"Okay, that might be true, but that's also mean!" Ollie had tagged along too, and he frowned at Alexander. "I just wanna help you. That's all I want to do, and you keep pushing me away."

"Don't you have a not-dead boyfriend to go cry over?" Alexander stormed into the bathroom and slammed the door behind him. He threw his shirt on the floor, angrily kicking his way out of his pants. He used Rota's tentacles to get the water going, adding a splash of magic to make sure it was scalding hot.

"Ouch." Ollie shouted through the door. "Hey! See, that's very hurtful!"

"Good! Take a hint!"

"Come on, little dude, please." Ollie opened the door and cautiously walked in, covering his eyes with his hands when he saw Alexander was naked. "Can we please talk?"

Alexander whirled around, wearing nothing but a sneer, and he glared up at Ollie. "I don't like you. I can't stand the sight of you. I wish I could leave you and never have to see your stupid face ever again and—"

Rota dove into Ollie's body, taking control and silencing Alexander with a passionate kiss.

"Mmph!" Alexander protested, smacking at Rota's chest as his strong arms wrapped around him.

I love you. I love you so much, Rota thought earnestly. *I know you're upset. This has wounded you deeply, and I know you are hurting. But it's not right to take it out on Ollie.*

Alexander wanted to fight, but it wasn't fair with how sweetly Rota was kissing him and holding him close. He curled his hands into fists, dropping them on Rota's chest as he kissed him back, squeezing his eyes shut to block out the tears trying to well up.

You lash out at everyone who tries to get close to you, and I understand why, Rota went on. *I know. I was there with you at Hazel....*

But you're right. It's not right to hurt Ollie, Alexander thought back, his stomach twisting up with regret. *I know it's not his fault.* He knew he was being an asshole, but he didn't know how to stop. It was instinct to shove everyone away, because that was safer. He couldn't get hurt if he didn't let anyone in.

It's okay. Ollie's thoughts joined theirs. *I just wanna make you happy. It's totally no big deal. I'm not mad.*

You should be. Alexander broke away from the kiss. "I don't deserve all of this, okay? I don't deserve someone like you."

"Like me?" Ollie spoke up, peeking open one eye. "What are you talking about?"

"You're just so *nice*. You don't have a mean thought rattling around your big stupid head!"

Alexander, Rota scolded.

"See?" Alexander groaned. "I can't even say something nice without being an asshole."

"It's okay." Ollie cracked a little grin. "I think it's kinda charming."

"You're so annoying." Alexander couldn't resist smiling back. He couldn't explain it, but there was something about Ollie that put him right at ease, and his shoulders felt lighter now.

"I know." Ollie hugged Alexander. "We'll get this figured out, okay? I'm gonna go work on that book, Rota is gonna do Rota stu-fahfah, and we won't have to deal with Stoker ever again. Any of us. No more invasion of personal living bubble or any of that."

Alexander was still a little awkward at hugging, but he tried to relax and hug Ollie back. He liked how Ollie's hands felt rubbing his hips, and he became very aware that he was standing there naked in his arms. "Yeah, or we could...." He cleared his throat. *You know.*

"Or what?" Ollie blinked innocently.

What is it, Alexander? Rota asked.

Alexander ran his tongue over his bottom lip, and he had a very clear idea of what he wanted to do next. He stood up on tiptoe, seeking a kiss.

Rota and Ollie both gasped in surprise, and they held Alexander tight.

We can finish what we started earlier with no more interruptions. Alexander dragged his fingers up into Ollie's hair, feeling brave enough to slide his tongue into his mouth. *Just us. Just... the three of us.*

Whatever you want, Rota promised. *We're yours.*

"Totally," Ollie mumbled against his lips. "Yup. So down. With that. Let's go do that."

"Hey!" Alexander gasped as Ollie picked him up and carried him right into the shower, wrapping his long legs around Ollie's waist. "What are you doing?"

"Fixing your brain!" Ollie declared. "You got all these bad memories with showers and stu-fahfah, so we're gonna fix 'em with a really good one!"

"You're getting soaked! Oh, for fuck's sake. You're making a mess!" Alexander tried to push the shower curtain back to block the water from spraying out onto the floor, but it was too late. He couldn't help but laugh, tipping his head back into the spray. "You're such an idiot."

"Yeah, okay!" Ollie grinned sheepishly. "The idea is sound, but maybe the exclusion needs some work."

"Execution?"

"Wait, who's getting killed?"

"Fuck's sake." Alexander laughed again.

Ollie shook his hair as water ran down his face and soaked his shirt. "Little help?"

With a flick of his hand, Alexander used Rota's magic to deposit the sopping-wet clothing in the sink. He leaned back against the shower wall, supported by Ollie's arms and a cascade of Rota's tentacles. He smiled warmly, seeing both Rota and Ollie looking back at him. He loved the feeling of their skin touching, both tentacle and mortal flesh, and he bowed his head for a kiss.

Ollie moaned when their lips met again, pressing into Alexander's arms and pushing his tongue forward. His cock was hard again, grinding against Alexander's, and his thoughts were a fog of happiness. *God, you feel so nice like this… I love how you kiss me. Your lips taste so fuckin' good….*

Take me. Alexander raked his hands through Ollie's curls as he tried to push his hips down. *Come on. Both of you… I want both of you in me again, like before.*

Whatever you want, my love, Rota replied sweetly. *We're yours.* He used his tentacles to help line Ollie's cock up, slipping him inside effortlessly. One of his slitted tentacles was right there with it, the tip sliding around before pushing in alongside Ollie's cock. *There, my love… there….*

Alexander groaned excitedly, letting himself be loud for once. It was okay. It didn't matter. No one was going to hear them, and he could let it all out. He spread his legs wide, his toes nearly touching opposite sides of the stall as Rota and Ollie pushed deep inside his hole. The ache was there, heavy and thick, and fuck, it was amazing when they moved together to fuck him.

The air was steamy from the hot water, and Alexander sent one of Rota's tentacles over to swat the showerhead downward and aim the spray away from him.

Yes, mmm, thank you. Alexander moaned, blissful and happy, clinging to Ollie's shoulders as he and Rota fucked him. Each thrust of cock and tentacle was fantastic, and they both felt huge in this suspended position. The tentacle could go so much deeper, and it twisted in such a delightful way that Alexander had no choice but to sob.

"F-fuck! Alexander!" Ollie gasped, slamming forward as if he could feel it too.

You're both so beautiful, Rota sighed. *There are such things I want to show you, the pleasures I can bring you.* One of his slitted tentacles was sliding back behind Ollie, pushing up against his hole.

"Yeah," Ollie panted. "Come on, Rota... please."

"Do it, Rota." Alexander whined when the tentacle pressed inside Ollie's body because he could feel it too, a new level of penetration to add to the already extraordinary pleasure he was experiencing. "Oh, by all the gods, fuck! Yes!"

Rota pumped his tentacles in and out of Ollie and Alexander, guiding Ollie's hips to pound into Alexander at the same relentless pace. Alexander was dizzy and squirming frantically, trying to relax so he could take it all. He could feel the snug heat of Ollie's body around Rota's tentacle and his own tight body hugging Ollie's cock like it was his own.

It was overwhelmingly hot, and when he kissed Ollie's lips, he was kissing both Ollie and Rota. He hoped they could feel how much this meant to him.

Rota tightened his tentacles around Alexander's legs to hold him in place while he fucked him, slamming the slitted tentacle in and out of his body with fantastic force. Alexander clawed at Ollie's back, his head smacking against the shower wall with a fierce cry. There was still a part of him that was afraid this was all going to disappear like it had so many times before, but there was no end in sight, not even when he was about to come.

Come on, my love, Rota urged. *Let yourself go... come for us....*

"Come on, baby," Ollie panted, latching on to Alexander's throat and sucking his damp skin eagerly. "I'm so fuckin' close too. Come with me. Come on, baby."

Alexander had no way to resist, and he took a deep breath, giving in to the fantastic pressure. He climaxed with a low moan, his cock pulsing between his stomach and Ollie's. He'd expected a quick rush, but his orgasm didn't fade away—it kept going.

He was frozen in the middle of an intense climax, his legs and hips twitching, lost to maddening bliss that showed zero signs of slowing down. He could feel Ollie's orgasm shuddering through him, the pump of his load deep inside, and how he too was caught in this endless loop of bliss.

It wasn't until Rota came, flooding both Ollie and Alexander's bodies, that the intense feelings finally began to dwindle. It was a smooth descent, like a leaf fluttering down to the ground, and Alexander went totally limp.

"Oh fuck," Alexander whispered, breathless and exhausted.

"I second that." Ollie grinned. "Oh fuck."

Alexander kissed him, and he moaned as the tentacle slipped out of his body. Even just having Ollie inside of him felt big and weird, and he clung a little closer for comfort.

You're both so beautiful, Rota praised. *Oh, Alexander. I love you so much... that was incredible.*

"We're not done," Alexander said stubbornly.

No? Rota chuckled.

"You know what I want." *The big one.*

"Well, let's give the boy what he wants." Ollie grinned wide. He pulled out gently, but he didn't let Alexander's feet touch the floor. He swept him up into his arms with some help from Rota's tentacles and carried him out to the bed.

Into the sheets they tumbled together, and Alexander didn't even care they were still wet. He pulled Ollie right back on top of him, and he kissed him hard. He was still turned on despite coming only a few moments ago, and he squirmed to get his hips in the right position. *Come on.... Rota. Now!*

So impatient, Rota tutted as his tentacles curled around Alexander's thighs and spread him wide. He had control of Ollie's body, and he used his hands to caress Alexander's stomach and hips.

"Yeah, it's just been a million years and only the third time having sex," Alexander grumbled, wiggling against the tentacles' hold. "Don't make me wait, you jerk."

"I won't," Rota promised with a kiss. "I'm all yours."

"Mm... lemme see it."

"Of course."

Alexander's eyes widened.

Okay, that thing was *huge*.

He swore it was as long as his forearm, and it had a defined pointed head with a tight slit at the tip. There were thick rows of ridges running over the top that reminded Alexander of the spikes Rota had on his back.

The ridges were arranged in neat lines and tapered upward from a thick knot to just underneath the bottom of the head.

Alexander had to touch it, reaching out to stroke the smooth underside and trace some of the ridges. The ridges were soft, flexible, and he shivered when he realized all of those were going inside of him. Fuck, and the *knot*. It had to be as big as his fist.

"By all the gods...."

"Your god." Rota smiled and fluttered Ollie's lashes. "Your god who has craved your touch for so long... I love you."

"I love you too." Alexander slid his hands over Rota's face that was Ollie's face, closing his eyes as he kissed him. He could feel the familiar sunshine sensation he recognized as Ollie bubbling up, but it seemed far away, as if he was trying to give them privacy.

Rota kissed Alexander passionately, sliding his arms beneath his body to hold him flush against his chest as the big tentacle slid between his legs. *Even after all these years, nothing could have prepared me for the heaven that is the feel of your body, the taste of your lips....*

Rota.... Alexander gasped when the pointed head bumped against his hole, and he tried not to tense. He breathed in shakily, hugging Rota's neck. *Take me, do it, fuck, do it fuckin' now, please—*

Patience, my love. Rota eased the head in, and he kissed his way down Alexander's neck. *I will give you everything you've ever desired, I promise you.*

Clinging to Rota's neck, Alexander whispered, "I love you."

"And I love you."

Alexander cried out when the big one—fuck, it was like a tentacle-cock, a *tentacock*—pushed in and lit up his entire body with sensation. He didn't know it was possible to be this full, and the flash of pain was so quick he barely noticed. He immediately wanted more. "Gods, yes. Give it to me!"

"Yes, my love... I will."

The tentacock moved in short bursts, and Alexander whimpered as each ridge popped over the rim of his asshole. Every single row created a burst of fiery sensation, and he couldn't stop panting, his tongue dry, and he moaned as the ridges rubbed against all the sensitive nerves deep inside his body. As the tentacock continued to thrust, the ridges seemed to flatten, and the slide in and out of his hole became slippery smooth.

Alexander dragged his hands to his stomach, and he groaned excitedly when he felt the bulge of the tentacock beneath his fingers. He was absolutely stuffed, the slightest movement causing an uproar of rapture that made him sob and his toes curl. The tentacles coiled around his thighs were pulling him into every thrust, and he swore that damn tentacock was up in his stomach now.

Hot tears were running down his face, and Alexander grabbed Rota's arms to help ground himself. He was afraid he was going to float right out of his body, his back arching off the bed as Rota continued to fuck him hard. He couldn't believe how wet and open he was, and he was far too aroused to even care how desperate he sounded when he begged, "Gods, please! Rota! Make me come, please. I wanna come!"

"Yes, my love," Rota growled. "I will make you come... over... and over again...." His tentacles lifted Alexander's legs up and pushed them forward, bending him right in half as he pounded the tentacock into him with new strength.

"Oh fuck! Rota!" Alexander shouted, gritting his teeth to take on the giant tentacock in this position. He was certain he was going to break, and the pressure down in his balls and in his dick was dancing the line between rapture and absolute torture. He needed relief, he needed to come, and he dug his nails into Rota's skin with a demanding growl.

Rota kept fucking him hard and fast, and the knot bumped insistently against Alexander's ass. Alexander wanted it, he wanted it so badly it was driving him insane, and he struggled against the grip of Rota's tentacles to push down, to slam onto it, to take it, to just fuckin' take it—ah fuck!

The knot popped inside, and the entire universe fell away, leaving nothing except Alexander's pulse throbbing around where that giant knot had stretched him to his very limit. He sobbed frantically, stars exploding before his eyes as he climaxed, the sound of thunder roaring in his ears as his pleasure pulsed over and over, just as Rota had promised.

He trembled all the way down to his bones, and his hips jerked as his cock spurted load after load of come. His limbs turned to cement, and he went limp, helplessly splayed across the bed as Rota fucked him into sheer madness. He felt the swell of the knot deep inside of him and the following rush of come bringing on another mind-shattering orgasm that made him sob.

And there, like a ray of pure sunlight, Alexander could feel Ollie too. His pleasure came over him like a warm blanket, soft and melting into his skin like butter. Alexander stretched and settled into the blissful feeling, utterly exhausted from being fucked so thoroughly, and he let out a triumphant and delighted laugh.

"I love you," Rota murmured, smiling brightly down at him. "Oh, my love. I love you so much."

"I love you too." Alexander was smiling so hard his cheeks hurt, and he kissed Rota, holding it for several long, tender moments as he enjoyed the slow crawl of their heartbeats winding down together. "Mmm... fuck, that was.... That was amazing."

"You're aware I still have two more tentacles capable of giving you pleasure, yes?"

"Fuck." Alexander laughed. "They can wait."

"Good." Rota chuckled, the sound fading into a thought as he left Ollie's body. *Because I am quite exhausted.*

"Mmm, me too."

"Me fuckin' three." Ollie flopped flat on his back. "I think I need a nap."

"I need a cigarette." Alexander reached out with Rota's tentacles to find his jacket. He glanced at Ollie. "You want one?"

"Nah, I'm good right now. Thanks, though."

Alexander got one lit up, took a long drag, and sighed with deep satisfaction. He hesitated for a moment, but then he slowly leaned back to rest his head on Ollie's chest. "Thank you."

"For what?"

"For giving me a good memory."

"Yeah?" Ollie wrapped an arm around Alexander, hugging him close.

"Mm-hm." Alexander took a long and luxurious drag from his cigarette, resting his hand on Ollie's wrist and enjoying the little flutter in his stomach. "Very good. Like. Wow."

Wow, Rota agreed.

"Wow is good, right?" Ollie beamed.

Alexander snorted. "Very."

"Oh, okay. Just checking."

"Idiot," Alexander said with an affectionate roll of his eyes. "You really are ridiculous."

"Yeah." Ollie shrugged. "But that's okay." He perked up and grinned. "'Cause I think you're startin' to like it."

"I've been accused of worse things, I guess."

You look so beautiful right now, my love. Rota was smiling. *You look... happy.*

"I am." Alexander closed his eyes. "I can't remember the last time I was this happy."

"When you were sixteen," Ollie said suddenly. "It was your birthday. Your parents worked all the time, and you never got to see 'em. Or maybe one would be home, but not the other... but for your sixteenth birthday, they were both there. And there was a cake, a super big cake."

Alexander stiffened. "What are you talking about?"

"The last time you were happy. I... I can see it."

CHAPTER 10.

"I CAN see a big cake." Ollie stroked Alexander's chest, and his eyes fluttered as if he was falling asleep. "Big cake with chocolate frosting, and they made some kind of sangria for everybody to drink. Not the kind with alcohol but, like, a kid-safe version because they remembered how much you hate soda."

"How are you doing this?" Alexander demanded.

"I don't know. I just… I see it. Like a movie." Ollie closed his eyes and scrunched up his brow. "A weird, blurry movie that's inside your head but then it's in my head."

To see all that is hidden, Rota said in awe.

"Is this real?" Alexander croaked, hating how broken he sounded. He couldn't believe this was happening, and he pushed himself up so he could look at Ollie's face as his heart hammered in his throat.

"Yeah…." Ollie smiled. "I can see some tall skinny guy with glasses and a lady with dark hair…."

Swallowing over the lump in the back of his throat, Alexander whispered, "My parents."

"They look real happy. I can't see any presents, though." Ollie's brow wrinkled. "That's all fuzzy. But everybody looks super happy." He opened his eyes and grinned. "I can see you. In a mirror. You're all covered in cake. Looks like there was a cake fight, and you seriously lost."

Alexander didn't even realize tears were running down his face until Ollie reached up to wipe his cheeks.

"Hey." Ollie was still smiling, but his gaze seemed unfocused, as if he was still seeing whatever memory his starsight had allowed. "Your eyes were brown…."

Oh, Alexander, Rota murmured, a wave of sweet comfort flooding their bond. *Oh, my love.*

Alexander swallowed again, trying to hold back a sob. *I never knew. I never even knew what color my eyes were…. I saw the pictures at Hazel, but me, Alexander, I never knew, I never saw them—*

"My love." Rota seized Ollie's body and wrapped his arms around Alexander, pulling him against his chest and kissing his hair. "Oh, sweet boy. I'm here. I'm right here."

I'm here too. I'm sorry. Ollie's thoughts sounded frantic. *Wait, I didn't mean to upset you, I didn't mean to hurt you—*

"It's okay, it's okay." Alexander clung to Rota, to Ollie, holding them as tightly as he could. He didn't dare cry. He refused to. He couldn't—

What's the matter, pretty boy? Aw, are you gonna cry for us? Aw, is the pretty little baby gonna cry? Come on, lemme see those tears. Lemme see 'em. Come on, just give me what I want—

"No," Ollie's voice said sternly. He sounded different, strange, not like himself at all. "No more." He pressed his hand between their bodies, his palm against Alexander's heart.

There was a jolt of pressure, and Alexander had trouble breathing. It was like Ollie was reaching right into his chest and going up his throat, tickling the bottom of his brain.

Alexander? Rota asked worriedly. *Ollie, what are you doing?*

Ollie didn't answer, and he kept his hand where it was. He seemed far away, and his expression was blank.

I'm okay, Alexander swore even as the feeling stole his breath away. *I'm okay—*

Alexander, Rota warned. *I can't take control—*

—I'm okay, I'm... what the fuck?

The voice of the taunting guard was gone without even an echo, and Alexander's mind's eye was flooded with a sea of color—the party. Balloons, streamers, the cake, his parents' smiling faces.

"How...?" Alexander inhaled shakily. "How is this possible?"

The memory was there, right there in his mind, his own sixteenth birthday party. Yes, there were pieces of it missing or unclear, but he could see his parents. Mom and Dad, Milton and Dianne Ward, smiling down at him and calling him—

"Landon," Ollie whispered. "Your name was Landon."

What did you do, Ollie? Rota asked urgently. *Alexander, are you all right?*

"I have no idea." Ollie grimaced, looking down at his hand as if it was going to bite him.

"He took one of my memories away." Alexander pushed Ollie back, but he did so gently. He needed space. And another cigarette. "And…. And he gave me one back. The one he was talking about. The birthday."

Ollie, please, Rota urged. *Let me…?*

"Oh, right. Yeah." Ollie nodded feebly. "Go ahead. Sorry for kicking you out. I don't know how I did that either."

Rota took over Ollie's body to wrap Alexander back in another tight hug.

"I'm fine." Alexander bristled at first. Physical contact was still not something he was used to, and it took him a moment to relax. He hugged Rota, burying his face into the crook of his neck. "I'm… I'm okay."

"I was worried. I didn't know what was happening." Rota's love was palpable, as was his worry. "I was scared."

That made Alexander smile. "My big, tough god of sap? Worried about me?"

"Worried about the man I love."

"Take a lot more than that to take me away from you." Alexander kissed him, framing his face and pressing close. He took a deep breath, waiting for the shaking in his hands to pass. He didn't even know when he'd started trembling.

It's okay, Ollie thought shyly. *We're here.*

"Thank you, Ollie," Alexander said, pulling back so he could look at Ollie's face and into his eyes. "Thank you for this… gift."

Rota's grip was slipping, and he faded away. *Thank you. I still can't believe it.*

"Hey, me either!" Ollie grinned. He was still hugging Alexander like Rota had been, and he hadn't moved. "I… I'm sorry. I'm not sure if I can do it again."

"It's okay." Alexander took a deep breath and chastely kissed Ollie's lips. *One memory is better than none.*

Ollie's hands tightened around Alexander, and he sighed, taking the kiss deeper. *I'd give them all back to you if I could. I'd fix everything….*

"Why?" Alexander blurted out, staring dumbly at Ollie. He was torn between falling right into those pretty green eyes to claim another kiss or running as far away as possible. His pulse was fluttering wildly, and he didn't understand how Ollie was doing this to him.

The only other person who had ever made him feel like this was Rota.

"Because you deserve it," Ollie replied simply. His smile could have lit up the whole damn city.

Alexander cleared his throat, and he sent Rota's tentacles over for a cigarette. He was blushing, and he absolutely hated it, quickly untangling himself from Ollie's arms. He'd had enough of feelings and emotions for one day. "So, uh. We have things to do. Very important things to do."

"Yeah?" Ollie perked up. "Like checking out those last two tentacles?"

"Like reading those books." Alexander snorted as he lit up.

"Oh. Right." Ollie looked as if he had actually forgotten.

Ah yes. Rota sighed dramatically. *Duty calls and all that. Although I will confess I'm also very interested in discussing what this is....*

"What?" Alexander asked.

Rota seemed to be smirking, and he said, *Oh, just remarking how very well you two seem to be getting along now. That's all.*

Alexander rolled his eyes.

"Well, it's whatever Alexander wants it to be," Ollie said firmly. "We can hang out like this. Or, like, hang out elusively—"

"Exclusively?" Alexander suggested.

"Oh yeah. That too. I'm, uh… just along for the ride, you know?" Ollie's side of the bond was teeming with a tender warmth that felt like anything but only wanting a so-called ride.

"We can talk about whatever this is or isn't or whatever it is later." Alexander glanced back up at Ollie and caught another bright smile, and his heart thumped. *But it's definitely… something.*

"Cool," Ollie said. "Mm, well, you guys get started on that reading stu-fahfah."

Alexander frowned as Ollie hopped out of bed, eyeing his naked backside. "And where are you going?"

"Well, I need a drink to make my brain read, and you need some leftover takeout. It's always better on the second go. So's Italian food. Trust me." Ollie winked. "Can't work on an empty stomach, right?"

Alexander laughed. "I guess not."

He is very thoughtful, isn't he? Rota mused.

"Yeah." Alexander's smile lingered as he watched Ollie stumble nude around the kitchen. "He's somethin'."

You really do like him.

"As much as I have tried not to, yes, I do."

Good. I like him too.

"You've been planning this," Alexander accused.

Me? No, I've been planning nothing of the sort. Hoping for something, on the other hand, perhaps a bit.

"I love you, you sappy-ass god."

And I love you, my grumpy brat.

"Hey, guys?" Ollie called worriedly from the kitchen.

"What is it?" Alexander asked.

"Uh, sort of a technical question, but I'm not sure if this is right. Are microwaves supposed to spark?"

"Oh, for fuck's sake."

Removing the fork from the dish Ollie was trying to microwave was an easy enough fix, and they got ready to settle back into bed to eat once the sheets were magically dried from their post-shower tumble. Ollie stayed unashamedly naked while Alexander opted to put on a fresh set of clothes.

When Ollie saw it was a pair of black sweats and a fitted black T-shirt, he teased, "See? Cool-ass vampire."

"Shut up." Alexander both loved and hated how easily Ollie could make him smile.

"Come on." Ollie patted the mattress where their leftover buffet was laid out. "Gotta feed that big ol' brain, yeah?"

Alexander plopped down in bed and helped himself to a few bites of everything. It was delicious. He twirled a thick bunch of noodles around his fork, declaring, "Tastes even better on the second go."

"Told ya," Ollie mumbled around a mouthful.

Alexander's eyes strayed over the bare curve of Ollie's hip, his soft cock, and he blurted out, "You really haven't been with anyone since you broke up with your boyfriend?"

"Huh?"

"You don't have to answer that. Shit, I shouldn't have asked."

"No, it's okay." Ollie shrugged. "It never felt right. Bein' with somebody is supposed to mean something, at least to me. Helping you guys meant something. It still means something. It means a lot to me actually, but uh…." He coughed. "Uh, and you guys… never…?"

"We tried." Alexander picked at his plate. "Not being able to touch is sort of an issue."

"Right. I guess finding somebody with starsight was a poop plan, and uh...." Ollie let the sentence hang.

"Scooping up some random guy just to get some? Yeah, not so much. I wanted my first time to be with Rota, whatever that meant."

Ollie choked. "Your first...? Like, *ever* ever?"

"That I remember. I don't know if I 'did it' before Hazel."

Neither do I, Rota confessed. *Though I am quite happy with our first time being our first together.*

"You're a god." Alexander put his fork down, laughing. "There were literally tentacle orgies. No offense, but the chances of you being a virgin are slim to none."

Gordoth the Untouched is a virgin!

"Not no more." Ollie chuckled.

"Right." Alexander strained to recall the details, but he hadn't been listening very well to Ollie when they first met. "Your... uncle?"

"Yup! My uncle Elwood. He took care of that whole untouched thing."

It's hard to imagine three old gods are living here on Aeon together, Rota said. *There could be more hidden that we don't even know about.*

"Plus all in the same town." Ollie crunched on a piece of fried broccoli and then took a swig of whiskey to wash it down with. "What are the chances?"

"It's not by chance." Alexander grimaced. "The veil between worlds has been torn here. It makes sense for gods to be drawn to this city because they can hear the prayers of mortals much more clearly."

"I knew that." Ollie frowned. "I think."

Alexander doubted that he did, but Gronoch had certainly known. It was why he had made his base of operations for the conduit program here, in hopes of eventually luring more of his kin down to unwillingly participate.

It did make Alexander wonder how many other gods might have similar dastardly plans and could be hiding here somewhere.

"Oh!" Ollie brightened back up. "That's why the cultist guys like to hang out here. They wanna dial up ol' Salgumel up with a good connection. Anywhere else the call gets dropped."

A brilliant comparison. Rota was smiling.

Alexander pushed the takeout containers out of his way and stretched out. He was full, and it was still dark outside. He wanted to go back to sleep.

"Those dudes suck," Ollie said. "Like, so much."

Agreed, Rota rumbled. *Starkiller asked us to keep an eye out for them when we traverse the worlds between worlds.*

"Yeah. They still haven't caught Je-fahfah. He's, like, their leader guy. Totally not nice at all. He killed me."

"You got killed by a guy named Jeff?" Alexander raised a brow.

"Does his name really matter?"

"Fair." Alexander slipped under the covers. "Well, if we find him, I'll kill him for killing you."

"That might be the most romantic thing anyone's ever said to me." Ollie batted his eyes.

Alexander snorted. "I'm going to sleep."

Tired, love? Rota asked.

"The sun is not up. Therefore, I am not going to be up."

Sleep sweetly. I love you, dear boy.

Love you too, Alexander thought back with a drowsy smile. "Staying up, Ollie?"

"Yeah, just for a bit. Get my drink on, see what I can see." Ollie leaned over and kissed Alexander's forehead. "Try to get some sleep, little dude."

"You too."

Alexander drifted, replaying the new memory of his parents' faces until he fell asleep. The party was in his dreams, but Rota was there, towering over the house and fumbling to cut the cake with his giant claws. Ollie was also with them, handing a slice of cake to Alexander, and everything was perfect.

He woke up to the sound of Ollie mumbling as he read, and he rolled over to groggily stare at him. He didn't know what time it was, but it was daytime now, and he couldn't believe Ollie was still awake.

And naked.

Good morning, my love, Rota greeted him.

Alexander grumbled.

"Oh, hey!" Ollie grinned at him. He sounded a little tipsy. "Good morning! You sleep good? You were out like a bulb. Did you know you snore like a little bunny? It's super cute."

Alexander grumbled again.

I fear Alexander is not much of a morning person. Rota chuckled. *He may need a few moments.*

"You want me to make some breakfast?" Ollie asked. "I can totally make us some breakfast. You liked my eggs, right? I can cook those again."

"Why are you always so happy?" Alexander groaned.

"Why are you so grumpy?" Ollie grinned.

"I'm fueled by spite." Alexander rubbed his eyes. "I'm going to the bathroom." He dragged himself out of bed, used the toilet, and freshened up. He caught a glimpse of his face in the mirror, and he could recall the memory of his reflection at the birthday party.

His younger self had been so bright and full of hope....

Alexander wasn't sure what he was now. So much had changed, and it was much more than the color of his hair or his eyes, or the bountiful binding marks carved all over his body. He wasn't that boy anymore, and sadly, he never would be again.

But that was all right.

He was Alexander now. He didn't know what Landon Ward's hopes and dreams had been, and he didn't care because he had some of his own.

First and foremost was getting Rota's body back.

Right after they solved the multiple homicides.

Fuck.

He came back out from the bathroom to find Ollie had cleaned up the takeout from last night and was cooking away in the kitchen. Alexander got settled back into bed with the books he and Rota hadn't finished, setting them across his lap as before.

Sleep well? Rota asked sweetly.

"Yeah." Alexander smiled and thought, *Better than I have in a long time.*

Good. Ready for some more reading?

Oh yeah. Can't wait. So exciting.

After a little while of Rota and Alexander reading through their respective books, Ollie brought over two plates of scrambled eggs and small bottles of juice.

"Thank you." Alexander was already eager for a break from the dry reading material.

"Yeah, no problem." Ollie sat down with him and nodded at the poetry book. "So, this poet chick had some pretty cool adventures with the gods, I guess? But nothing about the Fountain or the Kindress yet."

Alexander's stomach dipped. "Nothing?"

"No. But there is some other weird shit maybe worth mentioning. There's this one poem all about the god of legend and darkness and, like, some buddies of his. But, uh, I've never heard of him. Umbriech."

Alexander frowned. "Are you sure you're reading that right?"

"Yeah. I think. Yes."

That's strange. Rota floated over to peer at the book. *The God of Darkness is Xarapharos, not Umbriech. I've never heard of anyone by that name.*

"Look, there's a whole bunch." Ollie tilted the book up. "Umbriech goes o-fahfah to hang out with all his cool god buddies, Kalith, Drozzoth, Blariagnos, Starygoth, Davenos."

"That can't be right." Alexander took a bite of eggs "Who are they?"

"I don't know." Ollie hiccupped and shrugged. "But they're sure as hell in the poem."

"I don't suppose they have anything fun to say about the Fountain?"

"No. Sorry." Ollie rubbed his eyes. "But listen, they talk about hanging out by this stream."

What kind of stream? Rota asked.

"Says that Drozzoth and Kalith collected these tears and made a stream for Umbriech to do stu-fahfah in, but it doesn't say what stream or what kinda tears."

Alexander perked up. "Still. Tears. Could be talking about the Tears of Great Azaethoth."

It's worth a look, isn't it?

"Better than sitting here reading until our eyes bleed."

Ollie looked panicked.

"It's just an expression."

"Oh. I knew that."

"Eat your breakfast and get dressed." Alexander smirked. "Unless you're planning on exploring a new magical world naked."

Ollie grinned. "Could be fun. Get some air on my balls that hasn't had any balls in it in, like, a thousand years."

"Charming." Alexander rolled his eyes as hard as he could. He glanced up to where he sensed Rota hovering. "What is it?"

Are you sure we should be going before we've made any progress finding a purpose for those missing parts? Rota was frowning by the sound of it. *I know searching through these books is quite a task, but we will need to see Stoker later. I do not think he will appreciate us showing up empty-handed.*

"Fuck Stoker." Alexander stabbed his eggs. "This is the first lead we've had in weeks. We're going."

"Can we have nap time when we come back?" Ollie asked. "Can that be a thing?"

"Did you not sleep?"

"No. I wanted to keep reading, you know?" Ollie fidgeted a little, picking at his plate. "Kept hoping I'd find something."

Ollie was very determined to find the location of the Fountain for us, Rota said kindly. *He worked very hard.*

"And drank very hard."

"Thank you." Alexander shoved the last bite of eggs in his mouth because he didn't know how else to tell Ollie how much it meant to him that he was trying so hard. "Let's get ready, then, yeah? See what this Umbriech guy is all about."

"And I need pants, right?"

"Yes, Ollie. You'll need pants."

They finished eating, and Alexander changed out of the clothes he slept in for his usual combination of jeans, shirt, boots, and his faithful trench coat—all in black, naturally.

Only Ollie's pants had dried, so Alexander let him borrow one of his tank tops that was obscenely tight stretched over his broad chest.

Trying not to stare, Alexander asked hurriedly, "So. This stream. Where is it?"

"Here." Ollie took Alexander's hand and placed it directly on the page of the book. *Through the orchard, twisted and black, moistened by tears unshed—*

"*Moistened*? Really?" Alexander wrinkled his nose.

"Yes. Shush." Ollie cleared his throat and tried again. *Through the orchard, twisted and black, moistened by tears unshed, we traveled forward many days before heading back.*

Alexander could see the words in front of him like he was reading them himself, and there hidden between them was a location. It appeared as Ollie thought them, and Alexander held on to Ollie's hand as he used Rota's magic to open a portal. "Hang on."

They arrived in a blink to a terrifying small world. It was a plateau the size of Ollie's apartment, floating in the middle of absolutely nothing. There was dead grass, rocks, and an empty trench that may have once been a stream, but it was all dried up.

Taking a few steps forward, Alexander demanded, "What the fuck is this?"

"Uh." Ollie glanced around. "The... tears place?"

Alexander boldly strode across the short distance to the edge of the plateau and looked down. Nothing but more space, stupid empty space. He marched back up the dried-up stream bed and threw up a perception spell to look around.

This is most strange, Rota said worriedly. *We've been to hundreds of worlds, and we've never seen one like this.*

"You mean one that looks like it's falling the fuck apart?" Ollie scooted toward the very center beside the stream.

Yes. I don't understand what's happened here.

"Something bad." Alexander could make out the residue of a godly presence, something that reeked of death, and the echo of very powerful destructive magic. "Ollie, you see anything?"

"I can see myself tumbling over the edge into nothing pretty clearly." Ollie sat, hugging his knees. "But, uh, if you're talking about starsight things, no, not really."

"Great."

"Sorry." Ollie grimaced. "You know... it kinda does what it wants most of the time."

"Very helpful." Alexander kept walking up the stream, scanning as he went. He didn't see anything else helpful, and he snarled when he reached the other end of the plateau. "There's nothing here."

I wonder if it has to do with those gods....

"Drozzoth and them? The ones we've never heard of?"

Yes. Perhaps there is a reason we don't know them. Something very bad happened here, yes?

"I guess?"

There may have been cause to erase evidence of the gods' existence from mankind. That would include censoring their names from books,

*which would explain why we've never heard of them, and destroying
their places of worship like this one.*

"What could they have done that was so bad?" Alexander wondered
out loud.

Ollie snorted. "Maybe they—"

His voice abruptly cut off, and Alexander turned around to see
Ollie was gone. "Oh, what the fuck?"

A portal! Stoker!

"That son of a bitch!" Alexander charged over, reaching with
Rota's tentacles to find the trail. "It hasn't been that long! Why did he
take him?"

I don't know, but we must hurry.

"No shit."

Once he found the trail, Alexander was able to pull them right
through. They were standing next to a fuel pump at the gas station over
by where Will lived.

There was a dead body next to the pump, Will was on the ground
beside it, alive but bleeding, Ollie was standing there looking very
confused, and Stoker was holding Ollie by the back of his neck.

A large crowd was also forming around them.

"Well." Alexander made a face. "Fuck."

CHAPTER 11.

"YES, 'FUCK.' Very much so." Stoker was furious. "You took Ollie off world."

"Just for a second," Alexander argued. "Why the fuck did you steal him?"

"Because I felt him leave this fucking world! Pretty sure I forbid you from taking him—"

"I don't seem to remember that specifically."

"Sorry to interrupt," Rota cut in, speaking out loud so everyone could hear him, "but those people are getting closer, and they definitely had to have seen us teleport here."

"Ugh." Stoker tossed his head back, and everything froze.

The crowd advancing toward them, the people in their car at the next pump, and a person who was walking out of the gas station—they were all perfectly stopped, as if time itself had been frozen.

Alexander could still move, as could Ollie and Stoker, but everyone else as far as he could see was stuck. Even cars driving out on the street were frozen. There had to be some limit to it because some horns in the distance were honking angrily, but it was at least the whole block.

Holy fuck, he thought to himself. *Stoker did that?*

Yes, Rota thought back. *He is... very powerful. I know some gods could do this, but not on this scale.*

"You." Stoker pointed at Alexander. "Grab Lawrence."

"Who?" Alexander drawled.

"The man dead on the ground," Stoker snarled. "Grab his body!"

"You grab his body," Alexander spat back.

"I'm getting Will!"

"How about I get the body?" Ollie suggested.

Stoker squeezed the back of Ollie's neck. "No, I'm not letting you out of my sight."

"Fuck!" Alexander growled. "How about I get Will *and* the body, and you let Ollie go?"

"No." Stoker narrowed his eyes, dragging Ollie over with him to scoop up Will like a rag doll. "Let's go. Now." He vanished with them both.

As soon as he was gone, time began moving again, and the crowd closed in quickly.

Uh, Alexander.... Rota sounded nervous.

Several people were shouting, a woman screamed, and there was a snap of a nearby camera from someone's cell phone.

"Oh, yay. No big deal. We're just standing here with a dead fuckin' body!" Alexander roared in frustration, grabbing a hold of the dead man's foot and reaching out to track Stoker's portal. "I fucking hate that guy."

I am also not a fan. Let's go.

Alexander teleported them away, following the trail and now standing somewhere in the Hidden World by the feel of the magic around them. It was a doctor's office, and a large man with jet-black skin and a crooked back was tending to Will on an examination table.

The large man was probably descended from one of the Mostaistlis, an everlasting race known for their deformed bodies and black skin they painted with elaborate designs. This man was not painted, and he was busy healing Will.

Will's eyes were closed, and his mask was gone. With the way his head was turned, Alexander couldn't see what he'd been hiding, but that wasn't where his focus was now anyway.

His eyes were glued on Stoker standing in the corner, his hand still on Ollie's neck.

"Hey, guys!" Ollie waved.

Alexander dropped Lawrence's foot, scowling. "What the actual fuck is going on?"

"Someone attacked Will and Lawrence," Stoker replied with thinly veiled impatience. "When I arrived, Lawrence was dead and Will very nearly. I thought I saw someone fleeing—"

"Why didn't you go after them, huh? That was probably the killer!"

"I was busy cleaning up the crime scene. Yes, I want justice, but not at the cost of my people being exposed."

"Says the teleporting happy jackass. Do you have any idea how many of those people saw us?"

"I don't care about the magic police coming to fine me for using unlicensed teleportation. I do care about them finding the body of an everlasting descendant."

"Whatever." Alexander held out his hand. "Give me Ollie back."

"No." Stoker glared. "You cannot begin to imagine how very upset I was that while in the middle of cleaning up the blood of a very dear friend I felt Ollie vanish from this plane. He's staying here with me—"

"The fuck he is." Alexander made the room tremble.

"No."

Easy, my love, Rota soothed. *Let's not be too hasty.*

"How about we all take some deep breaths?" Ollie suggested. "We weren't trying to run away or nothin'."

"Why were you off world, then?" Stoker demanded.

"Looking for something," Alexander replied shortly.

"You were somewhere no one has been for a very, very long time."

"Pffft, like you fuckin' know what that place was." Alexander wished he could roll his eyes harder.

"Umbriech's Glen." Stoker seemed to enjoy Alexander's surprise. "A stream of tears not shed at funerals. Rather grim, but he was a deity of darkness, so it's to be expected. His world was once connected to Babbeth's, the God of Death."

Through the orchard, twisted and black, moistened by tears unshed, we traveled forward many days before heading back. Babbeth's Orchard. Rota snorted. *It makes sense—*

"Good for you, Stoker. You know some fancy stupid god stuff no one cares about." Alexander groaned loudly. He did not give a single fuck about any of that. "Why don't we pop back to that little crime scene with Ollie and try to track down the killer, huh? Before the portal fades completely."

"The person running away didn't use a portal." Stoker glanced over to where the doctor was working on Will. "They were on foot."

"They…." Alexander could barely comprehend it, and he dug his hands into his hair. "They were on fucking *foot*, and you, a powerful fucking witch, couldn't catch them?"

"Oh, I'm so sorry—" Stoker's voice was sugary sweet before rising to a furious shout that shook the entire room. "—I was distracted by watching one of my wards die in front of my fucking eyes!"

"Boo hoo," Alexander growled savagely. "That's your problem, not mine."

"Oh, it's yours now because you're not getting this lovely little ginger back until you catch this killer." Stoker raised his hand as if to snap his fingers.

"Don't you fuckin' dare." Alexander squeezed his hands into fists, and the room rattled hard enough to open a cabinet door and knock a framed picture off the wall.

Alexander, please calm down, Rota urged.

"You fuckin' calm down!" Alexander growled, not caring no one could hear Rota and this made him look unhinged. "I'm not calmin' shit!" He whirled back on Stoker. "This piece of *fuck* thinks he can just keep pulling our strings? Nah, no, no more. The last asshole who did that to me was a god, and—"

"Oh yes. He's dead now, I know." Stoker was not impressed. "But you don't have Starkiller here to help you, now do you?"

"I don't need him to deal with you," Alexander promised angrily.

"Don't be so sure." Stoker narrowed his eyes, and Alexander swore they were glowing—

"Stoker," the doctor spoke up. "I've lost him."

"No." Stoker let go of Ollie, now rushing over to Will's side. "What's happening?"

"He lost too much blood," the doctor said. "There's nothing I can do."

"No!" Stoker roared as he grabbed the doctor by his collar. "I have given you everything I have! There is no way he can die!"

"I can't!" the doctor cried. "He's gone! I can't bring back the dead, I can't—"

"Wait!" Ollie surged forward. "I can help!"

"What?" Stoker snapped.

Ollie, Alexander warned. *Don't!*

I'm not going to show my starsight! Just trust me! Ollie grabbed Stoker's hand and put it on Will's still chest. "Listen to me. I know a spell. If you're the tiniest bit godly like I fuckin' think you are, this will work."

"What?" Stoker flinched at Ollie's touch, but he didn't pull away.

"Heal him while I call his soul back!"

"No!" Alexander shouted. "Ollie! Come on! Fuck Stoker and his little friend! He's going to take you—!"

"That doesn't matter if I can help save Will!" Ollie nodded at Stoker. "Hurry up! We don't have that much time!"

Stoker's hands turned a brilliant shade of purple, and light sparked from Will's chest. "Whatever you're going to do, do it now, Ollie!"

Ollie closed his eyes, and he focused on a spell. *Please, please, please work....*

He's an idiot, Alexander spat inside his head. He didn't care Ollie could hear him insulting him. He wanted Ollie to know how stupid he thought this was.

Ollie is trying to help, Rota said. *He's just—*

We could have made a deal! Alexander scowled. *We know what Ollie can do! We could have traded his freedom for that—*

"It's not working!" Stoker snarled, his voice overtaking the ones he couldn't hear.

"Shut up! I got this!" Ollie scrunched up his face. *Hey. Could use a little backup here, guys.*

Make a deal, Alexander challenged. *That kid's life for your debt.*

"No!" Ollie growled. "Just do it!"

"Why should I?"

"Because it's the right thing to do!" Ollie pleaded. "Please!"

Alexander, Rota urged. *Please, for the love of Great Azaethoth. Let us help him—*

"No," Alexander snapped.

Then let me help him! Rota roared. *All this hatred for being a puppet, for being a slave—*

"And I said never again!"

Yes? Then what does that make me to you? What does that make me when I can do nothing without your consent?

Alexander scoffed, and he was suddenly struck by a wave of shame. Rota was right.

And Alexander was an even bigger asshole than he'd feared.

Rota... I....

Let me help Ollie! Rota cried. *Now!*

Without hesitation, Alexander raised both of his hands to channel the full power of Rota's magic into Ollie's spell. He gave everything he could, even as the marks on his arms burned and his fingers sizzled.

"There!" Ollie cried out triumphantly, taking the offered magic and working it into his spell. "Stoker, don't stop! Don't stop! Whatever you do—"

Will bolted up with a strangled gasp, pushing away their hands and wheezing. "The fuck, what the fuck?"

"Will!" Stoker grabbed Will's shoulders to steady him. "Hey, hey! Breathe. All right? Just breathe for me."

"Hey." Ollie took a few steps back and grinned. "Cool, it worked."

Stoker stared at Ollie. He was grateful, certainly, but he also seemed suspicious. "How did you do that?"

"It's my uncle's spell. A light to lead a soul home." Ollie beamed at Alexander. "Just needed a boost to make the light a little bigger."

"Thank you." Stoker looked at Alexander. "And you… for whatever it is you did."

"Yeah. Whatever." Alexander crossed his arms and focused Rota's magic to heal himself. It didn't feel right taking it now, not after that, but he was hurting.

We'll talk later, Rota said quietly. He could probably feel Alexander's guilt. *Go on. Take what you need.*

Will covered the burned side of his face with his hands, asking urgently, "My mask?"

Stoker handed it to him. "Here." He turned away to give Will a moment to put it back on, and he sneered at the doctor. "You. Out."

The doctor appeared very happy to leave, slamming the door behind him.

"Will, can you tell me what happened?" Stoker asked briskly.

"Did I… was I dead?" Will patted his chest. "Did I die?"

"Only, like, a third of the way!" Ollie said cheerfully.

Will's eye widened.

"You're safe now," Stoker assured him. "Now, please. Tell me what happened. Who did this?"

"I…." Will shook his head. "I was with Lawrence. I was headed home. We stopped at the gas station. He was going to get me something to eat…." He looked over toward the floor.

Lawrence's body was magically gone, though a smear of blood remained.

"And then what?" Stoker pressed.

"I don't know. Someone hit me… stabbed me?" Will touched his chest. "I don't know. There was all this pain, some weird light, and then I woke up here."

Stoker was clearly disappointed Will couldn't recall anything useful, but he patted his shoulder all the same. "Thank you."

"Lawrence is dead. Isn't he?" Will bowed his head.

"Yes. I knew he was in trouble, and I came as fast as I could. He was already dead, and you were well on your way when I arrived."

"Did you see… did you see who did this?"

"Oh, he did," Alexander was quick to point out. "He let them get away. While they were on foot."

"That could have been anyone." Stoker rolled his eyes. "It might have been an ordinary person fleeing a bloody crime scene—"

Will grimaced.

"A crime scene, by the way, I was trying to clean up when you idiots—" Stoker's wrath resurfaced, aimed at Alexander. "—decided to go vacationing in a magical world!"

Alexander practiced rolling his eyes as hard as he could, and he leaned against the wall. "Whatever. Why don't you just use your magical gangster powers and check the security cameras at the gas station?"

"Oh. Wow. Why didn't I think of the most obvious thing to check?" Stoker drawled. "I already tried. The cameras there haven't worked in months. There's nothing to see."

"What about magical evidence, huh?"

"That gas station is frequented by dozens, if not hundreds, of customers every day. The trails are countless. All I have is a glimpse of someone running away, large, probably over six feet, and—"

"Marbles!" Will gasped. "Hey! I remembered! Me and Lawrence saw Marbles at the gas station too. He came over to talk to us, and he was asking me about hot dogs."

"Hot dogs?" Stoker made a face.

"From the gas station."

"Marbles is a pretty big dude." Ollie shrugged. "Maybe that's who Stoker saw running away."

"There. He did it. Guilty." Alexander pushed away from the wall. "Let's go now."

"Marbles is one of our own." Stoker snorted. "He has no reason to hurt one of us. He could have been running away from the killer." He looked over Alexander expectantly. "Then again, I suppose we can't rule anyone out."

"Let me guess. You want me to go have a 'chat' with Marbles?"

"No, that would be bad." Will frowned. "They don't like you."

"Hmmph."

"Then I'll go," Stoker said briskly. "I grow tired of these games with the ever-resistant staff of that fetid little bar."

"Hey! No! No, they really don't like you either. Let me do it." Will perked up. "I've known Marbles and Jackie for years. They'll talk to me. If Marbles saw something, he'll tell me."

Stoker made a face.

"I wanna know who's hurting all my friends," Will insisted. "Please. Let me help."

"You literally just died." Stoker made a face. "You're covered in blood."

"Lemme go change and slap one of your watchman spells on me." Will slid off the table, reaching for Stoker's jacket and then giving it a sharp tug. "Come on. If anything goes weird, you can come find me."

"You will have six hours, starting now—"

"Hey, give me twenty-four at least!"

"Five."

"Twenty?"

"Four."

"Wait, wait, why do you keep going down?" Will pouted. "That's not how this is supposed to work."

"It does when I'm in charge. Four hours or none."

"Fine, yes. Bossy."

"Go talk to Marbles, get some answers, or else I will. He will not enjoy it, I assure you, so make sure he knows that it's in his best interest to cooperate." Stoker eyed Alexander. "As for you—"

"What?" Alexander narrowed his eyes. "Catch the killer or you won't give me Ollie back? How about I take that idea and shove it right up—"

"No." Stoker shook his head. "In light of Ollie's quick thinking and your assistance…." He waved his hand. "I'm forgiving his debt."

"Seriously?"

"Yeah?" Ollie grinned brightly. "You really mean that, Stoker?"

"Stay off drugs, Ollie." Stoker's smile was almost fond. "I still expect your assistance with bringing the killer to justice. I am beginning to suspect their motives may be darker than we first suspected."

"Why?" Alexander frowned, thinking, *What does he know that we don't?*

"Lawrence was a Deverach," Stoker replied. "His teeth were removed. They're used for one very specific thing in magic. Breaking the barriers. Like those of the mind, like hypnosis and—"

"Breaking the veil between worlds," Rota spoke out loud.

"Like if someone wanted, say, oh, I don't know, to go wake up a god?" Alexander scowled.

"Yes," Stoker confirmed. "And there's one god in particular who has a very passionate fan club."

"Salgumel." Alexander swallowed back a mouthful of bile that the name conjured. "You think this all might be part of an attempt to contact him?"

"Who else?"

"Sure. Yeah." Alexander huffed. "I love saving the world. It's great."

"Focus your little ritual scavenger hunt on any spells written for Salgumel. As with Tollmathan and Gronoch, there may be other gods here trying to awaken him, not to mention the cultists who have been quite active these past few months."

"Cultists? Seriously?"

Remember what Starkiller said, Rota reminded him. *Perhaps they're a bigger threat than we—*

"It's an angle we must consider," Stoker said firmly, his voice overtaking Rota's.

Rota sighed. *Being unseen and unheard is very difficult—*

"Report to me at once if you find anything," Stoker went on, once again overlapping Rota. "Will, remember, you have just four hours to talk to your little friends before I do. What precious bit of patience I had has been spent. This is it. And Ollie—"

"I'm staying o-fahfah drugs," Ollie said proudly.

Stoker sighed. "Yes, you are."

"You're letting us take Ollie?" Alexander asked. "Just like that?"

"I trust even you understand the importance of making sure no one awakens Salgumel," Stoker drawled. "Check your books. Find the ritual. Quickly."

Alexander grabbed Ollie's arm and pulled him close. "Yeah, we're on it."

"Hey! Wait." Will raised his hand. "Ollie? Alexander? Thank you. For, you know, saving my life."

"Aw. You got it, little guy." Ollie grinned. "Anytime."

"Remember," Stoker warned. "I expect results very soon."

"Whatever." Alexander used Rota's magic and took them back home in a blink, letting out a frustrated sigh. "Fuck, I hate that guy."

Ollie yanked his arm away, pouting down at Alexander. "Yeah? At least he cared about saving Will."

"Yeah, just to see if he knew anything about the murder!" Alexander scoffed.

Alexander, my love.... Rota sighed. *You were most unkind.*

"*Me*? I was trying to get Ollie the fuck out of there!"

"And let Will die because saving him might not benefact us?" Ollie shook his head. "No, come on." He stomped over to the kitchen. "That's fucked-up."

"Life is fucked-up." Alexander stalked in behind him.

"Stoker just forgave all of my debt for helping!" Ollie argued. "See? Being nice is good!"

"That was pure luck. Being nice is what gets you into shit, and it can get you killed."

"That's a terrible attitude, little dude." Ollie helped himself to a bottle of clear liquor, maybe vodka, and he wagged a finger at Alexander. "Not cool."

"You're an idiot." Alexander wanted to strangle him. "Life is not all puppies and rainbows and big stupid smiles! Life is fucking pain and people trying to use you—"

"You mean like you're using me?"

Alexander flinched.

Ollie, that's not true! Rota protested passionately.

"Maybe not for you, but it sure is for him." Ollie kept chugging, pausing to add, "It's just like how you use Rota, right? You use everybody to get what you want—"

"What I want is Rota's body back! I want him to be whole again! What I fucking want is to be *happy*!" Alexander shouted, snarling now as he snatched the bottle away from Ollie. "My entire life was fuckin' stolen from me! Do you not get that? And all I'm trying to do is—"

"Yes! I know!" Ollie yelled back as he tried to grab the bottle. "I'm in your head, jerk-face! All you want is to get Rota's stupid body back for some sweet ancient god loving and live happily ever after and...." He paused. "And...."

Get out of my fuckin' mind! Alexander growled. *Get out, get out, get out, get the fuck out!*

Alexander hadn't been thinking about anything in particular.

Maybe just how handsome Ollie looked when his face was flushed like that, perhaps how it was actually a little thrilling to see him lose his temper and show such passion—oh gods, no.

Ollie's lips twitched up into a smile. "You…. You like me?"

"No!" Alexander immediately snapped.

"You do!" Ollie gasped, triumphantly whisking the bottle away and running back toward the bed. "You like me! You really like me!"

"No, I fuckin' don't!" Alexander gave chase. "You're fuckin' drunk—"

"I'm always drunk—"

"I do not like you! You're an idiot!" Alexander stalked around the bed toward Ollie. "You're soft and stupid and you're way too happy all the time—"

"And you *like* me!" Ollie declared in a singsong voice as he jumped over the bed to get away from him. He tipped up the bottle and backed toward the kitchen. "You like me, you like me, you like meee!"

You know it's true. Rota was smiling so smugly, that bastard. *He can be quite charming.*

"Fuck you. Fuck you both." Alexander raised his middle fingers. "Fuck you both so hard."

"Only if you apologize, like, so much!" Ollie finished off the bottle, and he swayed a bit and then caught himself on the counter. "You were a giant jerk. Jerkiest of jerks."

"Apologize for what?" Alexander spat. "For trying to do the right thing?"

You were doing what was right for you, Rota corrected. *I know how much you've suffered, my sweet love. I lost my life too. I've lost even more in a way, because I cannot even take control of my own self—*

"You know I would never make you do anything that you didn't want to do!" Alexander pleaded, his guilt creeping in and extinguishing his rage. "I love you. I would never do that! I'm not him! I'm not Gronoch."

I am well aware. I know that… but I still do not have the freedom you so often have taken for granted. I am bound to you, love. Yes, our goals are the same, but you would have us walk a much darker path if I did not question your actions.

"You mean the path that actually gets shit done."

The path that takes your humanity as payment, love.

"Oh, for the love of the gods, you overdramatic sap."

"He's right." Ollie found another bottle to sip from. "You would have let Will die."

"Yeah, but only to prove a point to fuckin' Stoker!" Alexander argued. "The man who was going to lock you up for your stupid drug debt!"

"Don't you get it?" Ollie hiccupped. "Doing stu-fahfah like that makes you into a guy that is super hard to like. Like, wow, so hard."

It's true, Rota said. *You're not the boy I fell in love with, you know. I love you, I always will, but I worry. The things you're capable of... they trouble me.*

Alexander really did not appreciate how these two idiots were tag teaming him now. "I am capable of whatever it takes to get your fuckin' body back and to make sure we can be together. I don't care about the rest."

Maybe you should, my love.

"Yeah, because I have some strong feelings about having hot three-ways with unrepentant murderers." Ollie hiccupped again. "Like, that's a big no."

Excellent word usage, Ollie!

"Thank you." Ollie tipped the bottle in Rota's direction.

"Shut up." Alexander groaned, reaching up to try and snatch the bottle away with a snarl. "We can worry about what a bastard I am later. Us. Ritual. Now."

"Apologize!" Ollie held the bottle up high.

"Come the hell on!" Alexander huffed, glaring up at Ollie. There was no way he could reach it without using magic. "Give me that and get to work, you fuckin' giant moose."

"I am a moose who would like an apology."

"I'm sorry," Alexander ground out. "Happy?"

"Always! But I don't think you meant that."

You didn't sound very sincere, Rota chimed in.

"We have bigger things to worry about than me being an asshole!" Alexander snapped. "You guys heard what Stoker said. Hello! Bad ritual, could be waking up Salgumel."

"Oh yeah. The ritual with the things, and the…." Ollie's eyes closed. "The… thing…."

"Ollie?" Alexander expected Ollie to fall over, and he put his hands out to steady him. It wouldn't have been too surprising with how much he'd had to drink in the last few minutes.

Eyes still closed, Ollie wandered around Alexander and over toward the pile of books by the bed.

"What is he doing?" Alexander whispered.

I don't know. Starsight-ing… something?

Ollie reached down into the books, grabbed from the bottom of a stack and pulled out a thick tome. He didn't seem to notice the other books falling over. He flipped through the pages of the book he'd selected after setting it down open on the bed. He blinked, his eyes fluttering. "Oh, whoa. That was weird."

"What happened?" Alexander came over to look at the book, and he scanned the open pages. "Holy shit. It's the ritual."

CHAPTER 12.

"IT HAS all the ingredients from the victims," Alexander said excitedly. "Look!"

It's a ritual to speak to Salgumel! Rota exclaimed. *To send a prayer to his ear! Ollie, you've found it!*

"Oh, cool! Fuck yeah, starsight." Ollie pumped his fist. "Hey, does this mean we can go to dinner?"

"What?" Alexander sputtered.

"I'm hungry. And you owe me a date. Oh, and an apology. Like, a nice one."

"For fuck's sake."

"Dinner is a super nice way to say you're sorry, because there's food."

"We are not seriously doing this right now." Alexander picked up the book. "We need to go see Stoker."

I agree. Rota huffed.

"Thank you."

I also do not believe your apology was sincere.

"Hey! Look, can we maybe talk about how Ollie found the ritual we've been looking for?" Alexander shook the book at Rota. "Hello! It has all the ingredients. The teeth, the horns, all of it. And oh, surprise, it's a ritual for trying to summon Salgumel."

You still need to apologize, Rota scolded. *I think both Ollie and I deserve a proper apology for how rude you were, and... oh.*

Alexander could feel Rota leaning over his shoulder. "What's wrong?"

We're missing an ingredient.

"What?" Alexander could read most of the ritual, the language being a common Salgumel dialect that was very popular, but there was a section at the bottom written in another form of godstongue he couldn't make out. "A *conbusitae* husk...? I don't know that word. What is that?"

I'm not sure, love. It says the potion must be put into the conbusitae husk, and then it will.... Hmm. I believe that next word, "loquie," is "speak," so then the husk will speak to Salgumel?

"Ollie?" Alexander tilted the book toward him. "Any idea?"

"How should I know?" Ollie scratched his head. "I just needed to find the ritual, so my brain said hey, it's over here."

"You can't read this?"

Ollie emptied the bottle, burped, walked over, and stared down at the book for several moments.

"Well?" Alexander prompted.

"Toasty."

"Huh?"

"It says toasty."

"Your starsight is so stupid."

"Well, you're stupid, you like me, and we're going to dinner." Ollie smiled, and it was frustratingly adorable. He just kept smiling, as if he was daring Alexander to refuse.

"After we bring this to Stoker." Alexander slammed the book shut.

Then dinner? Rota chuckled.

"We'll see." Alexander narrowed his eyes. "He's still expecting us to find the killer, by the way."

"Okay. So. I have an idea." Ollie headed back to the kitchen to set the empty bottle down. He missed the counter twice before finding success, then turned to face Alexander with a clumsy flourish. "How about we don't go see Stoker right this very second?"

"Why not?"

"Because he's thinking we're gonna be working on the ritual, and I totally bought us some serious time to go grab dinner." Ollie beamed proudly.

"That is so stupid. Why are you so stupid?" Alexander groaned.

Ollie does actually raise a good point. Rota gently nudged Alexander's shoulder. *We've only just left Stoker. Do you not think he would find it strange if we return with the identity of the ritual after only a few minutes have passed?*

"Yeah, that." Ollie pointed. "That's exactly what I was thinking."

"Sure it was." Alexander rolled his eyes.

"We should totally kill some time before we go back to Stoker, like, the kind of time for eating dinner." Ollie wagged his eyebrows. "What do you say, huh?"

Well, I think it's an excellent idea, Rota said cheerfully. *Otherwise, Stoker may be suspicious as to how we were able to locate the ritual so quickly.*

"Or maybe he'll think we got lucky." Alexander snorted.

We don't want him to wonder about Ollie, do we?

Alexander sighed. "No."

Good. Then we have time to go out to dinner with Ollie. Once we're done, we will go see Stoker and start again on the search for the killer. Yes?

"You're both idiots."

Alexander couldn't deny the appeal of a date, but he wanted to get this murder mess resolved. Finding the ritual confirmed the cultists could be responsible for the killings by giving them a motive, but it also raised more questions.

Like, how did the cultists know where to find all the everlasting people? From what Alexander could tell, they wore varying degrees of glamour or lived inside Stoker's little world to stay hidden.

There were spells that could see through glamour, of course, but the cultists would have had to know the everlasting people existed to look for them in the first place. Even Sages thought they were gone, either off living in Xenon where the Asra rule after rebelling against the gods, gone with the gods into their dreaming, or died out on Aeon.

Ollie kept looking at Alexander with big stupid puppy eyes, and Alexander didn't want to upset him or Rota. He'd already done such a good job of that earlier, and he finally gave in with a very begrudging grumble.

"Oh, I'm sorry. What was that?" Ollie batted his eyes.

"Yes! I said yes!" Alexander wanted to smack him with the book. "Let's go before I change my mind."

"Yay!" Ollie tackled Alexander in a giant hug, smooching his cheek.

"Who the fuck actually says 'yay'?" Alexander only made a small effort to push Ollie away.

"Me." Ollie hugged him close. "Hey, let's swing by my apartment. I should change."

This is so exciting, Rota gushed. *Oh, would you like to change clothes too, Alexander? Something a bit dressier perhaps?*

"No," Alexander replied flatly.

You're no fun.

"Come on, come on, come on!" Ollie was practically giddy. "Let's go!"

"Ugh, it's not even close to dinnertime!" Alexander protested.

"Close enough! I'm hungry. And drunk. Drungry."

With a long-suffering sigh, Alexander summoned Rota's magic to transport them to Ollie's apartment. He watched Ollie stumble toward his bedroom, and he took a seat on the couch to wait.

I wonder what he's going to wear, Rota said.

"Maybe it'll be something with rubber ducks. Oh! Maybe palm trees."

I'm sure he will look very handsome.

"Whatever." Alexander closed his eyes and leaned back, listening to Ollie banging around in the other room. "I can't believe I'm doing this."

I think it's marvelous.

"You're nuts." Alexander resisted a smile, finding it faltered on its own when he remembered what Rota had said to him earlier. "Do you...."

What?

Do you really think I treat you like a slave? Alexander had to think the question, unable to ask it out loud.

Oh, my love. Rota's familiar ghostly touch moved over Alexander's cheek. *No. You do not.*

"But you feel like one. Don't you?"

Rota sighed. *At times, yes. It is frustrating not to be in control. That, however, is a reflection of our situation and not your treatment of me.*

"I never ask to use your magic. I just sort of... make you do things."

I like to think of it as our magic, love. It would be a bit troublesome to ask me for permission every single time you need to use it. But perhaps....

"Maybe I can start asking sometimes? Would that make me less of an asshole?"

It would be a good start. Rota was smiling.

"I love you."

I love you too.

"I'm sorry." Alexander inhaled sharply. Those words did not come easily to him, especially to say them so sincerely. He tried to push as much of his emotion into their bond for Rota to feel as he could.

I know. I forgive you, my love. Rota's response was a wave of love, warm and sweet, and left no doubts as to how he felt.

Alexander raised his hand, reaching for Rota, seeking him out with his thoughts. *Touch me. Please.*

Rota met his fingers with a cool, ghostly tentacle. *Mm, didn't think you'd want this anymore.*

"What?" Alexander slid his fingers through Rota's wispy flesh. "Touching me like this?"

I thought perhaps you'd prefer me in the flesh, so to speak.

"That's nice, but this? This is ours. Just me and you."

Me and you... and now Ollie.

Alexander smiled. "Yeah. Me, you, and the idiot." He couldn't stop the flutter in his belly, and he knew Rota felt it.

He's very special.

"In many ways." Alexander glanced to the bedroom door. "Should we check on him?"

Ollie popped out as if on cue, wearing a surprisingly demure floral printed button-up shirt, khaki slacks, and brown sandals. "Ready!"

You look wonderful, Ollie!

"Thanks, Rota." Ollie's cheeks noticeably pinked up.

"Yeah." Alexander stood and tried not to stare. "You look good." He smirked. "No rubber ducks?"

"Huh?" Ollie glanced at his shirt and then laughed. "Oh, well, I do have some boxers with flamingos." He wagged his brows. "Maybe if our date goes well, you can see 'em."

Blushing, Alexander mumbled, "Let's go."

"Wait, where are we—"

Alexander wanted to get out of the awkward situation as fast as possible, and he took them to the only restaurant he knew.

The Hot Pot.

Ollie blinked, looking around the alleyway Alexander had brought them to before he recognized it. "Oh! The Hot Pot! Fuck yeah!" He grinned. "You're gonna love this."

"Let's go." Alexander wished he could stop blushing, and now his whole face was burning.

"Hey. Uh." Ollie's smile turned shy. "Can I, like, maybe hold your hand?"

Alexander's face had promptly burst into flames, he just knew it, and he managed to choke out, "Yeah, whatever."

You two look adorable, Rota gushed happily. *I wish we had a camera!*

"Shut up," Alexander muttered, his heart tumbling against his ribs as Ollie took his hand.

It's so cute I could almost forget you didn't ask me permission to bring us here.

"Fuck!"

Rota laughed. *I'm only teasing, my love.*

"You can ask him when it's time to go home," Ollie suggested as he gave Alexander's hand a little squeeze, leading him up to the front doors of the restaurant.

"Wait." Alexander scowled. "How do you know what we're talking about?"

"Uh...." Ollie's eyes got comically wide. *'Cause I could totally hear everything you guys were talking about even though I totally tried not to, but then I kinda wanted to, but I know that's rude, and it was totally an accident—*

"Hey, hey!" Alexander tugged on Ollie's hand. "It's okay. Just... ugh...." He struggled to find the right thing to say. "Shut up."

That was the sweetest "shut up" I've ever heard, Rota cooed.

"You shut up too."

"It was sweet, wasn't it?" Ollie let Alexander's hand go so he could open the front door for him.

The inside of the restaurant was dark, decorated in red and splashes of gold with colorful lanterns hanging from the ceiling. A silk screen created a wall between the currently unoccupied hostess stand and the rest of the restaurant. There was a long bar, a section with large u-shaped tables built around a big hot plate, and a small dining area with regular tables and chairs.

It didn't seem very busy, probably because it was still early, but there was a small group seated at one of the u-shaped tables while a chef smacked rice and eggs around on the hot plate.

Alexander froze.

He had no idea what to do here.

He didn't have any memories of eating at a restaurant, and a sliver of panic slid up his spine. He didn't know how they were going to get to a table, much less which table it was going to be. He could see actual fire being thrown around by that chef. Was that even safe, what was—

"Hey, hey." Ollie grabbed his hand again, guiding him back a step away from the podium. "Are you okay?"

My love? Rota sounded concerned. *What's wrong?*

"I'm fine," Alexander lied. "Let's sit. Please." His eyes found an empty table in the corner away from all the activity beside the windows. "Like, over there. Way over there."

Are you sure? You don't want to watch the man cook?

"No. I'm good."

Ollie seemed to understand, bringing Alexander's hand up for a quick kiss. "Maybe next time, huh?"

"Yeah." Alexander forced himself to smile. "Next time."

The hostess appeared, and she greeted them with a friendly smile. Alexander barely heard Ollie talking to her, letting himself be led to the table he wanted back in the corner. He was so eager to sit that he nearly bulldozed Ollie, who was trying to pull out his chair for him.

"Thanks." Alexander let Ollie help him scoot in, and he ran his fingers through his hair. He was sweating.

"Yeah, no problem." Ollie sat across from him. "Do you, uh, want me to order for you?"

"Yes. No." Alexander took a deep breath to calm his nerves.

This was idiotic. He'd fought a god, and he was freaking out over a perfectly harmless meal.

"Hey! Let's play a game!" Ollie suddenly exclaimed.

Alexander stared at him.

"You know, to help you get your mind o-fahfah stu-fahfah."

What sort of game? Rota asked.

"Uh. How about questions?"

What's that?

"We ask each other questions." Ollie grinned.

"That's it?" Alexander scoffed.

"Usually there's alcohol involved. And you drink if you don't wanna answer a question."

"Alcohol is vile."

"Have you ever had a mixed drink before?"

"Mixed with what?"

Ollie's smile was now downright devious. "Oh, do you trust me?"

"No."

"Well, trust me anyway! I know you don't like soda, but you like fruit juice, right?"

"Yes."

"So, just trust me!"

The waiter approached then, introducing himself as whatever his stupid name was, and Alexander pretended to read the menu to avoid any and all eye contact. He vaguely heard Ollie talking to him, but he didn't put the menu down until the man left with their drink order.

"What the hell is a piña colada?"

"It's a drink and what I got for you. And you're either gonna love it, or you're gonna hate it." Ollie chuckled. "If you don't like it, then you can kick me in the balls."

"What? Why?"

"I dunno. It might make you mad."

"The drink?"

"Coconut does that to some people."

I understand it to be a divisive flavor, Rota said.

"It's fine." Alexander picked at the corner of the menu. He saw the noodle-and-chicken dish Ollie had picked out when they got takeout from here, and he settled on having that.

"Good choice," Ollie said. "I'm havin' the same thing. Oh, and with egg rolls."

"Get out of my head."

"Sorry. I'm all drungry, and you think super loud."

"How about we play your stupid game, hmm?" Alexander propped his chin in his hand, glancing over the restaurant. He was calmer now, and the anxiety was receding.

He could do this.

It was just a date.

The first date he could ever remember being on with a beautiful young man who liked him and he liked back and he had no idea what he was supposed to do—oh gods.

So much for not being anxious.

"Go ahead. You can ask me somethin' first." Ollie beamed. "Ask me anything."

"Why are you so damn happy all the time?" It was the first thing that popped into Alexander's head. "Really."

"Oh, I don't know." Ollie shrugged. "I guess because I got tired of crying all the time and being sad over my ex. I thought if I could pretend to be happy long enough then maybe it would stick."

"Did it work?"

"Okay, that's technically two questions, but I'll let you slide this time since you're new at this." Ollie winked. "It works most of the time. It's been easier, you know, since meeting you and Rota."

Alexander ducked his head to hide the new blush coming over him. "Yeah, okay. Who asks something now?"

"That's now three questions, little dude."

I'd like to ask Ollie something, Rota piped up.

"Go right ahead."

When we are intimate together, I sense such great pleasure when I penetrate you—

"Oh, for the love of all the gods!" Alexander cringed.

No one can hear me, shush. He said I could ask anything!

Ollie covered his mouth with his hand to smother a laugh. "It's totally okay. Uh, go on?"

Their waiter reappeared with their drinks, glancing between them with a curious expression. He must have thought he'd missed a funny joke. "Are we ready to order?"

When I penetrate you, your pleasure is so great, Rota went on. *I've been dying to know something.*

"Uh-huh." Ollie nodded, though it wasn't clear who he was responding to.

"Whenever you're ready." The waiter looked at Ollie expectantly.

Maybe you should order first.

"What?" Ollie blinked.

Order?

"Your order, sir?" the waiter prompted again.

"The fuckin' food, Ollie," Alexander hissed.

"Oh right!" Ollie grinned, that familiar dopey grin that made Alexander's insides melt a little. "Food. On it."

Alexander hid in his menu again while Ollie spoke to the waiter, and he decided to go ahead and try the weird yellowish-white drink Ollie had gotten him. He took a tiny sip, and wow, okay, that was actually delicious.

Apparently, he was a fan of coconut.

He'd downed nearly half by the time the waiter left.

"Like it?" Ollie asked.

"It's okay." Alexander smiled a little.

Looks like a little more than "okay," Rota noted.

"Yes, it's good." Alexander swept his hair back from his face. "Thank you, Ollie."

"No problem." Ollie slurped his own drink, something bright blue with sugar around the rim of the glass, and he glanced toward Rota's general direction. "Okay, now ask me. I'm all ears."

Is receiving pleasure your usual preference?

"I mean, pleasure is pleasure, but yeah." Ollie grinned shyly. "What about you, you godly stud? You like givin' the pleasure?"

Indeed. I never realized how much until recently, of course, but I do believe I am a "giver."

"This is my life now," Alexander said to no one in particular. "Talking about sex in restaurants. With coconut drinks."

"Your turn!" Ollie declared gleefully.

"Can I just chug this and not answer anything?"

"No, that's cheating. And that question was lame, so you're getting a do-over."

"I don't know what to ask." Alexander took another drink of his piña colada, wishing it would grant him some inspiration. "This is stupid."

"Just ask whatever comes to mind!"

"Fine. What did you want to be when you grew up?"

Ollie was surprised at the question, and he laughed. "Me? Oh, I don't know. An artist or something."

"Seriously?"

"Yeah. I always loved drawing when I was little. I was actually in school for art when, you know." Ollie pointed at his head. "All that happened."

"The starsight."

"Yeah. Stopped going after that. Stopped a lot of things. I still sketch stu-fahfah, but uh, I don't paint or anything now like I used to." Ollie shrugged it off, but Alexander could feel a glimmer of pain. It passed quickly, and his usual cheerful smile was back in place in a moment. "What about you? Same question."

"I...." Alexander had no idea.

"Right. Sorry." Ollie grimaced. "That was dumb of me. Uh. Favorite color? No, wait. Let me guess. It's black, isn't it."

Alexander's upper lip twitched into a smile. "Maybe we could just talk now?"

"Oh. That could work."

Perhaps we could talk about that apology you owe Ollie? Rota mused, a hint of a smile in his voice. *Just a thought.*

Alexander made a face and drank more.

"We ain't gotta do all that right now." Ollie shook his head. "Dates are supposed to be fun."

"No." Alexander fidgeted with his straw. "Rota is right." He took a deep breath. "I'm sorry. I know… I'm an asshole. And maybe I could be better about things. It's not in my nature to trust people."

"I hope eventually maybe that gets better." Ollie offered a sympathetic smile. "Not everybody in the world is out to get you. Some people really do wanna do the right thing."

"I used to be like that…." Alexander didn't know why he felt like sharing. Maybe it was the alcohol. Maybe it was the need to tell someone else, anyone, what he'd been through.

Alexander? Rota was concerned. He already knew what Alexander was thinking of, of course, and he slid a ghostly tentacle over Alexander's shoulder.

"It's okay, Rota." Alexander lifted his glass and drained it.

Ollie could obviously feel the rising emotions, and he started to say, "Hey, if you don't want to share—"

"No. I think I do." Alexander set the empty glass back down. "It was before I was bonded with Rota. Gronoch and his cronies had to get me ready to be a conduit. The marks took time… and I wasn't the only one there."

"There were… others?" Ollie leaned forward, his hands moving over the table.

Alexander didn't take them. "Yeah. I shared a room with one. Called him Vee. He was number eighteen. X-V-I-I-I. That's how we got our names. From our numbers. I was L-X-I-X. Lex, Alex, then Alexander. It wasn't like we had much else to talk about, and figuring out new names for ourselves helped pass the time in between operations.

"Vee had been there a long time. A lot longer than me. And he was getting desperate to escape. He used to be a locksmith, you see, and he had this crazy plan. He was gonna get us both out." *Stupid, stupid, it was so stupid, I should have never believed him.* "Long story short, he figured out how to get out of our room. Out of the hallway. All the way to the elevator. We had a real chance to escape."

Rota slipped into Ollie's body, and he moved one of Ollie's hands closer.

Alexander took it now. "It went bad as soon as we got into the hallway. This wall came down between us, this grate thing. It wasn't even magical. It was mechanical. They didn't need much to keep us from escaping since we were all Silenced. All Vee had to do was come back and unlock it. There was a door right in the middle of the fucking thing, a hatch I could have crawled through...."

Ollie offered his other hand.

Alexander could feel it was Ollie offering now, and he took that one as well.

"But he left me." Alexander decided to wrap up the story, hating how weak the memory made him feel. "I helped him, I thought we were friends, and he watched them... come for me.... He knew what they were going to do to me for trying to escape, and he just left...." His eyes were hot, and he squeezed Ollie's and Rota's hand.

What have we here? L-X-I-X, I do believe you're ready for the next stage of our program. Don't you all think so? Oh yes, indeed! Now it's time for some real pain....

Blood.

Agony.

And the torture continued even after the surgery, there in the showers beneath scalding hot water just because his captors wanted to be particularly cruel. That was where he found the edge of a drain cover was sharp enough to cut his wrists.

I can't do that again, I can't, I can't, they won't stop, they're never going to stop—

No more pain... no more....

"That's when Rota found you," Ollie whispered solemnly. "But how did—"

Their waiter showed up then with their order, politely waiting for them to break apart before setting the food down. "All right! Here we go, guys! Enjoy!"

Alexander quickly tucked his hands in his lap. The food smelled wonderful, but he didn't have much of an appetite now.

"Thank you so much," Ollie said to the waiter. "Can we get another round of drinks and some more white sauce, please? Thank you." He waited for him to leave before he looked back to Alexander. "So."

"So." Alexander kept his head down. "That's why I have a tiny issue with trusting people."

"I'm sorry."

"Yeah. I'm sorry too." Alexander knew Ollie meant the apology, but he didn't know what else to say. The ensuing silence was miserable, and he struggled for anything to break it and found nothing.

Not even Rota seemed to know what to say, having left Ollie's body and now silently hovering by Alexander's shoulder.

"So." Ollie cleared his throat. "Are we not gonna talk about how your number was sixty-nine, totally the coolest number ever?"

Alexander laughed. He couldn't help it. He finally looked back up at Ollie, finding that same stupid smile that always made his insides do funny things. "How do you even know that? You're an idiot."

"I know stu-fahfah!" Ollie smirked smugly. "Made ya' laugh."

"Thank you." Alexander smiled in return as best as he could. "For that, and for still liking me… even when I'm an asshole."

"It's all part of your charm."

He is quite charming, Rota agreed sweetly, *when he wants to be.*

"Fuck off." Alexander gave a good roll of his eyes.

"Hey." Ollie offered his hand and gave Alexander's a big squeeze when he accepted it. "I may not be able to totally understand what you guys went through, I know it was beyond fucked-up, but I do know this cool story about a turtle, and…."

"A turtle?"

Ollie's gaze drifted out the window beside them, and his eyes widened. "Uh, problem."

"What?" Alexander snorted. "Did the waiter forget to bring your crayons?"

"Yes. Wait, what? No!" Ollie shook his head and pointed out the window. "Look!"

Will was right outside, being led down the sidewalk by a man in a long coat. Will appeared to be sleepwalking, judging by his bowed head, closed eye, and shuffling gait.

The man in the coat had a large bandage over his cheek.

Who is that? Rota asked.

"That's Will—" Ollie started to reply.

"We know that's Will!" Alexander snapped. "Who's the other guy?"

"Oh. Right." Ollie gulped. "That's Je-fahfah."

"Who?"

"The guy who killed me."

CHAPTER 13.

"RUN THAT by me again?" Alexander watched Je-fahfah or Jeff or whatever his name was walking down the sidewalk with Will away from them.

"Right, so, I was a sacrifice?" Ollie chugged his drink, holding up his finger until he was done. "He's the one who did the stabby stabby."

And what is he doing with young Will? Rota demanded.

"Can't be anything good." Alexander stood, and the room spun a little. That was weird. He shook it off. "Let's go."

"What about the food?" Ollie motioned at their plates.

Alexander scowled.

"No. Right. Saving Will. Much more important." Ollie stood up and reached for his wallet. He hastily dropped some cash on the table while Alexander hurried outside.

At least Alexander tried to.

The spinning was worse when he walked, and he had to catch himself on the wall by the door before he fell. His vision wouldn't focus, his head was way too light, his cheeks were hot, and….

Oh, by all the gods, he was drunk.

Tipsy, really, but it made any kind of coordinated movement awful.

Alexander, are you all right? Rota sounded alarmed.

"I'm fine!" Alexander barked, startling a couple who was entering the restaurant as he pushed past them outside. He ignored the spinning in his head and looked around. "Which way did that guy go?"

Turn right. He went that way.

"Thanks."

This man is one of the cultists Starkiller asked us to look for. This more than confirms that the everlasting people were being murdered for the ritual, yes?

"As opposed to a series of Lucian-inspired hate crimes?" Alexander drawled. "They both suck."

Well, yes… but this "sucks" slightly less perhaps?

"No, I think this is worse."

Really?

"Can we have our bigot serial killer versus the end of the world debate later?"

"Hey!" Ollie was jogging to catch up to them. "So, I'm bad at math, but I think I left Lee a super good tip." He frowned. "Or a really bad one."

"Who?" Alexander snapped, turning his head to keep an eye on Jeff's head above the crowd.

"Our waiter? His name is Lee."

Alexander groaned. "Focus. Ollie! Tell me everything you know about that Jeff guy!"

"He likes stabbing people?" Ollie scratched his head. "Uh, he's a jumper. It's how he got away last time. He ported after I came back from the dead."

"Shit." Alexander moved around the people on the street and kept his eyes on Jeff. He wanted to be far enough away not to be noticed but close enough to snag the trail if Jeff teleported. "Why isn't he porting now, then?"

Stoker's watchman spell, Rota said. *Perhaps he saw it and knew not to go off world or else Stoker would be alerted like we were with Ollie.*

"So, where the fuck is he taking him?" Alexander turned right to keep up with Jeff, and he spotted him crossing the street. Traffic was light, but Alexander still had to wait for a break before bounding after him. "Shit, shit, shit."

"We're heading away from downtown." Ollie looked around. "I swear, it's almost like we're heading back to the bar—"

"Should we grab him now?"

"Why are you asking me?" Ollie blinked.

"Good point. Rota, should we grab him now?"

We should try to contact Stoker, yes? He wanted to be notified immediately.

"Fine." Alexander growled. "Ollie, try to call Stoker. Let him know we found the killer."

"Do we really know it's Je-fahfah, though?" Ollie made a face. "Look, he's stabby and all, but we haven't actually seen him do anything—"

"Less talking! More calling! Now!"

Rota gasped. *The toasty husk.*

"What?"

Will. He was burned, yes? He is the toasty husk, the burned vessel, for the ritual.

"Oh!" Ollie laughed. "Those words make a lot more sense than what I read."

"So none of this has been about targeting everlasting people except for ingredients," Alexander said.

It seems that way.

"Still doesn't explain how Jeff knew where to find them all."

"He's got some wicked witchy powers, little dude," Ollie said with a grimace. "I'm just sayin' maybe he was able to figure out a way to track them down. Also?" His grimace deepened, and he held up his phone. "I'm not getting a reply from Stoker. It's going to voicemail."

"Fine! We'll port over to his stupid fancy place and port right back. Ollie, you stay here and keep following them—"

"What if something goes wrong? What if he sees me?" Ollie's eyes widened, and a spike of fear filled the bond.

"The same bond that lets us share emotions and weird uncomfortable sex questions? It links us together. We'll find you." Alexander pulled Ollie down for a deep kiss, reassuring him with a flood of affection and determination. *I promise.*

"You should drink piña coladas more often," Ollie said cheerfully, pink and happy when they parted. "That was nice."

"Shut up."

"There was tongue—"

"Ollie! Go! Before you lose them!" Alexander straightened himself out and wiped off his mouth. "We'll be back as soon as we can." He paused. "Rota, may I please use your magic—"

Yes, of course! Let's go!

"Fine. Shit. Just trying to be nice." Alexander summoned a portal and stepped behind Ollie to help hide what he was going to do. He went to leave, but it was like hitting a brick wall face-first.

Literally hitting a wall, because he had stepped forward and smacked into the wall of the building they were standing next to.

"What the fuck?"

"What happened?" Ollie hissed. "Why are you still here?"

The theater, Rota replied quickly. *There is a shield over the building, maybe even over the whole block, that is preventing us from porting there. It's one of Stoker's own design, I'm sure. I did not sense any way to get inside without a key of some kind.*

"Can you guys port, like, right next to it and walk over—"

"New plan because they're getting away!" Alexander snapped impatiently. A few moments and they risked losing sight of Jeff and Will entirely. "Me and Rota are going to grab him and jump, and you're going to take Will through another portal. Do you understand? Keep trying Stoker and keep Will safe. Tell him we're going to the fields."

"Who? Will?"

"No! Stoker. Tell Stoker that." Alexander resisted the urge to shake Ollie. "We took Stoker there before. He'll know how to get there."

"Should I call my uncle? Or Sloane? Like, for backup?"

Alexander scoffed.

"Fine, mister tough guy." Ollie shoved his phone back in his pocket. "I can take him to Dead to Rites. Jackie and Marbles can help me keep him safe until we get Stoker."

"Good. Great. Let's go." Alexander dove back into the stream of pedestrians and made a beeline for Jeff and Will. *You ready, Rota? Two portals. One to the fields, one to the bar.*

I am ready, my love.

"All right." Alexander continued to advance, and Will and Jeff were only a few yards away now.

So, what's the plan once we subdue him, hmm?

"Kick his ass. Ask questions."

Shouldn't we try asking questions first?

"Maybe."

Alexander....

Fine! Alexander switched to his thoughts so Jeff wouldn't hear him sneaking up on him and arguing with himself. *We will try talking first. Happy?*

Very.

Reaching forward, Alexander called on Rota's magic to open the two portals. It was risky on a busy street like this, but if he did this quickly enough there was a good chance no one would notice. It would be nothing more than someone brushing by and then vanishing into the crowd.

He grabbed Jeff's shoulder and pulled him back, using a wave of Rota's tentacle to shove Will back into Ollie's arms and safely into the second portal. He tightened his grip on Jeff and lassoed him up with more of Rota's tentacles to drag him into the portal that led into the fields.

Jeff struggled violently, and Alexander let him go early so he could watch him drop in a heap on the ground. While Jeff was dazed from the fall, Rota's tentacles returned to bind him firmly as Alexander affixed a silencing ward to his forehead.

"There we go." Alexander took a few steps away, reaching into his coat pocket for a cigarette. "Hi. I bet you're wondering what you're doing here."

Jeff did appear rather confused. He sat up and touched his forehead, making a face when he felt the ward. He glared at Alexander and stumbled to his feet. "Oh, you have no idea who you're messing with."

Alexander snorted and lit up, waiting until he'd taken a long drag and exhaled before replying, "You're Jeff, but I'm going to call you fuck face. You're a real big fan of Salgumel and like murdering everlasting people."

"Who the hell are you?" Jeff raised his hands, putting his index fingers and thumbs together to form a triangle for a perception spell.

Alexander calmly waited for him to finish mumbling the spell and realize that it wasn't going to work while he was silenced. Alexander used a perception spell of his own to look over Jeff while he was still smoking.

Mortal, a weak aura of something—wait, wow, what was going on with Jeff's face?

Beneath the bandage was something… rotten.

What is that? Alexander urgently asked Rota.

As best as I can tell, it's… death.

Alexander did not like how shaken Rota sounded.

"You silenced me!" Jeff accused.

"You're a genius, fuck face," Alexander replied dryly. "Got anything else to share with the class?"

"Oh, I know who you are now. The smartass conduit." Jeff snorted and dropped his hands. "Wow, you're just adorable. Did Gronoch take you shopping at Hot Topic if you were a good boy?"

"Wow, you're hilarious, fuck face."

How does he know about Gronoch?

Who cares? Alexander thought back and spoke out loud to Jeff. "How about you go ahead and confess to killing everybody, huh?"

"Killing who exactly?" Jeff shrugged. "You're gonna have to be more specific."

"Uh, hello. All the everlasting people you butchered for your little ritual to dial up Salgumel."

"Me?" Jeff laughed. "You idiots. I just paid for the parts."

Alexander paused. *Rota?*

As far as I can tell, he's telling the truth. I don't understand—

"Now, if you'll kindly fuck off, I'm gonna go find what you've done with my damn vessel. Him I might have to kill, but I haven't yet, so why don't you let me go do that, and then you can try to kill me back, hmm?"

"Yeah, no. Sorry, fuck face." Alexander took another drag and leaned back, catching himself on part of Rota's side as it solidified to brace him. "You're staying here and hanging out with me while we wait for Stoker to come have a chat with you. You can plead your crazy shit out with him."

"Stoker?" Jeff laughed again. "Right. Of course he would send someone like you to come find me. To cover his ass."

"I know you're baiting me into asking you more stupid shit while you're trying to think of a way to get out of here." Alexander narrowed his eyes. "But we got some time to kill and you're definitely not escaping… so what the fuck are you talking about?"

"He didn't tell you?" Jeff snorted. "The book. The grimoire that has the ritual in it for summoning Salgumel with the *conbusitae* vessel? I bought it from Stoker."

Oh dear.

Wait, wait, wait. Alexander kept his face calm even as his thoughts ran wild. *Stoker didn't know he sold a book to a crazy fuckin' cultist?*

Perhaps he sold the book to him for another reason?

"I can see the wheels in your little brain over there just a turnin' away." Jeff smirked. "Trust me. Stoker knew exactly what he was giving me."

"He probably didn't think a fuck face like you could get the parts." Alexander flicked the ashes off his cigarette and arched one brow. "So, how did you do that, fuck face?"

"You're asking all the wrong questions." Jeff chuckled, and he reached up to the bandage on his face as if to adjust it. He turned away to hide whatever it was he was doing from Alexander's view.

Rota? Alexander stood.

On it. Rota lumbered over to peer around the other side.

"You should be wondering about whose side of the war you want to be on when the time comes and Salgumel arises," Jeff continued as he dropped some strips of medical tape on the ground. "Like, hmm, do I wanna side with the stupid mortals who are all going to be wasted to make way for the new world? Or do I wanna be with the faithful and actually be spared?"

"Hard pass." Alexander tossed away his cigarette, burning away the filter into ash. *Rota?*

He's taking off the bandage, Rota replied. *It's, wow, all right, it's quite awful. It's a big nasty rotten handprint burned into his flesh, and he's pulling something... out of the hole.*

Gross. What?

A healing totem? A very old one, very ancient... I don't understand why he's taking it out.

"Too bad." Jeff turned to face Alexander again and gave him a full view of the terrible injury. It was indeed a handprint burned into his cheek, and the glint of his teeth was visible through the wound. "We could have used you. You know, it's what you were made for after all."

"Fuck you." Alexander lit up another cigarette with a scowl.

Alexander, Rota warned.

Yes. I know I need to quit—

Alexander. Rota was nearly frantic. *Look. The hole.*

Alexander puffed and tilted his head. *Huh... is it...?*

It is.

It's getting bigger? Alexander watched in horror as the seeping black rot of the wound worked across Jeff's face, eating his skin as it went.

He was howling and sobbing in pain, but he let it go on and on, and the necrosis devoured his flesh right to the bone. It was horrific, disgusting, and Alexander didn't understand why Jeff was doing this—at least, not until it spread over his brow.

"The ward!" Alexander leaped forward, but he wasn't fast enough.

The sickness, whatever it was, ate right through the silencing ward as easily as the skin beneath it, and Jeff shouted an incantation that created a thick shield all around him.

Alexander snarled and focused Rota's magic on breaking it apart, snapping, "Oh, real cute. Just let your face cooties eat up the ward!"

Panting from obvious exertion, Jeff had dropped to a knee and popped the totem back into his cheek. The decay receded until it was but a handprint again, and he leered up at them smugly, his teeth gleaming between his lips and the nasty hole in his cheek. "You don't even know what this is, do you?"

"Your fuckin' fucked-up face?" Alexander could sense a weakness in the shield, and he raised his hands to channel even more of Rota's magic there.

"I have been touched by the first child of Great Azaethoth," Jeff declared. "I carry his power. You may stop me from performing this ritual, but if I find him? Then nothing else matters."

That made Alexander pause.

There was no way that was true. It couldn't be.

"Just remember, conduit. You coulda been on the winning side." Jeff winked. "Too bad, huh?"

"Fuck you, you're not going anywhere!" Alexander hissed as Jeff added another layer to the shield, preventing him from breaking through. *Rota! The spell Stoker cast at the theater?*

Yes?

Can we cast that, but in reverse?

Oh! Of course! Rota understood what Alexander wanted to do immediately and showed him the words for the new spell, weaving them in and out through the bond so it could be cast quickly.

Try as he might, now Jeff wouldn't be able to teleport out, though someone could still teleport into this world.

Alexander kept working at the shield, and he very much enjoyed the surprised and equally horrified look on Jeff's face when he realized he couldn't leave. "Problem, fuck face?"

"This isn't going to stop me!" Jeff snarled.

"What are you gonna do? Rot the spell away with your face hole?" Alexander snorted. "How about you tell me where the Fountain is at, hmm? Maybe who was doing your everlasting grocery shopping for you?"

"Oh, I'm sorry. Were you expecting me to monologue and explain all the details of my nefarious plans?" Jeff scowled and rolled his eyes. "No, I don't think so. All you need to know is that I am going to find a way to awaken Salgumel, and you can't stop me!"

"Or I could just kill you now. Choices!" Alexander finally broke the shield and sent in Rota's tentacles, stabbing them through Jeff's chest and stomach to curl around his vital organs and squeeze.

Gurgling, Jeff clawed weakly at the invisible appendages, and he went to both knees in agony. "Ah… ah, gods!"

"Now. let's try this again." Alexander smirked. "Where is the Fountain, huh? Tell me where it is right—"

Jeff lurched forward despite the obvious pain he was in, whispering a spell and pushing Alexander back.

Alexander didn't understand what was happening, and he gasped as he felt one of the binding marks on his arm break. He backed away, tearing at his sleeve to find pooling blood. Another one broke and tore a scream from his lips because the shattered mark had been somewhere inside his chest. "Oh, you bastard!"

Alexander! No! Rota cried. *The bindings! I can feel them. They're all weakening. They're going to break!*

"You're not so tough," Jeff sneered. "And you're not the only one who can reverse engineer a spell. Just like you switched the teleportation ward to stop me from leaving, I switched up my healing totem's magic to heal your wounds… including scars like those pretty little marks."

Alexander, no! Rota wrapped his tentacles all around Alexander, trying to stop the healing magic from working to no avail.

"Rota… I…." Alexander screamed as another mark broke and healed, leaving behind a gaping welt, and he could feel Rota slipping.

"Now." Jeff stood and dusted himself off. "There may be some side effects. Was never very good at healing spells. Maybe you'll figure out how to stop it before one of the marks on your heart or some other vital organ breaks, maybe you won't. Good luck." He raised his arms, twisting his fingers and casting a spell to tear down the teleportation ward.

Alexander barely noticed. He was too busy trying to find the healing magic working against him and stop it, but the pain was excruciating. It was beyond even the anguish of when the marks were put into his skin, and he groaned, watching in horror as he coughed up a splatter of blood.

"Farewell, conduit." Jeff smirked. "I don't think we'll be seeing each other again."

"Oh… no… you don't…." Alexander focused the great reservoir of Rota's power and reached out to grab a hold of Jeff's leg as he went into the portal he'd just opened.

Jeff vanished. His bloody leg remained.

That was a small comfort when Alexander was coughing up more blood and his entire body was on fire, another broken mark making him scream. "Rota... how... how do we stop it?"

I don't know! It's not offensive magic! There is no targeting to break! Rota held Alexander against him, making himself solid so he could embrace him. *My love, I don't know what to do—*

"What now?" A loud pop of a portal had Alexander's attention, and he saw Ollie rushing toward him. "Oh, Ollie... what are you...."

"Saving you!" Ollie dropped beside him, his eyes glimmering with tears as he took in the bloody mess. "I felt you! Through the bond! Magical sex bond! I just, I just followed it, my starsight did its weird-ass thing, and I'm here! What is happening? Wait, oh crap, and whose leg is that?"

"Might be... dying...." Alexander gritted his teeth and shuddered. "Fuckin... Je-fahfah...."

Jeff cast some sort of healing magic on Alexander, and it's destroying the binding marks. If any of the marks on Alexander's vital organs break—

"Shit! That fucker! God, I really do not like him!" Ollie held Alexander close, his hands turning red with blood as he felt over the wounds. "I'm thinking! I'm trying to think!"

"Now would be a great time... to use that starsight...." Alexander laughed weakly, but the sound was stolen when he howled in pain from another broken mark. "Fuck! Rota... I... I'm losing you."

Alexander, my love. No. No, no, no. No, you don't. Hold on. Ollie, please, do something!

"I'm trying! I'm fuckin' trying!" Ollie hollered. "I'm...." His eyes glazed over as if he was suddenly in a trance, and he reared back and slapped Alexander across the face.

"The fuck!" Alexander growled. To his surprise, the stinging of his cheek was now the only pain he felt. The marks were creeping back into his flesh, and he could actually see each one reappearing as if nothing ever happened.

Ollie blinked and refocused. "Oh! Shit. What happened?"

You slapped Alexander, and that.... Rota seemed equally confused. *That somehow stopped the spell?*

"Cool! Why are they all silver-looking now?"

Hmmm. It must be something you did when you cast. There is an additional line next to the arrow now as well, you see. I've never seen a marking—

"Come on." Alexander got to his feet with a groan, scanning the world around them and scowling. "I wanna go find that Jeff asshole right now."

"Hey!" Ollie stood and pulled Alexander into a big hug. "Can we, like, enjoy the fact you're still alive for at least two seconds, please?"

Alexander didn't want to dwell on what had just happened, especially knowing what could have gone down if Ollie hadn't found them. "Woo. Yes. I'm alive. Thank you. Happy?"

"Always." Ollie grinned.

"Wait, hey, what did you do with Will?"

"I left Will with Marbles." Ollie frowned. "He was still kind of out of it? Like, I couldn't get him to wake up all the way. Marbles said he would try. He was super cranky. Jackie and the other guys had to go meet with Stoker."

Ah, so that's why we probably couldn't get into the theater. Stoker probably locked everything down to have the meeting.

"Whatever." Alexander sighed. "Can we chase down Jeff now, please?"

"Four more seconds of hugging and then yes."

"Fine." Alexander didn't mind the hug as much as he suddenly had the urge to sneeze. He pushed away, blinking at a dusty residue on Ollie's shirt. "What is that?"

"Oh, people."

What?

"What?" Alexander echoed. Surely that had to be another mistake.

"Marbles just got o-fahfah work." Ollie rubbed the front of his shirt. "He said he had some accident with the processor thingie and it spilled all over him, and then we hugged, which he hated, but it was more of me hugging him, and it got real awkward—"

"What the fuck does he do?"

"He works at the funeral home. At the crematory."

"At the...." Alexander frowned, and the realization crashed into him like a freight train. "Oh. No."

"It's totally fine. He said it would wash out—"

"No!" Alexander shouted. "The residue on the bodies? The burned residue?"

"Huh?"

"It's him. It's fuckin' cremated remains. The killer is fuckin' Marbles!"

CHAPTER 14.

OH, BY the gods. Rota gasped. *Something burned! The residue on the victims! Could it actually have been cremated remains?*

"Marbles couldn't have done this!" Ollie protested. "He's, he's one of the everlasting! You really think he'd do that to his own people?"

"People are assholes," Alexander said flatly. "Everlasting or not. Nothing would surprise me."

"But…." Ollie seemed lost. "It's Marbles. I know him."

"Come on." Alexander grabbed Ollie's hand. "If I'm wrong, then we have nothing to worry about. It'll be another dead end. No big deal. But if I'm right, you just left Jeff's last ingredient with his co-conspirator."

"Oh, well, fuck."

"Let's go." Alexander glanced up. "Rota?"

Yes. Absolutely. Asking for permission does not feel appropriate when a life may be at stake!

Alexander quickly opened a portal to take them to Dead to Rites. They arrived outside the front door and startled a man coming out with their sudden appearance.

"Hi!" Ollie waved.

The man stared. "Uh… hi?"

Ignoring them both, Alexander pushed by and marched forward into the bar. "Come on, Ollie!"

"In the back!" Ollie stepped around him to lead the way. "The door behind the bar by the shrine thingie."

There were a half dozen or so patrons present, and none of them seemed pleased to see unfamiliar faces. Alexander ignored them on his way to the bar, finding a young woman standing there pouring a beer.

When Alexander tried to walk around the bar to get to the door, he found himself being struck by a small blast of fire magic. He quickly deflected it with a wave of his hand before it could singe his coat, and he turned to glare at the woman.

"Y-you can't go back there!" she cried. "That's private! Ollie, what are you guys doing?"

"I wouldn't try to stop him." Ollie shook his head. "He didn't get to eat his dinner, and he's had a piña colada. I don't know what he might do."

The woman's jaw dropped. "Wha…?"

"I don't know either." Alexander shrugged. "Permission to open the door, Rota?"

The woman was more confused.

Yes, yes, go ahead, my love. Quickly now.

"I'm trying to be better, okay?" Alexander sent Rota's tentacles to open the door. It had a simple magical lock on it, wouldn't take long to break—

Alexander! Behind you!

Alexander threw up a shield right as a bottle came flying at him, followed by a blast of ice, and he glanced over his shoulder to scoff at the men who had thrown them. "Uh, excuse you."

"I dunno who you think are," the smaller of the two men growled, "but we—"

"May I have permission to violently shake that man?" Alexander asked.

The man scoffed. "Fuckin' excuse me?"

My love, I'm afraid asking me for permission every time you want to cast a spell is becoming a bit tedious, and this is a very urgent situation. How about you ask me when it's a particularly large amount of magic, hmm?

"Okay, *fine*." Alexander grabbed the man around his middle with Rota's tentacles, slammed him into the ceiling with a loud crack, and let him drop to the floor in a heap.

The bar was deathly silent, and no one moved.

"Good, we're all done now? Thanks." Alexander snorted and went back to opening the lock.

"Was that really necessary?" Ollie asked in a hurried whisper.

"He's alive." Alexander broke the lock and opened the door with a wave of his hand. "Let's go already."

The door led into a hallway stacked with cases of beer and spirits. There was an emergency exit at one end and two more doors at the other.

"Straight ahead." Ollie pointed. "That's the o-fahfahice. There's these super-duper protection wards—"

Alexander raised a hand, seeking out the wards and crushing them.

"Okay, there *were* wards," Ollie corrected himself. "Uh, please be careful."

"It's not me you need to worry about." Alexander stalked to the door and directed Rota to fling it open hard enough to tear it loose from the hinges. "Knock-knock."

The office was a cluttered nightmare of more boxes of booze, paperwork, and broken furniture. Will was stretched out on a worn sofa, not moving, and Marbles was sitting at the desk on the phone.

He hung up and snarled, "You again, huh? Shoulda known you were gonna be—"

"Blah blah blah. We're taking Will, and you can fuck right off." Alexander strolled over to the couch. He hadn't let his shield drop yet, and it was a good thing because he was struck with a bolt of lightning. It bounced off the shield and went up into the fan above his head, creating a shower of sparks.

"Holy shit!" Ollie yelled. "Marbles! Hey! No! It's okay! We just wanna get Will somewhere safe!"

"I can't do that." Marbles frowned, his hand raised and ready to hurl another bolt. "What have you done? Where's Jeff?"

"I can get you a leg," Alexander replied dryly. "I think it's a leftie. Want that?"

"How do you know who Je-fahfah is…." Ollie gasped as realization settled in. "Oh no. Marbles, no."

"Surprise, surprise," Alexander mumbled under his breath.

"It's you, isn't it?" Ollie sighed mournfully. "You're the one killing everyone?"

"Look at that. Stupid Ollie finally got somethin' right." Marbles stood, and the room was suddenly very wrong. "Why don't you two take a little break while I sort this out, huh?"

The walls were leaning over and melting, and Alexander watched the cheap wood paneling drip away to reveal sterile white walls. The very sight filled him with dread, and the dull thump of his heart sped up as the desk morphed into a stainless-steel operating table. The office had vanished, and he was somewhere new.

It was the operating room back at Hazel.

Everything was perfect, down to the *smell*, and Alexander backed up against the wall behind him. He couldn't see Will or Ollie, and he looked down at his arms to find he was wearing nothing but a hospital gown.

His marks were gone.

"Rota?" Alexander called.

Silence.

"No, no…." He gritted his teeth and clawed at his arms. "No, no, no." Terror ate at his insides, and he fell to his knees.

What's the matter, L-X-I-X?

"No… fuck you." Alexander gritted his teeth. "No! Fuck you, fuck you, fuck you!"

Aw, that's no way to be, little boy… come on….

"You're not fuckin' real." Alexander's head throbbed. He knew this was a spell, and even though he couldn't see the marks, he knew they were there. He took a deep breath, his fingers trembling, and he dug deeper into his arm. He dug until the pain registered, and he felt the edge of a mark.

Alexander! It was Rota. He sounded far away, but he was there.

Rota. Alexander took another deep breath to steady himself, and he stood. *I'm gonna need your permission to use a shit-ton of magic to completely wreck this asshole's little world.*

It is yours, love. Rota was smiling now, and he was there. He was back with Alexander, and he wrapped his tentacles all around him. *I am yours.*

"Good." Alexander popped his neck and stretched, letting the cool feeling of Rota's flesh envelop him. He reached out into the air around him, digging into the spell that was keeping them trapped in this illusion.

It was thick, powerful, and he had no idea how Marbles had created such a thing—and honestly, he didn't care.

Now, now, L-X-I-X, the phantom guard's voice warned, *I don't know what you think you're doing, but it's not going to work.*

"Maybe don't pick someone out of my brain whose head I personally crushed like a walnut," Alexander mumbled. He searched, and there, there was an edge of the illusion. It was faint, but it was there under the bottom of the table. "Rota! Now!"

I've got you, my love! Yes!

The rush of magic made Alexander's entire body ache, and he gasped sharply. It was dangerous to take so much, but he needed it to break this trap. He honestly couldn't tell if they were off on another world or if this was something Marbles had created in his head.

Roaring in agony as the magic tore through his skin, Alexander ripped back the illusion.

It crumbled into nothing, and they were....

The birthday party. They were at his birthday party, the memory Ollie had given him back, but there was no one else here except Alexander and Rota. The candles were burning on the cake; the decorations fluttered as a faint breeze came through, but they were alone.

It's another dream. Another illusion. Rota stayed close, his voice right in Alexander's ear. *This is a powerful illusion spell, and there could be many layers. You and I may actually be fortunate we do not have that many years' worth of memories to sift through. Rest for a moment, and—*

"No time!" Alexander barked. He swatted away a balloon that had drafted too close. "There's no telling what he could be doing to Ollie."

And Will.

"Ugh, yes, and Will."

If Marbles is collaborating with Jeff, they may be preparing to perform that spell as we speak—

"Well, last time I checked, Jeff only has one fuckin' leg now, so hopefully that slows him down." Alexander was about to summon a new wave of magic to find a way to break out of here, but he heard the sound of someone crying. That wasn't part of his memory. "Rota?"

I will go look. Stay here. Keep searching.

Alexander looked down and saw he was back in his own clothes again. He felt better, stronger, and he reached out with Rota's magic, trying to feel for a weakness.

Alexander! Rota called. *Here! Quickly!*

"What?" Alexander turned to follow Rota's voice, and he skidded to a stop when he saw the source of the crying.

It was Ollie, but he was a small boy, no older than eight or nine. He was sitting on the ground next to the house, leaning up against the wall and hugging his knees. "... please just turn the light o-fahfah... turn it o-fahfah... it's too bright...."

"What the fuck?" Alexander dropped beside Ollie and petted the top of his head. "Hey. Ollie. Hey. Wake up. It's me. Alexander." He frowned as Ollie jerked away from him. "What's wrong with him?"

He's trapped in a memory, the same as we were.

"Why the fuck can't he get out?"

Ollie's head suddenly popped up, and he said in a perfectly normal voice, "Okay! Is it time to read? I just gotta turn the light off." He screamed and ducked back down, sobbing again like before. "… please just turn the light o-fahfah…."

He appears to be stuck in a loop of some kind? Rota was frowning. *A highly traumatic memory, apparently.*

"Did he just say 'off' without the 'fahfah'?" Alexander blinked.

Perhaps we should worry about how we're going to get him out of here?

"We take him with us." Alexander gingerly reached down and picked up Ollie, glad that his tiny boy form translated into a tiny boy weight.

Ollie didn't fight, and he leaned his head against Alexander's shoulder. "Is the light o-fahfah?"

"Yup. You bet. Light's off." Alexander carried him back toward the table, draping him over one shoulder so he could reach back out to search for a way to escape. It was there, another weakness, hidden beneath the cake. "Here we go, Ollie. Just hang on."

It was easier to break this time, and Alexander managed to pant through the immense pain washing over him as they pushed through to the other side.

Careful, my love, Rota soothed. *You need to heal. Your hands….*

"I'm fine," Alexander grunted. His fingers were burning, but he ignored them.

They had much bigger problems.

Like a giant asshole wearing a white tuxedo sitting on a throne in a big garden full of roses.

Marbles was the one wearing said tuxedo, and he laughed. "Well, I am impressed. You actually managed to get out of all that, huh? Wow."

"And we'll get out of this one too," Alexander promised. "And then I am going to drag you kicking and screaming to Stoker. It's up to you in how many pieces."

"Don't you see what we're trying to do here?" Marbles scowled. "Don't you understand how much better the world is going to be once Salgumel awakens?"

"Nope." Alexander shifted Ollie, still a little boy, on his shoulder and used his free hand to feel around the room. There had to be another weakness like before, and he was going to find it.

"There won't be any reason to hide who and what we are once Salgumel has taken over again," Marbles declared. "The everlasting people won't be looked down on for being abominations. We won't have to live in the shadows, slaves to monsters like Stoker! We can be free! And happy!"

"Whatever."

"And murdering your own?" Rota rumbled, making himself heard. "That was acceptable for you?"

"I did what I had to." Marbles looked around and frowned, and then he hesitated. "I didn't... I didn't want to... but I kept finding them. I only wanted Will at first. I just wanted to get Will."

"The child?"

"You have any idea how hard it is to find a burned husk for this spell?" Marbles laughed. "And here we had little Will right under our nose all of these years. When Jeff told me what he needed, it felt like fate. I went after him, but every time one of the others got in the way. Eric, Brady.... Just another ingredient falling right into my lap. It was as if the gods themselves were guiding me, showing me the way, and so, yes, I did kill them. I had to. A few had to die so that Salgumel can live once more."

"Fascinating," Alexander drawled as he intensified his search. "Please. Go on."

"The rest of my people will understand in time." Marbles's confidence faltered for a moment, but he continued on firmly, "They will know the others didn't die in vain, and the sacrifices of our brothers and sisters will be remembered for all time. Their names will be in all the chants...."

Alexander, here! Rota cried. *I found a way out! It's through him!*

Alexander gave a nod to confirm he understood, and he gently set Ollie down by his feet. He patted his head, whispering, "Don't worry. I'm getting us out of here."

"Light is going o-fahfah?" Ollie asked quietly.

"Yup. Light's going o-fahfah."

Alexander, my love. Rota came closer. *Please be careful.*

Not makin' a promise I can't keep. Alexander managed a small smile, and he stretched out his arms to channel Rota's magic right at Marbles. He could sense the seam of the illusion there inside the apparition Marbles had created, and he sent out Rota's magic to seize the edges and pull them apart.

Marbles was holding them here with a magical anchor of some kind to keep the illusion in place. He may have been using his very own body to bind it in the same way Alexander's bindings held Rota to him.

All he had to do was break it.

"...and then Salgumel will welcome us into his many arms!" Marbles had been ranting away, but he stopped when Alexander grabbed at him. "Wait, no! What are you doing? You can't break this. I have you! I have you right where I want you!"

"Fuck... you!" Alexander spat, growling as he increased the flow of magic.

The damn seal wouldn't break. No, no, no, it just had to! It had to fuckin' break!

Alexander's hands were burning, the flesh peeling back, but he didn't stop. He could hear Rota telling him to stop, and for once he was glad Rota had no control over how he used the magic they shared.

They were getting out of here, no matter what.

They were all going to go on dates and drink piña coladas and laugh and be happy!

Even as the tips of his fingers burned down to the bone, Alexander poured every ounce of power into that tear inside of Marble's chest. He sent Rota's tentacles forward to claw around it, forcing it apart and slipping through to keep it open. He tightened his raw fingers into fists, and he roared as he unleashed the full wave of Rota's power.

The ensuing explosion made his ears ring, and his vision went white. He was falling, and he couldn't call on Rota to catch him. It seemed like he was falling for several minutes, but he finally hit the floor with a rather dull thud.

He was staring up at the ceiling in the office of Dead to Rites, and he couldn't feel his hands. When he turned his head, he could see Ollie, full-grown once more and unconscious, lying next to him, and he tried to reach for him.

That's when he realized why he couldn't feel his hands.

One was gone completely, and the other only had small fragments of bones sticking out from his wrist.

The pain hadn't yet registered, and his ears were still ringing violently.

He fought to sit up, and he could feel Rota's ghostly tentacles all around him holding him steady.

My love, my love. Rota whimpered. *My love, your hands, your poor hands!*

"It's okay." Alexander may have been shouting. He wasn't sure with the state of his ears. "Is Ollie okay?" He looked around and saw Will still dozing on the ratty sofa right as they had left him. He looked back toward the desk and saw a bloody pile of....

Oh, that had to be what was left of Marbles.

There were splashes of blood and viscera all over the walls and ceiling, and oh, gross, it was on Alexander and Ollie too.

Alexander held out what was left of his hands, and he tried to focus Rota's magic on putting himself back together. He watched as the bones grew first, followed by tendons and blood vessels, then the muscle and flesh. "Fuck, that's gross."

"Super gross," Ollie agreed drowsily.

"Ollie!" Alexander leaped on top of him, forgetting about his injuries. He clung to his neck and kissed his face. "You're okay!"

Ollie! Rota exclaimed. *Oh, sweet boy. You're all right!* He eagerly wrapped his tentacles around them both, fleeting as his touch was. *My boys. You're both safe. You're safe.*

Ollie grinned, that perfectly goofy grin, and he wrapped his arms around Alexander's waist. "Me? I'm great. You guys ain't ever getting rid of me." He sat up with a groan, gently cradling Alexander in his lap and trying to be mindful of his hands. "You okay? That seriously looks cool and all, but also like it hurts—"

Alexander kissed him. *Shut up, shut up, just shut up and kiss me.*

"I can do that," Ollie mumbled.

Alexander was glad his fingers were healed enough to run through Ollie's hair, and he gasped as Rota slipped inside Ollie. He was kissing them both, tasting them, and oh, that heat stirring between his legs was not the slightest bit deterred by the guts dripping from the ceiling—

"Well! Uh, sorry to interrupt," a familiar voice called out from the doorway.

Alexander turned to see who it was, and he scowled.

It was Sloane Beaumont, Starkiller himself, and he wasn't alone. Azaethoth the Lesser was here, plus two men Alexander didn't know.

One was an older pasty redhead, and the other was a handsome black man who looked as annoyed as Alexander felt.

"Hey, Sloane! Azaethoth!" Ollie waved. "Uncle Elwood! You guys got my text."

"You texted them?" Alexander groaned.

"Next time, don't send a bunch of screaming emojis and a beer, okay?" The older redhead snorted. "Maybe somethin' a tiny bit more fuckin' succinct."

"Excellent word usage," another voice now purred. "I'm surprised you knew that one, Detective."

Sloane made way for none other than Sullivan Stoker to walk in, who immediately made a face when he saw the bloody mess. He stepped around the bits on the floor as best as he could to go check on Will.

Alexander deduced the redhead was Ollie's uncle, Elwood Chase, and the man with him had to be Benjamin Merrick, who was really a god named Gordoth the Untouched.

"Blow me, Stoker," Chase said with a sweet bat of his eyes.

"Where is Marbles?" Stoker asked impatiently.

"Oh, he's here." Ollie glanced around the ceiling. "And there. And over there—"

"What in the *fuck* happened here?" Chase demanded.

Alexander stood and straightened his clothes, replying briskly, "Marbles is the killer. He was hunting the everlasting people, his own kind, to get the ingredients for Je-fahfah." He grimaced. "For *Jeff*."

Stoker's eyes narrowed.

"Yeah, the same Jeff you sold the book to that had the ritual in it? Ringin' any bells?"

Sloane gasped. "Hey, wait! You sold Jeff a book with a ritual to raise *Salgumel* and didn't think to mention that?"

"You slimy son of a bitch," Chase seethed. "I oughta slap cuffs on you right now."

"We have nothing to hold him on," Merrick grumbled. "He would walk."

"This room is disgusting," Azaethoth noted with a wrinkle of his nose. "I really don't like it in here."

"Look, we'll leave in a second," Sloane promised him. "We just gotta figure out why Stoker thought it was such a great idea to give Jeff a freakin' book to wake up your dad!"

"But it wasn't great. I believe the word you're looking for is 'stupid,' my sweet Starkiller."

Alexander rubbed his temples. "Whatever."

Time to go, my love? Rota asked knowingly.

"Yeah." Alexander copied Ollie's excited wave as he announced, "Well, now you all have fun figuring this shit out. We're going."

"Wait! Alexander!" Sloane pleaded. "We might have some questions—"

Alexander didn't bother waiting. He grabbed a hold of Ollie and blinked them the hell out of there as fast as he could. He took them home to the hotel, and he didn't let go of Ollie's hand.

"Hey." Ollie pulled him in for a hug. "I'm here."

Alexander ignored how disgusting they both were, and he let Ollie embrace him. He buried his face against his chest, sighing heavily. He was exhausted, sore, and he wanted a hot shower and to collapse right into bed.

Doubtlessly reading his thoughts, Rota agreed. *I believe that's an excellent plan, my love.*

"Ditto." Ollie kissed the top of Alexander's head. "I can't make any piña coladas, but I can probably pull o-fahfah a Long Island Iced Tea with all the booze you have here."

"Let's do that." Alexander closed his eyes. "But... hold me for a second first?"

"You got it."

I'm sure Starkiller will want to speak to us soon, Rota said gently. *He and the others will have many questions, and we do have such interesting news to share with them.*

"Fuck 'em," Alexander muttered. "What is there to tell? Marbles killed everyone, Jeff is one leg short and got away. Oh, and Stoker's an asshole."

I'm confident they know that last part already.

"What's the interesting news, then?" Ollie asked.

Jeff claimed his wound was the result of being touched by the first child of Great Azaethoth. The Kindress itself.

"Really?" Ollie gulped. "Well, that's freaky as fuck."

"You should have seen how he removed the silencing ward we stuck on him." Alexander grimaced.

"I don't wanna know, do I?"

"Probably not."

This could potentially confirm the existence of the Kindress. Jeff must have encountered it somewhere in his own travels between worlds. Perhaps even at the Fountain.

"And if that fuck face can find it, that means we can," Alexander declared.

"That's awesome!" Ollie grabbed Alexander around his waist and lifted him up for a big kiss. "This is gonna be so great! No more Stoker or crazy murder or any of that! Just me, you, Rota, and that big ol' book! I'm gonna read the shit outta that thing—"

"Ollie!" Alexander lightly smacked his shoulder. "Hey, hey, put me down!"

"Sorry." Ollie grinned and gently set Alexander back on his feet. "I got excited. I'm, uh, well, you know. And I'm maybe kinda hoping even after we find that Fountain and get Rota's body, maybe you guys will let me stick around. You know, keep hanging out together, even if you... uh... don't need me?"

As soon as Alexander saw the sweet, dopey smile, he already knew what his answer would be.

Rota agreed, judging by the rush of warmth in their bond.

"Maybe." Alexander ignored the fluttering in his chest as Ollie's smile grew. "We can talk about all that shit later. First things first."

"Ah." Ollie nodded. "Shower?"

"Shower." Alexander smirked. "I wanna see if you were lying about those flamingos."

"Oh, you're totally on."

CHAPTER 15.

OVER THE next two weeks, Ollie continued working on the translation of the poetry book. Alexander decided it would be wise for him and Rota to stay over at Ollie's so they would be close in case he made a breakthrough, although they all knew that wasn't the only reason. He got to sleep with Ollie and Rota every night and woke in bed with them each morning.

For the first time in a very long time, Alexander was happy.

Sloane was kind enough to give them a few days to recuperate, but he did come looking for answers about what had happened with Jeff. Chase and Merrick visited as well, though Chase seemed much more interested in interrogating Alexander about what his intentions were with Ollie.

Alexander let Ollie and Rota handle the talking on all accounts.

Rota was able to answer their questions about the case, specifically as to what happened while they were in Marbles's illusion. Ollie didn't remember anything, including the strange childhood memory that may have been responsible for his odd idiom. Alexander knew from personal experience some memories just weren't worth remembering, so neither he nor Rota pressed it.

They learned from their visitors that Jeff was nowhere to be found, still on the run, presumably with the ingredients for the ritual. Well, except Will of course, who was now Stoker's esteemed guest in the Hidden World and its first mortal resident. Stoker admitted to selling the book to Jeff but claimed he had only allowed him to have it because of the healing spells it contained. After all, with a face that was actively rotting, Jeff needed some incredibly powerful magic.

Plus, according to Stoker, he paid very well, and the idea of him ever gaining access to the rare ingredients required had never occurred to him.

Alexander had some doubts as to whether or not Jeff was telling the truth about the Kindress being the cause of his injury. Whatever messed up Jeff's face was certainly the most destructive magic Alexander had ever seen, but it only led to more questions he couldn't answer.

If Jeff had found the Kindress, why didn't he use it to wake up Salgumel?

Hell, why didn't Jeff ask the Kindress to remake the world and cut out the middleman? What was the point of bothering with the god of dreams if he had access to the true firstborn of Great Azaethoth?

Whatever.

Those were problems for Sloane and Detective Chase and Gordoth the Slut, or whatever his name was.

Alexander had his own problems to deal with, like waiting for Ollie to finish the translation and reveal the location of the Fountain so they could recover Rota's body.

Oh, and how to maybe ask Ollie to go steady.

Alexander didn't know how it was going to work with all three of them—people did this, didn't they?—but he wanted it. He knew Rota did too. The joy he felt seeing Ollie's dopey smile was only rivaled by Rota's own surge of happiness. The life they'd found together over the past few weeks was beyond anything Alexander could have ever hoped for.

After Ollie would exhaust himself translating, Alexander found one of his favorite things in the world was snuggling on the sofa with him watching horror movies while Rota tried to predict the ending. Ollie had started drawing again, and he would doodle in a sketchbook during the scary parts so he wouldn't have to see them. They had more dates, including a few at home so Ollie could teach Alexander and Rota how to cook. They all stayed up late so they could look at the stars, and Ollie was endlessly patient and adoring and happy and just so damn *Ollie*.

Alexander knew it wouldn't be perfect. He knew it wasn't always going to be like this. But for the moments when it was, those sweet moments where time itself seemed to stop and his heart swelled deep inside his chest until it felt like it was going to burst, it would be worth it.

It was just last night that Alexander had decided.

Ollie deserved an official answer, and Rota had left it up to Alexander to decide what to do about their "hanging out" situation. Alexander planned to put it off for as long as possible, naturally, but then he'd woken up from a bad dream to the sound of Ollie singing. There weren't any words to the tune, only a soft and soothing melody, and Alexander asked him why he was singing it.

"Somebody was yelling at you, and you were crying," Ollie had said. "In the dream, I mean. I heard you in my head. So I wanted to make sure you heard something nice whenever you woke up."

"Thank you" was all Alexander had managed to reply, and on Ollie went with his singing.

Soon Rota's rumbling voice joined Ollie's, and they sang together, strong arms and wispy tentacles rocking Alexander back to sleep.

When Alexander woke again the next morning with Ollie tangled around him and Rota's presence hovering on the other side, he knew this is what he wanted. He didn't have to be afraid of getting close to someone else or being hurt.

If there was any other soul in the universe he could trust his heart to, it was Oleander Logue.

Ollie, who was currently snoring away, drooling quite a bit, and had taken all the covers.

With a smirk, Alexander tugged the covers back in one swift pull.

"Mmmrrph?" Ollie groggily lifted his head.

"You took the blankets again," Alexander said.

"Oh. Sorry." Ollie wiped his mouth and then laid his head back down, hugging Alexander's middle. "Won't ever happen again."

That's what you always say, dear. Rota chuckled.

"Morning, Rota," Alexander said, smiling as Rota slipped into Ollie's body to add his presence to the hug.

"Morning, love," Rota spoke now with Ollie's voice and his own distinct rumble. "Did you sleep all right? We were worried."

"I'm good. Thank you. Both of you." Alexander snuggled in close, and he laughed when he felt Ollie's hard cock poking his hip. "Mmm, is that yours or Ollie's?"

"It's mine," Ollie mumbled with a sleepy little grin. "Sorry. Just woke up, and you're all warm and snuggly and very, very hot."

"Mmm." Alexander slowly pushed Ollie's hand down. The innocent press of Ollie's morning chubbed dick was enough to get him going, and he wanted Ollie and Rota to hop on board with how he wanted to start the day.

"Oh?" Rota caught on quickly and laughed. "Yesterday was not enough to satisfy you, my love?"

"Nope." Alexander directed Ollie's hand right to his own thickening cock, rubbing it through the covers. "Makin' up for lost time."

"Is that so?"

"And I'm just really fuckin' horny."

"Mmm, I see." Rota squeezed, and he shifted closer, bowing his head for a kiss.

Alexander grabbed a handful of Rota's hair and kissed him back hungrily. He was ready to go, to feel Rota and Ollie inside of him, to come over and over—wait, where was Ollie?

It was only Rota kissing him.

"Ollie?" Alexander asked.

"Oh, I think he fell back asleep." Rota snorted.

Alexander rolled his eyes and shook Ollie's shoulders. "Hey! Wake up."

Ollie's lashes fluttered as he resumed control, clearing his throat loudly. "Wait, wah? I'm awake. What are we doing?"

"Trying to have sex with you."

"Oh, cool." Ollie grinned. "Let's do that."

Alexander dragged him back in for a kiss, and there, now he could feel them both through their bond. Ollie's lips were softer somehow, sweeter, and Rota's tentacles pushed the covers out of the way.

"Mmm, my love," Rota whispered. "I want you so badly. My entire being aches with the need to be inside you and feel you quiver around me."

"What he said," Ollie mumbled as he kissed his way down Alexander's neck, repositioning himself on top.

Rota's tentacles tugged at their pajamas—a full set for Alexander, just sweatpants for Ollie—and quickly got them out of the way. He could probably feel how eager Alexander was, and his own desire was equally fierce.

Alexander pulled Ollie in for another kiss, and he hooked his legs around his hips. "Mmm, come on. I want you both. Now."

"I got you, baby boy," Ollie promised as he lined himself up, rubbing the head of his cock against Alexander's hole. "Rota?"

Of course, Rota spoke in their thoughts. He hadn't fully separated from Ollie's body, but they'd found sometimes it was less confusing in the heat of the moment for him to speak this way and let Ollie keep control of his own voice.

Alexander groaned softly as his hole opened up and magically stretched, wet and ready in seconds for Ollie's cock. He loved the heat as Ollie pushed in, and he gasped when he felt Rota was getting Ollie ready too.

"F-fuck, Rota!" Ollie moaned, his hips pushed forward by the added pressure inside of him. He thrusted a few times, falling into a steady rhythm once he was fully sheathed and kissing Alexander sweetly. *Mmm, fuck... you both feel so good... you always feel so damn good....*

So do you, Alexander thought back, bracing himself on Ollie's broad shoulders. *Gods... mmm... more. Give me more.*

Yes, my love, Rota purred. *I will give you more. Both of you. My beautiful boys. I will give you everything....*

The tip of a slitted tentacle was now at Alexander's hole, and he inhaled sharply as it pushed its way in beside Ollie's cock. The stretch was more comfortable now than it had been before, and he was able to breathe through it with ease. God, being this full and having that hot friction so deep within his body was absolute bliss. Ollie's cock could only venture so far, but Rota's tentacle seemed to go on forever, seeking intimate places no mortal could ever reach and forcing the most delicious sounds from Alexander's lips.

Rota was inside Ollie too, giving him the same great pleasure, pumping in and out of their bodies in perfect sync. He was guiding Ollie's hips so that even his cock was on rhythm, and more of his tentacles spread Alexander's legs and held them wide. *Ahhh, my boys... my perfect boys....*

Alexander tried to keep kissing Ollie, but he couldn't catch his breath. It was such an incredible ecstasy to be taken by an immortal, and he could feel the pressure between his legs rising to thigh-trembling levels already. Both tentacle and cock were fucking his slick hole perfectly, and he loved the throbbing slide against every delicate nerve inside of him. He was so close, his muscles tightening, heat rising fast, and ah—there!

It shouldn't have surprised him how quickly Rota could make him come, and every sweet pulse made him moan. Ollie was coming too, filling him with a hot load, and fuck, now Rota was coming, and Alexander was overwhelmed by the sensation of Rota flooding his body and Ollie's at the same time.

Alexander's climax went on for several mesmerizing moments, carried by his partners' pleasure and the magical thrust of Rota's tentacles. He greedily rocked his hips down just to keep it going for as long as he could, locking his lips with Ollie's and tasting Rota there with him.

By all the gods, it was always so fuckin' good.

Feel better now, my love? Rota asked with a smirk in his voice.

"Mmm, much," Alexander mumbled.

"Well." Ollie grinned. "Feel free to wake me up like that anytime."

Rota laughed.

"Yeah?" Alexander touched Ollie's cheek. He could see the silver in the scar there on Ollie's chest, so like the silver gleam some of his own binding marks now had. He summoned up all of his courage, riding the high of their coupling, and he asked, "And if I wanted to do it every day?"

"I just said feel free... oh!" Ollie paused. "Okay, so, it's early, and my brain isn't working great, but are you saying what I think you're saying?"

Alexander? Rota was smiling, and his happiness was practically bubbling. *Yes?*

"Yes," Alexander confirmed.

"Yes, what?" Ollie's grin was growing. "Yes, you want me to go make breakfast? Yes, you want to try playing *Battleship* later? Or, oh, do you mean you wanna watch *Hell's Kitchen* because Sloane is always talking about—"

"Yes, I want you to go out with me. Us. Me and Rota." Alexander sighed loudly. "I want us to be together. All of us. Okay?"

"Okay." Ollie squeezed Alexander's hand and leaned in for a tender kiss, his side of the bond warm with happiness.

"Wait, wait." Alexander shook his head. "That's it? You're not gonna make Rota ask you?"

I already did, Rota teased.

"You *what?*"

Last night. Yes, I know I'm not supposed to peek in that beautiful head of yours, but I was quite worried about your nightmare.

"After you fell back asleep, me and him talked for a little bit." Ollie seemed very pleased with himself. "He told me about your, uh, decision, and he asked me. We agreed to wait for you to say somethin', and well... here we are."

Alexander smiled, enjoying the fluttering sensation taking up residence in his chest. Being close with Rota had been the only thing that ever brought this on, but now he felt it with Ollie. He hadn't known Ollie very long, but....

It gave him hope this was going to be something that lasted.

"Yeah," Alexander said. "Here we are."

Ollie kept smiling at him, Rota was hovering so very close, and it was starting to feel awkward. Talking was not one of Alexander's strengths, especially things of a romantic, feelsy nature. He hated the quiet that was falling between them all, and he didn't know what to do or say or—

"So! How about I make us breakfast, huh?" Ollie piped up.

Alexander sighed in relief. "Yeah, that would be great."

After smooching Alexander's cheek, Ollie carefully separated himself and got out of bed. He brought towels to clean up what Rota's magic had left behind—which was nothing, really, but Alexander suspected Ollie just liked taking care of him—and then grabbed a fresh pair of sweatpants and new pajamas with bright yellow ducks for Alexander.

"I'm gonna go now. You know. To make breakfast." Ollie waved, grinning back at Alexander for so long that he nearly smacked into the doorframe on his way to the kitchen because he wasn't paying attention to where he was going.

Alexander lay back in bed, clean and snuggled in the oversized atrociously hideous pajamas, still riding the high of being freshly fucked and smiling.

I love you, Rota said.

"Mmm, love you too."

Happy, my love? Rota asked.

"Yes." Alexander's smile widened. "Very."

Good... because there is something I need to tell you.

"What is it?"

The topic of discussion last night—

Ollie suddenly screamed.

"Fuck, what now?" Alexander bolted up and ran toward the kitchen, preparing himself for anything. He skidded to a stop when he saw Stoker standing there by the counter, appraising the mess with a wrinkle of his nose.

"Ollie, I'm going to send a maid over to clean this up," Stoker scolded. "This is abysmal."

"It's, it's really not that bad," Ollie stammered from where was, poised as if he was ready to climb up the side of the fridge. "I mean, sure, there might have been something there, living in my sink, but I've really been trying here lately!"

"Oh great. Stoker." Alexander groaned. "What do you want?"

"Just wanted to pop in and check on everyone." Stoker smiled with faux sweetness. He eyed a sketchbook on the cluttered kitchen table and flipped through the pages. He paused on one Ollie had drawn of Alexander sleeping in bed with Rota's tentacles floating around him. "How sweet. Ollie, you really are quite talented."

Ollie grinned. "Aw, thanks."

"Hey. Hello." Alexander waved. "What are you doing here, Stoker?"

"I thought you'd be interested in knowing how well I'm getting on with the staff of Dead to Rites now," Stoker replied. "They were quite happy that I was able to solve the mystery behind the murders—"

"You?"

That bastard is taking all the credit? Rota scoffed. *How rude!*

"Of course, they weren't pleased it was one of their own, but such is life." Stoker stepped away from the sink. "And I wouldn't say it's rude to take full advantage of the situation. I need them to trust me, and you provided me with a wonderful opportunity."

"Great." Alexander scoffed. "Now get out." He paused. *Wait, Rota, did you say that shit about him being rude out loud?*

No? Rota sounded worried. *I did not.*

"A very dear friend of mine once told me to act dumb," Stoker drawled. "That way no one will ever expect anything out of you. I don't believe in acting dumb, per se, but I definitely prefer not to play all my cards until I absolutely have to."

"You asshole." Alexander scowled. "You could hear us? The whole time?"

"Mm-hm. I think my favorite was 'dickweed in a three-piece.'" Stoker smirked. "Also, that kiss? Do you have any idea how awkward it was to watch?"

"Wait, if you knew we were lying, why didn't you say anything?" Ollie asked Stoker urgently.

"Because I believed it would be more beneficial to let your little game play out." Stoker smirked again. "And I was right. You proved yourselves to be quite powerful and resourceful." His eyes fell on Alexander. "I'd like to offer you and Rota a job. It seems Jeff has made quite a fool out of me, and I simply cannot have that. Plus, ending the world? Quite bad for business."

"No shit," Alexander griped.

"So, will you accept?"

"What about Ollie?" Alexander realized if Stoker had been listening to all of their psychic conversations, then he had to know Ollie had starsight.

"What about him?" Stoker smiled. "As far as I'm concerned, he picked up a neat trick from his uncle and saved young Will's life. That's all."

"I don't trust you."

"Good. I don't trust you either."

"What the fuck are you?"

"A businessman who has many places to be." Stoker tilted his head. "And perhaps, one who was a touch too arrogant to see the threat he'd created before it was too late."

"A touch?" Alexander scoffed loudly.

"Yes." Stoker narrowed his eyes. "I will admit my hubris is why I didn't suspect Jeff, which is why I am determined to make this right and bring him to justice."

"Is that you admitting you fucked up?"

"I am only human, after all." Stoker smirked. "So, is that a yes?"

"We'll think about it," Alexander replied flatly. "Now get out."

"I hope you do." Stoker waved. "Now, you should really see about getting these wards fixed. Wouldn't want any other uninvited guests."

Alexander flipped him off.

With a bow and a smug smirk, Stoker vanished.

"Fucker."

"Are you gonna do it?" Ollie asked hesitantly.

"Work for Stoker?" Alexander snorted. "Yeah, fuckin' right. I'd rather choke on a concrete dildo—"

If he wants us to help him stop Jeff and the other cultists, perhaps it is worth speaking to him, Rota cut in. *It is a noble cause, is it not? Certainly Starkiller and the others would welcome our help as well. A combined effort between all members of the Super Secret Sages' Club would be—*

"The what?"

"It's what Sloane and them call us," Ollie explained. "You know, everybody that's in the know about gods bein' awake and, like, real, and doin' god stu-fahfah. We could help out. You know, do helpful things."

"I don't like doing things for people. Or people." Alexander sighed loudly. "Can we maybe talk about this not right now?"

Right. Of course. We must continue our earlier conversation.

"About what?"

I was trying to tell you that last night the topic of discussion wasn't only the future of our relationship.

"Yup." Ollie nodded. "It was also how to tell you that I finished the book and—"

"What?" Alexander gasped.

This was it. It was going to happen. They were going to get Rota's body back, and they would all be together. Even when Rota was restored, Alexander knew he still wanted Ollie with them.

"Why didn't you guys tell me?" Alexander demanded.

"But we just did?" Ollie appeared very confused.

"The book!" Alexander groaned. "Did you find it? The Fountain?"

That's the problem. Rota sounded sad.

Ollie's face fell. "I read the book. I... I read it twice just to make sure. There's nothing in there about the Fountain."

"What?" Alexander snapped angrily. "No! That can't be right!" He turned and headed to the bedroom in search of the book.

"Alexander, I'm really sorry." Ollie followed. "I even had Rota help me with some of the super big words, and there's nothin'. Like at all."

The book was there on the bedside table, and Alexander snatched it up. He thrust it into Ollie's arms, glaring at him. "Read it again."

Alexander, please calm down, Rota soothed. *It's all right. We will keep searching—*

"Read it again," Alexander pleaded as bile rose in his throat. "Come on. Please."

"I can't," Ollie said quietly. "I tried so hard. It's just not there. There is nothing on those pages about the Fountain or even the Kindress."

Alexander jerked when Ollie reached for him, and he wished he could control how angry he was. He walked a few steps away, and he suddenly took hold of the book with Rota's tentacles and then tore it into pieces.

"Alexander!" Ollie cried.

Don't, Rota warned. *Just... just let him be for a moment.*

Page after page fluttered to the ground until only the heavy gold cover was left, and Alexander got to work on that too. He grabbed it with his bare hands, aligning his fingers with Rota's tentacles to tear at the metal plating until they were bleeding.

This is so stupid! Alexander screamed inside his head. *It's fuckin' stupid! I hate it! It's bullshit! We fought so hard for this. We searched and searched and for fuckin' nothing! It's not fuckin'—*

The thick cover was hollow.

"What is that?" Ollie tiptoed closer.

Alexander pulled at the side of the broken cover, and a single page fluttered out. "The fuck?"

"It's from the book." Ollie kneeled, reaching for a chunk of the torn pages and the new page. "I thought this one part was just messed up because it was old, but look." He lined it all up together. "See?"

What had appeared to be a frayed seam behind the title page was in fact the original home of the page.

"What does it say?" Alexander dared not get his hopes up, but there had to be a reason it had been hidden like that.

"Okay, it's way early, and I'm weirdly sober, but uh...." Ollie focused, squinting as he read, "With all my love to the gods, old and new, lost and found, and blah blah blah. Okay, it's like... a dedication page? No, wait, it's like an autograph."

"Fuckin' seriously?"

"Happy... uh... naming day to Jake the... Gladsome?"

"Who?"

"Hang on. There's more... oh."

What is it, Ollie? Rota pressed.

"So, you know how people used to write names and dates and where a photo was taken on the back?"

"Huh?"

"Just go with it. This was signed by Wilhelmina Pickett in the three hundred and eighty-seventh year of Great Azaethoth's reign to Jake the Gladsome at the Fountain of Great Azaethoth's Firstborn, the Kindress." Ollie stared at Alexander in shock. "This is it. The dedication. It's a spell. It's a doorway right to the Fountain."

"Wait, what?"

"Look!" Ollie offered the page for their inspection. "There are teeny tiny little words written inside the words! Like, the teensiest tiniest littlest words ever. They must have used, like, the world's smallest pen ever."

"Holy fuck." Alexander suddenly scowled. "How did you not know that was in the cover?"

"You know my starsight doesn't work that way, and you, sir, just told me to read it!"

"Okay, okay, it doesn't matter." Alexander took a deep breath. "We're going. Now."

"I don't have a shirt on—"

"Ollie! Please!" Alexander reached for him.

"Right. Uh. Hang on." Ollie closed his eyes and traced his finger over the words on the page.

They were there.

It happened in the space of a blink, and they were standing in front of the Fountain.

It wasn't even so much a fountain as it appeared to be a large stone well, and the world around them was a barren wasteland floating in the middle of space. The soil was cracked and dry, and several of the cracks ran off to create large ravines and caverns that fell off into absolute nothingness.

Alexander had forgotten to breathe, and he gasped now, clinging to Ollie's arm as he took it all in.

This…. This is the Fountain? Rota sounded distraught, his tentacles flailing as he floated frantically around them. *I don't understand….*

The destruction here was an echo of the other old world they'd visited, and the air smelled sour. There was still magic seeping through the ground beneath their feet, and it was certainly ancient and pulsing faintly. The focus of the power was definitely the Fountain, or well or whatever the hell it was.

"What the fuck happened here?" Ollie asked quietly.

"I don't care." Alexander took a deep breath and stepped forward. "Rota's body is here. Let's go." He didn't see anything around the Fountain itself, so he walked toward the broken edges of the world to search, his pulse thumping away.

"You guys… uh… I'll stay here." Ollie inched back to the Fountain. "Those giant drops into the big space nothing don't look like fun." He cleared his throat. "Uh, see anything yet?"

"No." Alexander walked quicker, checking in the deep ravines and the caverns. He walked faster and faster, and his heart pounded in his ears. He figured the body of an old god should be fairly easy to spot, and he couldn't stop smiling.

Any second now, they were going to find Rota's body.

I cannot wait to hold you, my sweet boy, Rota gushed.

"I can't wait to do a lot of fuckin' things." Alexander hurried to the next cavern. "Can you sense it at all?"

No, nothing. I'm not sure that I would.

"It's fine. We'll just keep looking." Alexander ran over to another ravine. He found nothing but more rocks and dust. He was getting more desperate, and a quick glance around them revealed there weren't many places left to look. "Shit."

Rota doubtlessly felt Alexander's growing dread, and he touched his shoulder with a ghostly tentacle. *Fear not. We're almost there.*

Alexander said nothing as he sprinted to the last ravine. He held his breath, hoping and praying that the terrible feeling in his gut was wrong, and he gasped when he looked down into the darkness and saw...

Nothing.

There was nothing here.

"What the fuck?" Alexander backed out of the ravine and scanned the land around them. He had checked every crevice and cave, and there was absolutely nothing here. He was having trouble deciphering the tornado of emotions swirling through him, but it was easy to settle on an old favorite.

Rage.

"We search for months to find a fuckin' way to get here!" he shouted. "We search and we search and we finally get that stupid book, and then what? What! It takes weeks to translate because oh, the very stupid page we need is somehow hidden inside the stupid fuckin' cover, and we finally get here... and... and!" He was shaking. "There's *nothing* here!"

Alexander, my love. My sweet, sweet love. Rota was defeated. *We have to consider—*

"No!" Alexander stalked back across the rocky terrain to the Fountain. It was a large well made out of dark stone, about ten feet across. Ollie had been sitting next to it, but he scrambled out of Alexander's way when he stormed over. When Alexander looked down, he was staring into more endless space. "What the actual *fuck?*"

Rota floated over. *It's... empty? No, it's more than empty.*

"What is it?" Ollie took a few cautious steps toward them.

"There's nothing," Alexander replied bitterly. "There's no bottom. No tears. No Kindress. No fuckin' nothing."

We have to consider that Gronoch was lying, Rota said. *He may have just said that to send us on this fool's errand.*

"He sounds like a real asshole," Ollie chimed in.

Alexander leaned against the well, bracing himself on the edge and trying to talk himself out of smashing it to pieces. Anger was still the easiest thing to feel, and he rationalized that it was better than giving in to his despair. "For a second, I really thought…."

I know, my sweet love. I know….

I thought we were going to be together. Alexander squeezed his eyes closed, and he couldn't stop the tears from slipping down his cheeks. *I just wanted all of us to fuckin' be together.*

"Hey, and we are." Ollie was there now, a bit shaky but determined as he wrapped his arms around Alexander's waist. "We're here, aren't we? All three of us." He shook his head. "Look, I know this isn't what you guys wanted, I know, but this is just a teeny, tiny setback."

Alexander grumbled. "A setback…? Months of effort for absolute shit is a *setback?*"

I appreciate the sentiment, Ollie, Rota said sadly, *but I'm afraid it's a bit more complicated than you realize. Hazel Medical is gone, as are all their facilities and employees, and Gronoch is dead. We don't know where else to look.*

"Well… uh…."

Alexander knew Ollie was trying to help, and he stood up straight from the well, wiping his hands off on his jacket. They were wet with tears, certainly having fallen while he was crying. "It's okay. Don't worry about it. What we have now is more than I thought we'd ever get, and—"

"Oh! Wait!" Ollie bounced. "Wait, wait, wait!"

"Fuckin' asshole!" Alexander chided, turning around to glare at him. "I'm trying to have a sweet moment here. I don't do that, okay?"

"But, okay, this is impotent," Ollie insisted. "Didn't you say Je-fahfah knew about Gronoch?"

"Yeah. Why?"

"Well, if Je-fahfah knew Gronoch, like, if they were cahooting together, maybe he knows something." Ollie offered a small smile. "I mean, it's worth a shot, right?"

Starkiller and the others are searching for Jeff for his many crimes, Rota said. *Even Stoker is looking for him now. Our efforts would definitely not be our own on this. We would have help.*

"You want us to work with those morons again?" Alexander groaned.

"Think of it like one big weird family sharing information to catch a super bad dude," Ollie said cheerfully. "I mean, come on. We got a fuckin' Starkiller, two gods, my kickass uncle, and us. So, then, that's, like, three gods, me, plus a kickass you, versus Je-fahfah. Come on. That ass doesn't stand a chance."

"You really think so?" Alexander hugged Ollie close, and he felt it when Rota joined them and warm tentacles spiraled around them to tighten the embrace.

Think of all we've done, Rota said. *We caught a serial killer, saved young Will's life, and we found the Fountain! Yes, it is not what we expected, but still, we found something most Sages don't even believe exists. We did that. Together. And together, we can do anything, my love.*

"We can do it," Ollie assured him. "Together."

"Together." Alexander buried his face into Ollie's chest and held on to Rota's tentacles.

Here in this impossible place with the god he loved and the mortal he was falling for….

He believed it.

Keep reading for an exclusive excerpt from
Insquidious Devotion
by K.L. Hiers!

CHAPTER 1.

"So," SLOANE drawled, his hands on his hips as he stared his husband and daughter down, "what have we learned today?"

"Ah! I know this one!" Loch grinned. "Not to make crème brûlée when you're home."

Pandora, their infant daughter, gurgled in what appeared to be agreement.

"No." Sloane shook his head.

"Hmm." Loch frowned. "Not to make crème brûlée while you're sleeping?"

"We have learned to make crème brûlée *never*."

Part of the kitchen was still smoking—the perils of a god and a little demi-goddess trying to cook together were many.

"I was able to put out the flames," Loch complained, "and the damage to the cabinets can easily be repaired."

"And what about our daughter? She could have been burned!"

"Ah! I have recently discovered that Pandora is quite fond of fire." Loch tilted his head. "As in, I discovered this about ten minutes before you woke up from your nap. Hmm, and there was something else I was going to tell you…"

Pandora wiggled out of Loch's lap where they'd been cuddling on the sofa, and she waddled over to Sloane. Although she wasn't quite four months old, she was as big as a one year old would have been, and she could walk quite well.

Sloane bent over to pick Pandora up, but he immediately recoiled when her hands burst into flames. "By all the gods!"

Pandora giggled and waved her flaming hands excitedly.

"No! Young lady! Absolutely not!" Sloane grabbed Pandora around her middle and blew out her hands, quickly checking them for any sign of injury.

Fussing, Pandora swatted at Sloane.

"Ah, that was the other thing I meant to tell you!" Loch grinned sheepishly. "She is also quite flame-resistant,"

"Seriously?" Sloane groaned. "We were already worried about babyproofing, and now we need to fireproof too?"

Pandora's hands were warm but otherwise seemed fine.

Sloane knew that life with an old god was going to be interesting, but he could have never prepared himself for the adventure of raising a child together.

Especially a child who had tentacles like her father and a penchant for mischief.

And fire now, apparently.

"Oh, my beautiful husband. Fear not." Loch waved his hand at the kitchen, and all evidence of the fiery disaster vanished. He stood to join Sloane and hugged him with Pandora between them, wrapping them up with a thick bundle of grayish-blue tentacles.

Pandora grabbed for one of the tentacles, her hands morphing into long purple tentacles of her own and curling around Loch's. She immediately pulled his tentacle into her mouth and began to gnaw on it.

"I will cast fire protection wards all over the apartment," Loch promised. "Nothing will catch fire here again, I swear to you."

"Probably should have done that a while ago." Sloane smirked.

Loch gasped. "Is that a slight directed at my cooking ability?"

"Just a tiny one."

"Hmmph."

Sloane leaned his forehead against Loch's, cuddling Pandora as he said, "Seriously. I just worry. Being a new parent is hard enough without having to freak out every ten minutes that she's learned some new kind of magic. What if she opens a portal?"

"Then we will go find her." Loch smiled. "She does have a watchman's spell on her, you know."

"What if she tries to summon bees?"

"You don't summon bees," Loch soothed. "You have to ask for their assistance in smiting your enemies. We've been over this before, my sweet husband."

Sloane groaned.

"I am Azaethoth the Lesser. I am an ancient, handsome, and powerful god. You are a Starkiller with the most gorgeous, luscious eyebrows in the universe. We have saved the world countless times and defeated many demented members of my family. I love you, and I know we can do anything together." Loch kissed Sloane's brow firmly. "Even this."

Sloane's heart fluttered, and he actually felt a little bit better.

They'd been through worse, after all.

Crazy cultists, murderous gods, and even that one time Loch lost his body at the post office.

"Thank you." Sloane kissed Loch sweetly. "You're right."

"I know."

"She's growing so freakin' fast and getting into absolutely everything, not to mention also terrifying me at every turn. But." Sloane took a deep breath. "We can totally do this."

"Of course we can." Loch beamed. "We can—ow!" He pouted, pulling the tentacle Pandora had been mouthing on away. "Hey! That is not for eating."

"What happened?" Sloane asked.

"She bit me." Loch sighed. "She now has teeth."

"Already?" Sloane tried to peek into Pandora's mouth.

Pandora grinned and offered a flash of a few shiny little teeth.

"Well then." Sloane cradled Pandora against his chest and kissed her cheeks. "I guess that means it's time to work on getting some baby food, huh?"

"Ah! I will prepare our daughter's sustenance, thank you." Loch turned up his nose. "Say what you will about my culinary abilities, but I am more than capable of providing for her."

"Uh-huh." Sloane headed into the kitchen. It still smelled a little burnt. He reached into the fridge to grab a bottle of formula, a special godly variety that Loch's mother, Urilith, had made for them.

"You doubt me?" Loch followed him, pouting now.

"Only a tiny bit." Sloane chuckled as he heated up the bottle with a swipe of his thumb. "I think it's very sweet, but are you really sure you can do all that? She's probably going to eat a lot, isn't she?"

"Most likely, based on her exponential growth, but it will not be a problem." Loch grinned.

"Because you're a god?"

"Yes, because I'm a god."

Sloane rolled his eyes and offered the bottle to Pandora, cooing, "Your daddy is very silly. Don't worry. I'll get you some baby food from the store."

"Oh! How you wound me!" Loch clutched his chest.

Sloane's cell phone rang.

"I'll make it up to you." Sloane scrambled to reach into his pocket while holding Pandora and the bottle.

"Here." Loch gently took her from Sloane as he chided, "Your father is a cruel, cruel man. Don't ever forget that, my darling spawn."

Pandora gurgled in reply.

Sloane chuckled as he retrieved his phone from his pocket. "Beaumont Investigations, how may I help you?"

"Hey, Sloane!" Milo Evan's voice greeted him.

"Hey, Milo!"

Milo was Sloane's best friend from college and former coworker at the Archersville Police Department. Milo's girlfriend, Lynnette, was expecting their first child any day now. They were a few of the small group of people who knew that Loch was actually a god and the true nature of Pandora's birth.

The exclusive circle was affectionately known as the Super Secret Sage Club. They knew that the Sagittarian faith had been right along, and that while some of the old gods were still deep asleep in the dreaming in Zebulon, a few were here on Aeon with them.

Sloane was married to one, of course, and he'd met many members of Loch's family. Loch's mother, uncle, and sister were all quite sane, but his brothers....

That was a different story.

"Everything okay?" Sloane asked. "How's Lynnette? Ready to pop yet?"

"Yeah!" Milo laughed. "She's okay! Super huge and beautiful and ready. Technically she's not due until next week, but I think she's ready to send our new kiddo an eviction notice. How are you and the rest of the godly brood? How's my little Panda Bear?"

"Oh, you know. The usual." Sloane glanced back at Loch and Pandora with a smile. "Setting fires, trying to burn down the apartment. Ah, and Panda has some teeth now."

"Already? Sheesh!" Milo laughed. "She's gonna be headed off to college soon!"

"Right? It's crazy." Sloane didn't mind having a casual chat with Milo, but it was a little odd for him to be calling in the middle of the day while he was at work. "So, what's up?"

"Yeah. Uh." Milo's voice dropped to a conspiratorial whisper. "We have got some high-level weirdness going on down here. Like, definite cultist type shenanigans."

Sloane's stomach flopped. "Seriously?" He frowned at Loch and put the phone on speaker. "What's going on?"

"Chase and Merrick had this super freaky case a while back where a guy drowned in the alley behind Dead to Rites. Like, drowned in salt water. From the ocean. The case went cold, but then it happened again."

"Another drowning?"

"Yeah. Last week. And well, then it happened *again* just today."

Loch's brow creased with concern, and he asked loudly, "Were there any butlers in the vicinity?"

"Uh, no," Milo replied. "Look, we think it's Daisy."

"Daisy?" Sloane echoed.

Daisy used to be a forensic tech at the AVPD with Milo, and she had secretly been a member of a cult dedicated to Salgumel, Loch's father and the god of dreams. Salgumel had gone mad in his dreaming, and the cult's aim was to wake him up and remake the world into one where the old gods would rule again—by destroying it.

And the cultists weren't alone.

There were old gods who wanted Salgumel to rise so they could reclaim what they'd lost.

Sloane and the other members of the Sages Club had already defeated two of Salgumel's sons, Loch's older brothers, for having the same nefarious desires as the cult. It was how Sloane had become a Starkiller, having been given a sword of pure starlight from Great Azaethoth himself, to strike the gods down and save the world.

But every time was getting harder.

The cult was growing, and they had no idea when any of them would strike next. They didn't know how many gods were in league with Loch's brothers, but they had to plan for the worst. After the cult's last attempt to wake Salgumel had failed, Daisy had vanished along with Jeff Martin, the cult's leader.

If she was back, that meant nothing but trouble.

"Yeah," Milo confirmed. "The newest victim drowned in a hotel, and we got a pretty clean shot of her going into the room and never leaving. I'm, like, ninety-eight-percent sure it's her. Chase and Merrick think so too."

Detectives Elwood. Q. Chase and Benjamin Merrick were also members of their little Sage club. Chase was mortal, but Merrick was actually Gordoth, the Sagittarian god of justice and Loch's uncle. Like Loch, Merrick used a mortal body as his vessel to hide in plain sight from the world.

They were partners at the AVPD and in their personal life, Chase having been quite proud of himself for taking "the Untouched" title from Merrick a few months ago.

"Any idea how she's making people... drown?" Sloane asked.

"No clue." Milo sighed. "We were kinda hoping you could swing down here and take a peek? Use that magical, ahem, starlight of yours and see if you got any ideas?"

"We will be expecting a consulting fee," Loch declared. "We no longer accept personal checks unless you have two forms of personal identification."

"Wait, wait." Sloane scoffed. "We can't go anywhere. What are we gonna do with our little Panda Bear, huh? We can't take her with us, and we can't exactly drop her off at a normal daycare center."

"Why?"

Sloane stared at Loch.

"Oh yes, right." Loch grinned. "Tiny demigoddess with tentacles who likes fire in a world where most people assume the old gods are myths and sudden evidence to the contrary might cause mass panic?"

"Yes."

Pandora giggled, and she then pulled off her bottle to coo, "Mafff panic!"

Sloane resisted the urge to slap his own forehead.

"Holy crap!" Milo gasped. "Was that Panda? Sweet little Panda Bear? Did she just talk?"

"Yes. Yes, she did." Sloane didn't know whether to be proud or mortified by Pandora's very first words.

"No mass panic, young spawn," Loch chided, one of his tentacles playfully booping her nose. "That is decidedly frowned upon in this house."

"Mafff panic!" Pandora declared as she swatted back at Loch's tentacle. "Maff panic, maff panic!"

"Ah! I know! I shall summon my sister!" Loch nodded. "She is more than capable of watching over our tiny godly spawn."

"Well…." Sloane reached over to pet Pandora's curls.

He had barely left her side since she was born—other than quick naps, quick runs to the store, and even quicker quickies with Loch—and he remained hesitant to leave her. If the cult was back, however, he knew they needed to help.

Fate of the world and all that.

"All right," Sloane said. "As soon as Gal gets here, we'll come. Just text me the address, okay, Milo?"

"Cool!" Milo replied. "Will do! See you guys soon!"

"Bye." Sloane hung up with a sigh. There was a knot of dread in his stomach, and he did his best to ignore it. "Well, here we go again."

"Go?" Loch asked. "Where are we going?"

"Going on another crazy adventure." Sloane kept playing with Pandora's hair. "Taking time off from working cases and being here at home has been… really nice."

"The midday naps spoiled you, didn't they?"

"They sure did." Sloane chuckled. "Could almost pretend everything was okay, you know?"

"Well, even though we haven't *seen* the cultists or any of my wayward relatives plotting, we know they're still out there."

"I guess there was a part of me that hoped they'd just give up, as silly as that is. They've been so quiet… which now that I think about it has me more worried."

"Why, my sweet mate?"

"Because it means they've probably been working on something big." Sloane grimaced. "Like drowning people. Why? What possible purpose could that serve?"

"I don't know, but we will figure it out."

"Maff panic," Pandora chimed in.

"And you!" Sloane laughed, grinning down at her. "You, little lady, are the most perfect and wonderful thing in the world. I'd much rather be here with you, dealing with fires and whatever else you decide to get into."

"Maffffff panic!"

"She's talking. How is she already talking?" Sloane scooped her up from Loch's arms, cradling her against his chest as he gave her back the bottle. "I swear that we're gonna blink, and she's gonna be a teenager."

"That is certainly a possibility," Loch mused, "but unlikely."

Pandora jerked her head away from the bottle, and she cried loudly.

"Aw, baby girl," Sloane cooed. "Hey. Hey, what's the matter?" He tried to give her the bottle again, but she pushed it away with a frantic wail.

"Oh, little spawn!" Loch fussed over Pandora with his tentacles, trying to comfort her to no avail. "What can we do, hmm? What's wrong?"

Pandora grabbed one of Loch's tentacles and promptly chomped on it.

"Ow." Loch clenched his teeth together as he grumbled, "I am hardly an expert, but I do believe she might be hungry."

"But she won't take her bottle," Sloane protested.

"Flesh! She hungers for flesh!"

There was a knock at the door.

"Gods. I hope that's Galgareth." Sloane passed Pandora over to Loch. "Here."

"Ah yes." Loch made another pained face. "Put her closer to the source of nourishment. Good idea."

Sloane hurried over to the door and then opened it, sighing in relief when it was indeed Galgareth. "Hey! Thank you so much for coming so quickly! And for knocking."

Galgareth was in her usual vessel, a teenager named Toby who liked piercings and dying his hair funky colors. It was purple and neon green currently, and he had a new ring in his eyebrow to accompany the ones in his lip and nose.

"Of course I knocked!" Galgareth grinned. "Who knows what kind of debaucherous things you two might be up to?" She embraced Sloane. "Mm, it's good to see you!"

"Good to see you too." Sloane happily returned the hug. "How are you? How's Toby?"

"Toby's good!" Galgareth gestured to her face. "Got a new piece of metal stabbed into his flesh to celebrate his birthday! He's seventeen now!"

"Happy birthday, Toby!" Sloane always found it a little weird to talk to Toby since Galgareth was always in control of his body, but he didn't want to be rude.

After all, it wasn't like with Loch or Merrick whose vessels were empty. Toby was a very devout follower of Galgareth and offered himself willingly whenever she came to Aeon.

"That's marvelous. Wonderful." Loch pouted miserably. "Can someone please assist me? Our spawn is attempting to digest me."

Pandora had a very firm grip on Loch's tentacle and was gnawing away.

"Oh!" Galgareth snapped her fingers. "I bet she's teething."

"You think so?" Sloane shut the door, frowning. "I mean, she did just have a bunch of teeth magically appear."

"Where's the bracelet Uncle Yeris gave you for a wedding present?" Galgareth asked. "It was made of amber. That'll work perfectly!"

Loch held out his hand, and the bracelet appeared. "Ah, you mean this one?"

"Yes!" Galgareth took the bracelet and then gave it to Pandora, urging her to take a nibble. "Here, little one. Try having a chew on this, hmm?"

Pandora's eyes widened, and she released Loch's tentacle to eagerly accept the bracelet.

Quickly retracting his tentacle, Loch took a step back and groaned in relief. "Oh yes. Thank you."

"I put a little smidge of healing magic on it," Galgareth said, smiling reassuringly. "That plus the amber should ease the ache."

"Goddess of serendipity, huh?" Sloane grinned. "Of course you'd remember the one magical thing we have that's perfect for teething."

"Don't forget I'm also the goddess of love and night too." Galgareth held her head high.

"We may want to find a substitute for her," Loch warned, carrying Pandora over to the small bassinet beside the couch to lay her down.

"Why?" Sloane followed to help tuck her in. "She seems to like it. Do we really want to upset a happy baby?"

"The bracelet carries my uncle's blessing." Loch stared at Sloane expectantly. "Protects whoever wears it from drowning?"

"Are you guys planning a beach trip soon?" Galgareth quirked her brows.

"No, but the case we're being called in on?" Sloane turned toward her. "All the victims are drowning."

"And Rose was spotted, right?"

"Rose?" Sloane frowned.

"Rose, Tulip, Lily…." Loch shrugged. "It's a flower."

"Daisy," Sloane corrected patiently. "Her name is Daisy, and yes, she was seen with the last victim."

"Here." Galgareth's tentacles appeared, and she touched both Sloane and Loch on their foreheads. "A quick blessing for luck."

"Thank you, Gal." Sloane rubbed his forehead. He happened to glance at Galgareth's shirt, and he saw something familiar in the colorful pattern.

The design was a wild sunburst, and there were words woven in between the waving rays of multicolored light.

"What's on your shirt?" Sloane tilted his head. "Well, what's on Toby's shirt?"

"Do you like it?" Galgareth laughed. "Another birthday present from some boutique clothing store in downtown Archersville."

"The words. Is that… Godstongue?"

"Yes! I haven't had a chance to read it all yet, but I believe it's a blessing for Salgumel."

"And they just slapped it on a shirt?" Sloane shook his head. "That's horrible."

"Trust me." Galgareth smiled sadly. "Seeing a sacred prayer to my father plastered all over uppity mortal merchandise isn't exactly my idea of reverent either, but maybe it's a good thing."

"How?" Loch wrinkled his nose. "Are we getting a cut of the profits?"

"Well, no, but if people want to know what their shirt says, they might start learning about the old ways to find out." Galgareth's smile brightened. "It might be enough to spark someone's interest and lead them to the gods."

"Conversion through fashion, huh?" Sloane grinned.

"You never know." Galgareth joined Sloane and Loch by the bassinet, and she leaned down to nuzzle Pandora. "Maybe this little one will even have her own worshippers one day, huh?"

"Mmm, yeah." Sloane chuckled to himself. "Anyone looking for help to start a large fire can call on Pandora, goddess of spontaneous combustion."

"That is not her official title," Loch scolded. "We haven't had her naming ceremony yet."

"It was a joke."

"Don't you two have a crime scene or something to go to?" Galgareth politely reminded them.

"Right." Sloane fiddled with Pandora's blankets again, watching her chew away on the amber bracelet. "Okay, she still has that bottle over there on the counter, and the formula Urilith made is in the cabinet by the fridge, and—"

"Sloane," Galgareth cut in. "I've got her, okay?" She smiled warmly. "Goddess, remember?"

"Yes. Sorry." Sloane bowed his head to kiss Pandora's forehead. "Be good for your Auntie Gal, okay?"

"Maff panic," Pandora whispered through a mouthful of bracelet.

"No mass panic. No."

"Maff?"

"No."

When Pandora pouted, she looked just like Loch.

"We'll be back soon, I promise." Sloane kissed her a few more times before finally pulling away. "Okay. I'm good, we're going. Lemme just grab my coat."

Loch cuddled Pandora with his tentacles and gave her a kiss. "Don't fret, my little one. Daddy and Dad will be back in no time to cuddle you, love all over you, teach you how to flambé—"

"No flambéing!" Sloane rolled his eyes as he put on his coat.

"Go on! Both of you!" Galgareth shooed Sloane and Loch toward the door. "Have fun at the crime scene!"

"Oh yeah," Sloane grumbled. "It's gonna be a real hoot."

The address Milo had texted was for a hotel near the university, and Sloane drove there with his stomach churning. Loch had taken Sloane's phone, claiming he wanted to play a game, but he was instead scrolling through Sloane's text messages.

"Lochlain has invited us over to feast with him and Robert for Dhankes," Loch was saying. "You have not answered him."

Lochlain Fields was Lynnette's brother, and it was his murder that first summoned Loch down to Aeon to seek justice. After his resurrection courtesy of Great Azaethoth, Lynnette made a ghoul copy of Lochlain's body for Loch to use. Lochlain was a talented thief and his husband, Robert, was a fence and broker for illegal magical items.

"I did so," Sloane protested. "I told him I'd get back to him."

"Which is not an answer."

"It's literally the first of October. We have all month to figure it out." Sloane glanced at Loch, and he frowned when he saw Loch swiping around more. "Now what are you doing?"

"You haven't spoken to Fred in almost two weeks. We should send him a message and check on his penis."

"We should not do that," Sloane replied firmly. "I'm sure him and Ell are doing just fine."

Best friend and fellow thief to Lochlain, Fred was a ghoul. While the secrets of true necromancy had been lost to the world—the miracle of Lochlain's resurrection aside—it was possible to bind someone's soul to a copy of their body before they died. The practice was rare, highly illegal, and ghouls had the unfortunate tendency to rot.

This created the need for ghoul doctors like Fred's boyfriend, Ell, who specialized in powerful magic designed to preserve and increase a ghoul body's longevity. It wasn't clear how exactly a ghoul could be intimate with another person, but Sloane had long decided that it was none of his business.

Loch, however, disagreed.

"But he's a ghoul. Things... fall off."

"I'm aware."

"But *how* do they mate? How?"

"However they want. Stop being weird."

"Hmmph." Loch typed something.

"You better not be texting him about his penis."

"I am... texting him about something else." Loch poked at the screen.

Sloane stopped at a red light and put the car in park. He then reached over to grab his phone. "Stop! Right now!"

Loch twisted away, using his tentacles to push Sloane back as he typed faster. "I'm almost done!"

"Oh, I swear by all the gods I'm going to kick your ass if you send him something about his dick—"

Loch cackled, and he easily kept Sloane's swinging arms at bay with his many tentacles. "Just a few more words... hmmm, how do you spell 'engorged'? The automatic correction is failing me."

"Dead!" Sloane laughed at the sheer ridiculousness of fighting a god over what was certainly a very lewd text message. "You're so dead!"

"It keeps trying to spell 'enforced'. Hmm. Oh, I know—"

"Loch, quit! Right now—" Sloane gasped as the car lurched forward.

"Hey!" Loch braced himself against the dash.

The car was still moving—no, it was being *lifted*—until the front grill was parallel to the street and hovering several yards up in the air. The only things keeping Sloane from falling into the windshield were his seat belt and a bundle of Loch's tentacles.

"Loch!" Sloane exclaimed. "What the—"

"This is very rude!" Loch griped.

Sloane watched in horror as *something* stepped into view in front of the windshield. It was massive, horrible, too many eyes and way too many legs, but wait….

No.

Too many *tentacles.*

It was a god.

K.L. "KAT" HIERS is an embalmer, restorative artist, and queer writer. Licensed in both funeral directing and funeral service, she worked in the death industry for nearly a decade. Her first love was always telling stories, and she has been writing for over twenty years, penning her very first book at just eight years old. Publishers generally do not accept manuscripts in Hello Kitty notebooks, however, but she never gave up.

Following the success of her first novel, *Cold Hard Cash*, she now enjoys writing professionally, focusing on spinning tales of sultry passion, exotic worlds, and emotional journeys. She loves attending horror movie conventions and indulging in cosplay of her favorite characters. She lives in Zebulon, NC, with her husband and their children, some of whom have paws and a few who only pretend to because they think it's cute.

Website: http://www.klhiers.com

A SUCKER FOR LOVE MYSTERY

ACSQUIDENTALLY
IN LOVE

K.L. HIERS

A Sucker for Love Mystery

Nothing brings two men—or one man and an ancient god—together like revenge.

Private investigator Sloane sacrificed his career in law enforcement in pursuit of his parents' murderer. Like them, he is a follower of long-forgotten gods, practicing their magic and offering them his prayers… not that he's ever gotten a response.

Until now.

Azaethoth the Lesser might be the patron of thieves and tricksters, but he takes care of his followers. He's come to earth to avenge the killing of one of his favorites, and maybe charm the pants off the cute detective Fate has placed in his path. If he has his way, they'll do much more than bring a killer to justice. In fact, he's sure he's found the man he'll spend his immortal life with.

Sloane's resolve is crumbling under Azaethoth's surprising sweetness, and the tentacles he sometimes glimpses escaping the god's mortal form set his imagination alight. But their investigation gets stranger and deadlier with every turn. To survive, they'll need a little faith… and a lot of mystical firepower.

www.dreamspinnerpress.com

A SUCKER FOR LOVE MYSTERY

KRAKEN MY
HEART

K.L. HIERS

"A breezy and sensual LGBTQ paranormal romance."
—Library Journal, "Acsquidentally in Love"

A Sucker for Love Mystery

It's just Ted's luck that he meets the love of his life while covered in the blood of a murder victim.

Funeral worker Ted Sturm has a foul mouth, a big heart, and a knack for communicating with the dead. Unfortunately the dead don't make very good friends, and Ted's only living pal, his roommate, just rescued a strange cat who's determined to make his life even more miserable. This cat is more than he seems, and soon Ted finds himself in an alternate dimension… and on top of a dead body.

When Ted is accused of murder, his only ally in a strange world full of powerful magical beings calling for his head is King Grell, a sarcastic, randy, catlike immortal with impressive abilities… and anatomy. The two soon find themselves at the center of a cosmic conspiracy and surrounded by dangerous enemies. But with Ted's special skills and Grell's magic, they have a chance to get to the bottom of the mystery and save Ted. There's just one problem: Ted's got to resist Grell's aggressive advances… and he isn't sure he wants to.

www.dreamspinnerpress.com

A SUCKER FOR LOVE MYSTERY

HEAD OVER TENTACLES

K.L. HIERS

A Sucker for Love Mystery

Private investigator Sloane Beaumont should be enjoying his recent engagement to eldritch god Azaethoth the Lesser, AKA Loch. Unfortunately, he doesn't have time for a pre-honeymoon period.

The trouble starts with a deceptively simple missing persons case. That leads to the discovery of mass kidnappings, nefarious secret experiments, and the revelation that another ancient god is trying to bring about the end of the world by twisting humans into an evil army.

Just another day at the office.

Sloane does his best to juggle wedding planning, stopping his fiancé from turning the mailman inside out, and meeting his future godly in-laws while working the case, but they're also being hunted by a strange young man with incredible abilities. With the wedding date looming closer, Sloane and Loch must combine their powers to discover the truth—because it's not just their own happy-ever-after at stake, but the fate of the world....

www.dreamspinnerpress.com